Shlomc

MW00474376

Shlomo Kalo

THE
CHOSEN

Book II: **THE PROPHET**

© All Rights Reserved
Y   D.A.T. Publications
Publishers and rights owner of Shlomo Kalo's works
POBox 27019,
Jaffa 61270, Israel
Fax: +972-3-5070458
Email: dat@y-dat.co.il
www.y-dat.com

Original Hebrew title: *HaNivchar*
4th Hebrew edition, 2011
First interantional English edition of the three books of THE
CHOSEN in one volume, 2014
First collaboration with Amazon CreateSpace, 2015

English translation by Philip Simpson

Cover design based on suggestion by Hagit Shani
Image: kwest/Shutterstock

ISBN: 978-965-7028-55-1

THE CHOSEN is available also in Hebrew and in Korean

In the previous part of THE CHOSEN...

Book I: THE YOUTH, gives an account of Daniel's early years. The narrative opens with the aftermath of the conquest of Jerusalem by the armies of Nebuchadnezzar, King of the Chaldeans. A group of Jewish youths is to be sent to Babylon, to serve in the court of Nebuchadnezzar, and Daniel and his close friends, Mishael, Hananiah and Azariah, are among those selected. He has time for a final visit to the prophet Jeremiah, who gives him his blessing, and must then part from his mother and his younger siblings and join the convoy. (His father was killed in the last battle in the royal palace of Jerusalem, after the king had fled.)

The convoy proceeds on the long and tortuous journey from Jerusalem to Babylon, with various adventures along the way, blended with reminiscences of the past. Daniel has particularly fond memories of Nejeen, his sweetheart since childhood. During this journey he hears for the first time eyewitness accounts of his father's death and also strikes up some unlikely friendships, which will prove significant, such as that with Or-Nego, a senior Chaldean officer and commander of the convoy. A few other Jewish youths, especially Adoniah, develop hostility towards Daniel.

On arrival in Babylon the four friends are given new names (Daniel becomes Belteshazzar; Mishael, Hananiah and Azariah are now -- respectively -- known as Meshach, Shadrach and Abed-nego) and must be educated for their roles in the service of the

King, learning the Chaldean language and the ways of the court, and honing their equestrian skills. This section of "The Chosen" ends when the four friends finally come face to face with Nebuchadnezzar himself and must answer his questions. While pledging to serve the King, Daniel insists that his first loyalty is to his Judean heritage. The King - cruel and capricious though he undoubtedly is - respects the young man's principles and promises him a responsible position in the imperial administration

Contents

NASHDERNACH

Working in the office of Nashdernach, the man appointed by the King to supervise his senior counsellors and reputedly an authority on the holy writings of the Jews, was fraught with tension. Runners came and went from early morning till late in the evening, even at times when Nashdernach was absent from the office, leaving their messages either orally, in which case the duty clerk made a written record with a stylus on finely crafted scrolls, or in the form of inscriptions on clay tablets, parchment or those thin, flimsy sheets of paper imported from Egypt, made from reeds and known as "papyrus".

For his part, the chief minister of the King's council made every effort to be present and to receive in person the dispatches arriving from all far-flung corners of the great kingdom, especially the oral reports, which were sometimes corrupted in transmission from one runner to another and from one clerk to another. If he suspected any such inaccuracy, the minister would personally interrogate the runner and force him to repeat the message over and over again, while a harassed clerk took dictation. If the several versions of the same material were inconsistent, as frequently happened, or even contradicted one another, a less common occurrence, Nashdernach would fume, abusing and berating the unfortunate runner and the fool who had entrusted him with the message, and sending him back the way he had come, accompanied by a runner of his own, who was instructed to report the minister's displeasure, demand an enquiry and return post haste with a clear and authenticated version of the original message.

At such times as this, the minister's extensive office was in a ferment: scribes and calligraphers running back and forth in search of more efficient styluses and better quality parchment, anxious to avoid any mistakes when taking dictation from Nashdernach, runners waiting tensely and changing places in the line, depending on how keen they were to be sent to that distant region from which the corrupted message had originated, secretaries consulting scrolls and tablets in search of all available information regarding the governors and agents of the Crown responsible for that particular locality. There were quieter days too, days of routine when no unrest had been reported in any of the regions and the provinces on account of some or other demand on the part of the King or those governing on his behalf; no one was complaining of an unreasonably oppressive regime or fomenting sedition.

A constantly irksome matter, naturally enough, was the tribute paid by conquered lands. Governors, chosen by the local populace, and agents acting on behalf of the Chaldean monarch, would sometimes make common cause with the residents of that territory or region or formerly sovereign state, and try every means at their disposal, from exploiting obscure points of Chaldean law to the offering of bribes, in the effort to reduce the tax to what they considered a more tolerable level. Thus for example, the merchandise sent in accordance with the treaty of submission, signed by the envoys of the King and representatives of the population of the vassal state, was not always of the quality explicitly required by the terms of the treaty. On the contrary, all too often these goods were of inferior quality, sometimes very inferior quality, so much so that Nashdernach took it upon himself to return them to the sender with a reprimand, a warning or even a threat, and this in spite of the expenses involved in returning the goods. And there were duplicitous agents who resorted to covering the inferior commodities with a thin top layer of goods of superior quality. If someone confirmed receipt of the merchandise without adequate inspection and reported it satisfactory, then the conspirators in the provinces had cause for celebration, while the people of Babylon had no option but to consume the flawed foodstuffs, gritting their teeth and swallowing the bitter pill. In many such cases Nashdernach demanded a thorough investigation of the issue, and the clerk who confirmed the receipt faced dismissal. In cases where responsibility was less easily assigned, the high quality material masking the inferior was simply sent to the palace for the use of the King and his court, and the remainder taken to the market and sold off cheaply – a highly unsatisfactory outcome. And if the business came to the King's knowledge, someone would pay for his carelessness, with a heavy fine or a lengthy term of penal servitude.

He was noted for his attention to detail and his diligence, qualities for which Chaldean clerks were not always renowned and especially – for his honesty. Whenever it was revealed, this uncompromising honesty aroused admiration – closely followed by jealousy, scorn and rejection. Nashdernach appreciated these qualities and came to depend on him when he needed to take decisions or prosecute somebody or other.

He did his work conscientiously and did not skimp on the hours of work, often staying on late in the office if some matter required urgent attention. And with this too he gained the esteem of Nashdernach and the jealousy of his colleagues. Furthermore, his handwriting was clean and legible and he wrote with remarkable speed to the minister's dictation which, in his angrier moments, tended to lack consistency and clarity, verging on the incoherent.

Late one evening a report of an imminent uprising in a remote southern province arrived on the minister's desk, this on account of a demand for the doubling of the rice quota sent to Babylon as tribute. The effect of the demand would be to add still further to the already wearisome burden of toil at every stage of the process – planting, harvesting, sorting, drying, packing and dispatch to the authorities in Babylon.

Nashdernach decided to send a punitive expedition to ravage the province and reduce its "feckless" inhabitants, as he called them, to "poverty and penury", and the only question in his mind was the scale of the expedition required, bearing in mind the expense involved and the need to obtain royal approval.

Nashdernach approached him as he was engaged in transcribing an illegible text onto clean parchment, gave him a sharp look with his oily, bloodshot eyes and asked him:

"Will one battalion suffice?"

"To start with," he replied.

"What's that supposed to mean – 'to start with'?" – Nashdernach retorted, angry and surprised.

"The first act of suppression will only be the beginning," he explained calmly, adding: "The revolt will spread, and people won't bother rebuilding the straw huts that have been torched; instead they'll set ambushes for Chaldean soldiers and attack them. This is their territory and they know all its dark corners, every tree and every stone, and if it comes down to guerrilla warfare the rebels will have the advantage and you'll have to send another expedition, and then another."

"In the end, the rebels will be crushed!" the minister declared, disbelieving the other's words, despite the confident tone in which they were spoken.

Ignoring the interjection, he continued:

"And on top of everything, you'll lose all the rice – all of it!"

"Expenses, expenses – and no revenue!" – Nashdernach grumbled.

Instead of answering, he went back to deciphering the ancient text.

The minister turned and began pacing up and down his spacious office, lit with numerous oil-lamps, his hands clasped behind his back. He was wearing a brown robe and a cloak of superior fabric, with no embellishment other than the silver medallion hanging on his chest, the symbol of his eminent status in the service of the King.

Having measured the length and breadth of his office once again, Nashdernach finally stopped by his desk and asked him:

"And what would you do in my place?"

"Without presuming to put myself in your place," – he looked up and calmly met his supervisor's gaze – "I would rescind the excessive demand for doubling of the rice quota."

"What makes you say it's 'excessive'?" – cried Nashdernach.

"The rebellion that it's provoked."

"They're just a bunch of idle no-hopers!" – Nashdernach complained.

"If they were idle no-hopers they wouldn't have completed even the original quota, and they wouldn't now be in such a mutinous mood, spoiling for a fight."

"If I reverse the decision," – the minister tried to explain – "I shall lose face in the sight of those barbarian populations, and they'll try to wriggle out of their existing obligations! Other lands and provinces will learn from them and follow their example, and the whole apparatus will unravel, with disastrous results!"

"The opposite is the case," he retorted evenly.

"How so?" his supervisor queried, a sceptical glint in his eyes.

"Only a strong ruler is capable of admitting his mistakes, and such an admission will arouse only esteem and respect in the hearts of the peoples under his sway. If you withdraw the excessive demand, you will gain the affection and appreciation of the local populations, and you will save the costs of a punitive expedition, and not run the risk of incurring royal displeasure. In addition, you will again receive the quota of rice as agreed in the treaty of submission, and it is very likely, that if you succeed in winning over the people of this province with incentives or expressions of your appreciation for their efforts – they themselves will decide to add to the existing quota, even if they don't go so far as to double it."

"You have a brain in your head!" exclaimed Nashdernach, clasping his fingers tightly behind his back. The minister turned sharply, sat down facing him and said to him:

"Listen to me, Belteshazzar! Put that work aside and listen!"

He did as he was asked, carefully folding the document and placing the work in progress under an ivory paperweight, then looked up at his supervisor serenely, his tranquil eyes cleansed from all the vanities of the world.

"Your advice is the best that there is, but that doesn't mean that I have to accept it and put it into effect! Not at all!" exclaimed Nashdernach. "However sincerely we may wish to do what is right – we are compelled to act in ways contrary to honest reason. And why is this?" he asked, and continued his impassioned speech without waiting for an answer: "It's because of the need to preserve this skin of ours," – and he pinched the back of his mottled hand – "We are concerned for our skin because there's no one who can be trusted! You have to understand – this idea, so logical and sensible, will be whispered in the ears of the King and presented in the most unfavourable light, as a sign of failure, the plan of an abject and spineless minister who can't manage his own affairs and worst of all – it will be taken as a slur on the honour of the King and a token of flawed loyalty. Pay close attention to what I'm telling you," Nashdernach stressed – "Disloyalty to the King, betrayal of the King's trust, well, you know the rest! Hard labour for the remainder of your life, confiscation of property, wife, sons, daughters, parents – on the streets!" He struck the table with his fist, so hard that the stylus left on it leapt into the air and fell to the floor.

He bent down, picked up the stylus, replaced it on the table, and responded:

"The esteemed minister is gravely mistaken!"

"What is that supposed to mean?" – once again Nashdernach fixed him with that oily stare of his, expressing wonderment and considerable curiosity.

"There is someone who can be trusted."

"Who?"

"God."

The minister froze in his seat and his fleshy mouth gaped open, like the mouth of a fish. A long moment passed.

"Who is this God that can be trusted. Are you referring to Bel or to Marduk? They both have a habit of abandoning their devotees in times of adversity."

"Neither one nor the other."

"Who then?"

"The God who created everything, who rules over everything, and who loves us as a father loves his children."

"And why then, if such a God indeed exists, who loves us as a father loves his children, and who created everything and rules over everything, why, I ask you, has this father-God cast us down to flounder in this Hell?"

In his deep, limpid eyes, a bright glow flashed for a moment, and he answered the minister Nashdernach, senior counsellor to King Nebuchadnezzar:

"Because people don't put their trust in him!"

Nashdernach pondered this, and after a long silence, he rose from his seat and resumed his pacing, back and forth, his step vigorous, hands clasped behind his back.

He returned to his copying work, and was on the point of finishing it, when Nashdernach called to him from one of the corners:

"And you trust in Him, who created everything and rules over everything, who loves us as a father loves his children?"

"With all my heart and all my might!" – was his clear and resonant response.

And sure enough, the minister Nashdernach changed his mind and decided against sending a punitive expedition. Instead he sent a deputation of conciliators who informed the inhabitants that the King, the valiant and the wise, the compassionate and the merciful had see their misery, and being well aware of their devotion to him and valuing their loyalty, he had decided to release them from the increased rice quota and even, in recognition of the respect and the warm feelings of esteem in which they held the King, to forgo the standard quota of rice for the current year, as a gesture of the goodwill, appreciation and gratitude that the King felt for them.

When the messenger-runner returned from the remote province he was so emotional he had great difficulty giving his report, describing how those unfortunate people had received the astonishing news, how they had hugged and kissed him and carried him shoulder-high, how they decided there and then, using their own meagre resources, to erect a temple to King Nebuchadnezzar, the wise and the valiant, the compassionate and the merciful, the one and only, and to worship him as a god, since only a god – those unfortunates claimed – could understand their feelings and the depth of their poverty, know of their oppression and bring it to such a conclusive and satisfactory end.

And the messenger-runner broke down in tears when he tried to describe the moving scenes to Nashdernach, sitting at his table, and all the clerks of the office listening to his disordered words; even those who were supposed to be recording them were utterly distracted from their task by the strength of the feelings that had gripped them.

Even the oily little eyes of the chief counsellor to the King of Babylon filled with tears that he was powerless to resist, and they glided over his round ruddy-red cheeks, and were absorbed into his bushy beard, flecked with silvery threads.

Finally, in a voice still defying his attempts to control it, the minister asked the messenger to leave the room, and not to return until he had composed himself; only then should he make another effort to dictate a succinct report for the benefit of the scribes.

When the minister's instructions had been followed,

he rose to his feet and, snapping his fingers pleasurably behind his back, he approached him, leaned towards him and said:

"It seems, after all, He is worthy of our trust!"

IN MISHAEL'S LODGING

A year passed. And it came about one day that all of them, he and his companions, happened to be in one of the royal assembly rooms. The King's senior advisers were about to convene a meeting in this room, and their Jewish clerks had come to prepare the tables. Adoniah was there too, although he often left Babylon to travel to strange and distant lands where he traded in all the commerce of the world, from shoe-laces to slaves and concubines for the royal palace. Through all these dealings, he had made a handsome profit for himself.

One after another they entered the room, unable to restrain their joy at the unexpected reunion.

"Hananiah!" cried Mishael, almost embracing his friend.

"Mishael!" cried Azariah, and hurried towards him. The three of them exchanged handshakes and jovial slaps on the shoulder – and at that precise moment, although through separate doors – he and Adoniah made their entrance.

Adoniah hurried towards him and shook his hand vigorously, with surprising sincerity, then turned to the others and repeated the exercise, with warm handshakes, and even a slap on the shoulder for Azariah.

"How I've missed you, my friends and brothers!" he exclaimed – "And how good it is that God has brought us all together. My feet have trodden the wide open spaces of the world, places I never imagined I would go to, places I never knew existed! All those nations and tongues and peoples and principalities, living and subsisting on this continent of ours that is so full of surprises.... and most of all – I have missed you!" He turned to him again, this time with a convivial slap to the shoulder. "For some reason," he went on to say, his speech light and fluent – "It seems to me I haven't behaved towards you the way I should, and this has pinched my guts and weighed heavy on my heart! Anyway, blessed is the hour of our meeting, and this opportunity that I have to confess to you the sin I committed against you!"

"You're talking a great deal of nonsense!" he retorted. "I don't reckon you have ever sinned against me in anything!"

"Oh, I've sinned, you need have no doubt of that!" Adoniah insisted, the cheerful look on his face still bright, and growing brighter from moment to moment.

"And I tell you this too, my friend and brother!" Adoniah cried, shaking his hand again, a clownish grin flexing his fleshy lips: "I'm going to sin against you some more!"

The other three advanced, as Adoniah went on to say:

"You were good-looking even as a boy and now you've gone from strength to strength, what a brilliant career! Who would believe it? A courageous young fellow, a high-ranking courtier and a man of God as well! The frivolous young girls who chase me around would be scared off by you, living angel of God that you are, pure and unsullied, noble and brave, never to be tripped up by the sins of the flesh, and invincible – seeing that God Himself, in person, defends you and stands by your side, keeping you secure against evil or adversity! And why does God the all-powerful do this?" cried Adoniah, turning to Mishael, Azariah and Hananiah and answering his own question: "Because there is no one more worthy of it than him – no one! And who could possibly be jealous of such a man, doing everything in his power to dig a pit before his feet, to set a trap into which he will fall? This surely belongs to the dark side, the side that leads astray and causes delusions, the side of hypocrisy and seething anger, the serpent from the Garden of Eden, in other words, the side – to which I am totally committed!"

Hananiah intervened, his voice, in normal times so evenly modulated, turning harsh and almost menacing:

"All you're doing is fooling yourself! This power that you speak of can do nothing when it is revealed, in the open. It depends on cunning and deceit, and dark corners!"

"And perhaps," Adoniah interrupted him, "I really am cunning beyond belief and sufficiently degraded, a genius in that regard, to deceive you all and in particular, to arouse the superior compassion of Belteshazzar, and to blunt his eternal vigilance. Ha-Ha-Ha-Ha!" He shook his head with its mass of rust-coloured hair and beard and added: "I'm warning you – don't trust me!" Suddenly he turned more serious and wiped from his eyes the tears brought on by his wild laughter. "Don't trust anyone and take good care of yourselves, especially you!" – he pointed at him and laughed again.

He did not respond, but maintained his composure. Adoniah went on to say:

"You make me so angry, the anger of flesh and blood! Always the chief player, always in control of yourself, always standing in the right place, following the right road, always standing tall, to put it plainly – always a prig!" He turned to the remainder of his audience and asked gaily: "Don't you agree?"

"No!" the three companions replied with one voice, and as if they meant to protect him with their bodies, moved in closer and stood as a barrier between him and

Adoniah.

"You seem to be drunk!" Azariah hissed between his teeth.

"Drunk, but not on wine!" Adoniah declared.

"What then, if not wine?" asked Hananiah and almost regretted his question, but the answer was not slow in coming.

When Adoniah spoke, his voice had changed and was calm and measured, although the arrogance of his mood was undiminished:

"On hatred!"

And suddenly, in an unexpected movement, Adoniah skirted the barrier of the three friends and stood facing him, fixed flashing eyes on him and asked:

"And you?"

"What?" he retorted in a clear, authoritative voice, not budging from his place.

"How much do you hate me?"

"I don't hate you."

"Pity me?"

"No."

"Afraid of me?"

"No."

"Despise me?"

"No."

"And you make no distinction between me," he hesitated for a moment, then completed his sentence – "and these, shall we say?" He pointed to the three friends, with a sweeping gesture of the hand.

"I do make a distinction."

"Them you love and me – you hate!" cried Adoniah in a tone of triumph, like one who has caught his quarry or exposed another as a liar.

"I think of them with pleasure, and of you – with great

sorrow!" he declared.

Adoniah stood with head bowed and made no reply.

Mishael exploited the pause to issue an invitation:

"Come to my room this evening. I have some wine from the homeland, which we can drink with a clear conscience!"

In Mishael's lodging a surprise awaited them: besides the kosher wine, Gershon was sitting there – grey-haired now but looking fit in his clean clothing.

"You're all growing beards!" he cried, clearly finding the reunion an emotional experience – "Only a little while ago your faces were so smooth!"

They looked into one another's faces and perhaps for the first time realised they were no longer boys but men, young men with incipient beards.

"And have any of you taken wives yet?" Gershon asked curiously.

It emerged that Mishael, Azariah and Hananiah were soon to be betrothed to Jewish girls, precious finds indeed.

"There's no place for bachelors in the Chaldean administration!" Azariah explained.

"It's an immutable law," added Mishael.

The three of them had searched, and found in the environs of the city of Babylon a devout and decent Jewish community. The fathers of this community had no objection to marrying off their eligible daughters, knowing that the prospective grooms were not only Jews but were also functionaries in the service of Nebuchadnezzar.

"And what about you, Adoniah?" Gershon asked.

"I intend to marry a beautiful Egyptian princess, whose father, the prince, was taken captive by

Nebuchadnezzar. The price that I shall pay for her – is her father's ransom!"

"And how can you afford the ransom? After all, a prisoner of such distinction will command a very high price!"

"The ransom will cost me nothing!" – Adoniah chuckled.

"How so?" Gershon persisted.

"The man who is holding him owes me a favour!" he declared, amused by the stony expressions of the others, and adding: "That's how things work in the wonderful world of commerce – you repay good with good, and evil with evil! As it says in our Holy Law – *an eye for an eye, a tooth for a tooth!*"

"And what if she induces you to change your religion?" Gershon went on to ask.

"Either she'll induce me, or I'll induce her. We are neither of us renowned for our faith or for our zealous observance of commandments!"

"Egyptian women turned the head of King Solomon, the wisest of all men!" – Mishael commented earnestly.

"Then I shall gladly follow in his footsteps!" – Adoniah chuckled again and sat down at the table.

Gershon was given the seat of honour at the head of the table, and he blessed the bread and the fruit of the vine and one after another they all read from the scroll of the Psalms that Adoniah had succeeded in salvaging from the homeland. Then they sang their favourite anthems and finally, resumed their personal conversations.

He asked Gershon about his work in the office of the royal calligrapher, and he answered willingly, as all listened attentively, telling them how he had already been promoted on account of his experience and his expertise;

all agreed he had no equal in the skilled use of the sharpened Egyptian stylus, and in determining the quality of parchment and in mixing the ingredients of ink in the correct proportions, producing the colour required to make the text leap from the page, so that the reader would not only read and understand and be informed, but would also derive enjoyment from seeing the script, as a work of art in its own right. In the same way, a person who is fond of natural beauty or of weapons of war will enjoy the sight of a field or a forest or, *mutatis mutandis*, a sharp sword or a dagger, a bow and arrow or assorted spears. As for Chaldean writing, it was not complicated at all; on the contrary it was simple and easy to copy – and very satisfying. It was of course a cuneiform script, Gershon went on to explain, clearly glad of the opportunity to demonstrate his intimate knowledge of the subject, unlike the complex Hebrew script. Nevertheless – Gershon concluded with a smile and a conspiratorial wink – he preferred the Hebrew alphabet with all its complications to the pale and uninteresting Chaldean equivalent.

"And why is that?" Hananiah wanted to know.

"Because of the spirit that the Hebrew letter embodies."

"How so?" – Mishael expressed his sincere bemusement and added: "What makes you say that the letter embodies a spirit?"

And Azariah declared:

"The letter is dead and there is no spirit in it, never mind a living spirit!"

"You're wrong there!" Gershon answered him – "the letter is alive, and every language has a living spirit of its own!"

"What is the spirit of the Chaldean language, and what does the Hebrew language tell you?" asked Azariah, utterly baffled.

"The spirit of the Chaldean language is a spirit of arrogance. It is sure of itself, and it has a solidity to it and yet – it lacks depth and profundity. The spirit of the Hebrew language on the other hand, aspires to the heights and is always trying, trying and trying again to reach the sky, the firmament which is the foundry of the language!"

"As the people, so is the language, and as the language so is the people!" – Hananiah tried to simplify the issue for himself, a faint spark of gratification in his voice.

Adoniah commented:

"If you carry on with this line of conversation, discussing the comparative merits of languages and peoples and nations and races, praising your own people and disparaging the Chaldeans, treating them with such open contempt – you'll be accused of insulting the nation and its monarch and fomenting sedition – and before you know it you'll be on your way to the copper mines in the bowels of the earth…"

"This is just a private conversation, between friends!" – Gershon retorted.

"Walls have ears!" – Adoniah put a finger to his lips as if warning of the dangers of idle talk and added: *"He who guards his mouth and tongue, is guarded against adversity* – so said the wisest of men!"

"In this room," he interjected, "there are ears of flesh and blood only." He meant to reassure Gershon, who responded:

"I spent long enough among the tanners on the Euphrates to learn what hardship means. No human being on earth could imagine what is going on there! No man sent down to the Euphrates to scrape animal skins for the Chaldean King will come out of there alive…"

"Except you, apparently!" Adoniah remarked with

emphatic scorn.

"That was by the grace of God, the living God, the God full of mercy," declared Gershon reverently, with an involuntary inclination of the head.

"Why don't you tell us something about the Euphrates and the tanners?" Hananiah suggested.

Gershon looked at him again with a question in his eyes and, receiving his silent acquiescence, without hesitation and without a stumble, launched into his harrowing account:

"The river is broad at that point, so you can hardly see the other side, and it is shallow near the bank. The river bed is covered with stones and projecting rocks, creating all those swirling currents, and as if the currents weren't enough to cope with, the tanners have to stand barefoot on these stones and rocky surfaces from before dawn until the first star rises in the evening. There they stand, without pausing for a moment, scraping the crude skins fresh from the beasts, and causing serious injury to their feet. To begin with, you feel intense pain. As time passes, the pain is numbed, but walking becomes a very complicated process. You can tell a tanner by the way he walks – slowly, ponderously, picking up his feet like a goose. Here's the evidence!" – and with a quick movement, before anyone had the chance to protest, Gershon pulled off his shoes, unfastened the rags and revealed to the assembled company his bruised and battered feet, blackened toes deformed and folding under themselves, the very bones distorted. All looked on, and shuddered.

"What vicious beasts these Chaldeans are!" exclaimed Adoniah.

"How can you walk with your feet in that state?" asked Azariah.

"I manage, and every day I thank the living God for

releasing me from that Hell, alive and with only this disability to cope with. God is full of grace and all powerful, doing great and marvellous things, going down into the depths to rescue those that He loves from the hands of the wicked, performing miracles and wonders. He is compassionate and kind and I shall bless Him and praise His name for as long as I live, and that's all there is to say!"

Carefully he wrapped his feet again and put on his shoes.

"Is there more to tell?" asked Mishael.

"And why don't the tanners leave that terrible place and seek employment elsewhere?" asked Hananiah.

"They have guards there, and overseers – guards with weapons at the ready, to prevent anyone leaving and overseers with whips – long, thick, black whips made from buffalo tails. A single blow from one of those could knock a healthy man to the ground. Somehow, my Lord rescued me from these floggings, but there are very few who can endure them. The overseers are fond of lashing the bare backs of the tanners, as we stand there naked as the day we were born in the dirty, frothing water, a wooden scraper in one hand and in the other – a vile-smelling animal skin."

"Didn't they supply you with clothing?" he asked.

"The new tanner is given a shirt, a loin cloth, a strip of coarse, untreated wool to wrap around the head, and a pair of shoes. But all this stuff disintegrates within a few days, leaving him without even a scrap of material to preserve his modesty. No other clothing is supplied. One issue is supposed to last you for life – not such a long time, admittedly.

"I never knew a tanner who endured this back-breaking toil for more than seven years. I was the oldest of them all, and no one expected me to last long. Within six months, a year at the most, they reckoned the overseer's whip would knock me down – and I wouldn't get up, not ever. They're a heartless, merciless lot those overseers; wild, ravening creatures are paragons of compassion compared with them!

"There were times when the work was proceeding to the full satisfaction of the overseers and the guards, and not one of the tanners was doing anything to disrupt the routine, all working in silence without looking up or attempting to move paralysed limbs, from before dawn until evening, and then one of the overseers cracks his black whip over a tanner who has caught his eye, and this merely as a means of relieving boredom or as he himself would put it, for the sake of exercise. The overseer's cronies come hurrying along to join in the fun, howling with raucous laughter, and the whips lash the body of the chosen victim until he collapses on the spot, falls in the water and usually doesn't come up alive…"

"It's as if you've described to us a scene from Hell," cried Hananiah – indignation, horror and revulsion blending in his voice.

"Hell is precisely what it is!" Gershon declared, adding: "In the evening they dole out a tiny portion of broth, broth made with rotten, foul-smelling rice or beans that don't smell any better. And sometimes that's the only ration. And then you sleep in straw booths on flimsy mats the colour of the ground, and just about indistinguishable from it, like garbage that's been left uncollected, to fester."

"It's a nightmare you've described!" Adoniah exclaimed.

"What can we do to ease those dreadful conditions?" – Azariah tossed the question into the air and unconsciously turned towards him.

One after another Mishael, Hananiah and Gershon followed his example, as did Adoniah, whose quizzical look was tinged by a strange air of tolerance, of one who recognises his own weakness and makes no attempt to conceal it.

He answered them solemnly, in a quiet but resolute voice:

"God will show us what to do, and soon!"

"And why has this God of yours left it so long, and why is He still waiting?" – the mocking note returned to Adoniah's voice.

"Because people don't turn to Him!" he answered him in the same tone, controlled but vehement.

"And if they turned to Him, would they be delivered?" Adoniah persisted.

"It is written: *The Lord is near to all who call upon him, all who call upon him in truth.* Every appeal to God that is truthful is answered at once, and in full!"

"And how can this God of yours satisfy the ravenous hunger of those wretched slaves?" Adoniah demanded to know, his tone provocative.

"He will send down manna, manna from Heaven!" he declared calmly.

"I've been roaming about this strange world of ours for more than a year. My horse's legs have covered vast distances, and it seems there is not a remote corner anywhere in which I haven't set foot. I have travelled to regions that have no language and no name, I have seen upright and honest children of the Torah, and scoundrels and buffoons who call themselves saints, I have known people of indelible faith whose lot in life is far from lavish, but never have I seen with my own eyes manna descending from Heaven!" Adoniah concluded, grating notes of anger creeping into his voice.

"Our fathers saw it," he answered him steadily, adding: "They ate of it and were satisfied."

"And instead of praising and thanking God," Gershon interjected hoarsely – "they began complaining and longed to return to the servitude of Egypt!"

"And these people that you happened to meet – honest and upright, people of faith and lovers of God," – Hananiah turned to face Adoniah: "Were they in a state of distress or of abject misery?"

Adoniah gave the matter some thought, his eyes straying to the smooth white ceiling.

"I'm not altogether sure…" he faltered, his head lowered – "but if I'm doing my best not to offend against the truth, then I have to say that in all my life I have never seen people so happy in their lot, so hospitable, always prepared to sacrifice something of their own for another. And you have to take care not to express any kind of wish in their presence!" Adoniah laughed a bitter laugh.

"Why is that?" asked Azariah.

"Because they'll move heaven and earth to make it come true! And if you're foolish enough to admire your host's shirt, you won't be allowed to leave the house without it – even if it's the only shirt he has and he's left with just a loincloth!"

A broad, radiant smile spread over the faces of his audience.

"You're not as unpleasant as you sometimes pretend to be!" – Hananiah approached Adoniah and slapped his shoulder.

"How do you make that out?"

"You're telling the truth, and you have described those godly people just the way they are!"

"And perhaps you're the gullible one, Hananiah, falling so easily into the traps that I set for you!"

"I don't think so, my friend and brother!" Hananiah smiled a gentle and reassuring smile – "And I am sure that when the time of testing comes, you will pass it with honour, as befits a son of our holy race, this race of prophets and kings and saints."

"Don't be quite so confident!" Adoniah retorted and turned to him: "And you, do you share Hananiah's child-like trust in me?"

"I do – and more!" he declared without hesitation.

Adoniah looked down again, and after a moment's silence turned to him and said:

"It slipped my mind completely!" – and he raised his hand as if drawing up a memory – "When I was in Jerusalem a girl approached me, not the kind of girl one normally meets on one's travels – and I'm talking about the purity in her face, the quiet courage in her dark-blue eyes, the seal of wisdom shining on her smooth forehead – and she asked me if I was going to Babylon and if I knew Daniel, son of Naimel, former minister of the royal household, and if so she wanted me to pass on her regards and best wishes, and if possible, this modest gift as well…" He thrust his hand into the pocket of his gown, pulled out a small packet and handed it to him.

With trembling fingers he unwrapped the bundle and found in it a parchment scroll and a tiny seven-branched candlestick made of silver – a real work of art.

His hand closed around the parchment scroll. He felt tears springing to his eyes, and made an effort to curb them, with some success. He took the candlestick and showed it to the assembled company. The skilfully beaten silver caught the flickering glimmer of the oil-lamps and grease-lamps in the room, shining with a pure radiance and reflecting the light back to those looking on, a gentle and conciliatory light.

"Did she ask about me?" – he turned to Adoniah, and the latter replied to him in a deliberately casual tone, in an effort to show complete indifference and the self-confidence which he so conspicuously lacked:

"She asked, oh yes – she asked!"

"And you told her?"

"I didn't want to disappoint her, and superb raconteur that I am, I could have told her a great deal about you. There is plenty to tell after all! On the other hand, I didn't want to confuse her either, and she was clearly preoccupied at the time, to say the least!"

He gave Adoniah a sharp, inquisitive, probing look until the latter flinched, recoiled involuntarily and fell silent.

"So what did you tell the girl?" asked Azariah, with a distinct edge of asperity to his voice.

"First of all," Adoniah grinned – "Nejeen isn't a girl any more, not the girl she once was. The years have passed and the girl has become a woman. A young woman of exceptional feminine beauty, whose equal is not to found anywhere on this earth, or possibly even in the Heavens above," and to the astonishment of his audience he attempted to reinforce his words with the most bizarre of arguments: "If a thief happened to be in her presence, a habitual thief, and he glanced once at her face if only for a moment – he would turn from his evil ways and return everything he had stolen to the rightful owners, or donate it to charity, and go to the Temple of God, and bow down before the Holy Ark, and fall face down on the floor in the fullest repentance. Such is the beauty of Nejeen of the house of Gamliel, and this is its special nature! However, I am no thief and am therefore absolved from repentance!"

"You're not answering the question, Adoniah!" – Azariah pressed him.

"Don't be so hasty, dear friend! Everything in its time! Didn't the wisest of men say, there is a time for everything? A time for peace and a time for war, a time to love and a time to hate? Well, I told the aristocratic young lady, Nejeen of the house of Gamliel, who it seems is also related to the royal family, about her sweetheart, who is doing great things in Babylon!" His sarcasm was venomous, and intended to hurt.

"Be careful what you say, Adoniah!" he warned, his voice icy.

"I haven't accused you of worshipping the spirits of the night," Adoniah retorted – "control your temper! It's true that you've visited the shrine of Bel," he continued with an air of secret, contemptuous pleasure, – "but you haven't changed your religion yet! I, on the other hand, stand accused of contemplating a change of religion for the sake of a foreign lady, the diametrical opposite of your Jewess... Well, so it goes, we differ in nature and in taste, and in the kind of people who are drawn to us, differ fundamentally..." Adoniah sighed a bitter sigh and added as if in conclusion: "Such is the way of the world and there's no remedy for it!

"'I know him!' I told her," he resumed his account, "and I had the privilege of seeing her wondrous exaltation of spirit, the brightness coming to life in her eyes, the brightness of fearless nobility, fine breeding, and for this reason I was quick to stress: 'I know him well! We both travelled to Babylon in the same convoy, and we studied in the same school. We even competed, at the behest of King Nebuchadnezzar, in horse-racing and steeplechasing, and as you can well imagine – he was the victor!'" Adoniah smiled a thin and calculated smile, was silent for a moment to deepen the impact of his words and add to the tension among his listeners, before continuing:

"Obviously, in this instance she needed to invest a lot of effort in the attempt to hide the surge of sublime emotion – and in my humble opinion, she's not accustomed to feelings of any other kind – that took hold of her.

"For her part, she was sure she had succeeded in curbing and concealing her emotions before it was too late, and I was happy to pretend to be unaware of her state of mind, because at that time it was my wish and my firm intention to reassure her and if possible – to cheer her up as well. The fact is, it is inconceivable that any creature should try to injure and offend one such as she, and if ever such a strange creature were to be found, he would deserve the soundest of thrashings. And yes, this is what I tried to do, I suppressed my noble inclination to make her happy, I tried to grieve and injure her – and I was soundly thrashed! Utter failure! And how did I try?" – he asked and answered for himself: "I tried by telling her of the Chaldean beauty who seduced Beltezhazzar (I revealed to her the proud Chaldean name that he bears) and led him to the temple of idolatry, the shrine of Bel, the Babylonian deity, and how they stayed there much longer than would be reasonably expected, and I stressed the point that all this information came from first hand, since I personally followed them there and waited, and waited a long time for them to emerge from the temple, and in the end, when there was still no sign of them, I gave up and left the place.

"I was sure I had succeeded in plunging a poisoned arrow into that sensitive heart, most wondrous of hearts... but not a bit of it!

"She turned to me and asked me why I had acted this way, and why I had followed them. Had I been appointed their bodyguard? And here I can tell you for sure that in

35

her voice there was a clear intention to hurt me and to teach me a lesson, and expose my shameful behaviour to public view – and a threat like that always throws me off balance and sometimes numbs all my senses too. And that is what happened in this instance, and I turned to her and told her in all sincerity:

"It's because I'm jealous, my lady, I'm envious of him! Everywhere he outshines me and outclasses me, whether it's horse-racing or landing the best jobs, or making an impression on well-connected Chaldean women, and I'm sure you can't blame him for that! However, I shall fulfil my errand, if you still consider me suitable, if my conduct has not made you reconsider!' And what do you think she said? Can you have the slightest inkling of her response?" And without waiting for a reply he continued: "She said, 'Esteemed Sir, I trust you!' And that was it! With those words she trampled my soul into the dust! For a moment, I wanted to jump off the wall, but I didn't have the nerve!" Adoniah bowed his head, looked away and continued: "After we had parted company I thought of throwing the little package away, but then some instinct told me there might be something valuable in it and rather than discard it, I should take it to a silversmith and make some money from it. I opened the package and saw it was indeed a charming piece, but of little value. And I went further and read what was written on the parchment, I couldn't resist the impulse! And you," – he turned to him – "you can read it to us if you like, or shall I? Anyway, it says 'Love is stronger than death'."

He gave him a tolerant look, not particularly sympathetic but also devoid of hatred or abhorrence.

"You can pity me!" Adoniah resumed – "Pity me as much as you like. I'm more deserving of pity than any other creature in the world, and yet I don't ask for your compassion, I despise it. You can call me a scoundrel and challenge me to a duel with swords or spears or bare hands, or with bows and arrows – and I won't accept the challenge because I know perfectly well that you are superior to me in all these skills. But the day will come that I am longing for, when I shall tackle you in the way you least expect. Remember that. Remember it well!"

"You're out of your mind!" Gershon cried – "Crazy!"

"Not crazy exactly, a little deranged perhaps!" Adoniah corrected him, with a hoot of raucous laughter. He poured the remainder of the wine into his cup, gulped it down thirstily and noisily to the very last drop, put the cup down and said:

"Jerusalem is going to rebel! Remember what I'm telling you! Zedekiah is leading the Jewish people to catastrophe. Jeremiah is saying this too, but he's just repeating what his God is telling him, whereas I'm reporting to you what my eyes have seen and my ears have heard. If you want to save the lovely Nejeen," he turned to him suddenly – "fetch her here and do it soon!" And saying this he rose from his seat, and swaying a little on his short legs, left Mishael's lodging.

Adoniah's departure seemed to clear the air for those remaining, and all breathed more easily.

"The man's a fool, and he's talking nonsense!" Gershon exclaimed.

He did not respond, although the others expected him to. In the equable stillness that reigned in the little room, he asked Mishael if he was enjoying his work in the legal department.

Mishael answered willingly, telling them of a new law which had been proposed by the council of sorcerers, wizards and astrologers and would soon be presented to the King for his approval. According to the new law, the death penalty was to be imposed on anyone expressing contempt for the government of Nebuchadnezzar, however mild or good-humoured it might be. Now they were having to draft the law with all its clauses, and the senior legal adviser was doing his best to tone down the more stringent provisions. What was needed was an agreed and precise legal definition of "contempt".

Azariah described his work in the buildings inspectorate of the palatial complex, and the difficulty of finding enough assistants, or rather skilled artisans, for the work that needed doing. And since Babylon was not richly endowed with building labourers of the calibre required, he had suggested to his minister that skilled workers should be brought in from Judah. It seemed his suggestion had been accepted, and a convoy would soon be on its way, to recruit the Jewish artisans who were so sorely needed.

Hananiah was the assistant to the King's senior adviser on educational matters, and the work in that office was most agreeable to him. An edict was soon to be issued in the name of the King, according to which every child of the common people who proved adept and knowledgeable, would receive a full education at the King's expense. Preliminary surveys had shown that at least one out of every hundred plebeian children would benefit from this scheme, being educated free of charge by the best teachers in the land.

Later he returned to his own room, dismissed the slave who was preparing to serve his supper, turned to face Jerusalem, put his hands together and said softly:

"O my father in Heaven, my God, shining in the hearts of all men, bringer of peace, joy, truth and freedom, You are the one and the only true God, God the all-powerful, whose name is love!

"You are the God of the humble and the upright, the brave and the pure, the undaunted, and anyone who is born of You, who reaches out to You – overcomes the world!"

He rose to his feet, undressed slowly and climbed into his bed with a clear sense that the self within him had faded away into nothing, and all that was left was that perfect happiness, that the language of humans cannot even begin to describe.

THE TANNERIES ON THE EUPHRATES

On the anniversary of the repeal of the stern edict imposed on that remote region, in the matter of the rice levy, the office of the King's senior adviser, Nashdernach, was visited by a delegation representing the region. After the repeated bows and salutations, the delegation presented to the minister and his office clerks a gift of choice swine-meat, smoked in the traditional manner of that locality, and reels of coloured fabric of the finest quality.

Nashdernach was moved and he warmly thanked the members of the delegation, extolling for their benefit King Nebuchadnezzar the wise, the merciful and the valiant, conqueror of the world, and he expressed the emphatic hope that the people of this province not only would not disappoint His Majesty in any way, but would continue to demonstrate with signs and tokens their loyalty to him, and their appreciation of his beneficence and his generosity, this King who had dealt with them as a wise and loving father deals with his children.

The members of the delegation, twelve in number, were also moved, assuring Nashdernach there had been no need to raise the points that he had raised, and as proof of this they revealed to him that they themselves, of their own free will, and with a deep sense of gratitude that would never be erased from their hearts or the hearts of their children after them, had decided to do everything in their power to exceed the quota of rice imposed upon them, and also to treat the rice with special methods handed down among them since time immemorial, thus producing the finest-tasting rice to be found anywhere in the world, normally set aside for themselves and for their families.

Nashdernach entertained the twelve members of the delegation to superior wine from the royal cellars and wafers dipped in honey from the royal hives, and sent them on their way gratified and in good spirits.

The delegation left the office, and Nashdernach rubbed his hands together with emphatic satisfaction and a broad smile, approached him and said:

"I think we'll carry on believing in Him!"

He looked up at his superior, who was leaning towards him, awaiting his response. He said to him earnestly:

"There is another place where reliance on God and trust in Him would bear fruit worthy of the name!"

"What are you talking about?" Nashdernach pulled up a chair and sat facing him.

"The tanneries on the river Euphrates."

"Ah!" the minister retorted: "That business was brought to my attention not long ago, when we debated it in the general council. The feeling is that there's nothing to be gained by maintaining that plant and its idle work-force... oh yes, they are idle!" he insisted, noticing the spark of protest that flashed in his eyes: "The poor level of production doesn't justify the expense. Someone suggested those barefooted workers should be sent deep under ground, to the copper-mines, and given the opportunity to show how industrious they can be. We didn't discuss it at length, as there were more pressing and complicated issues to address, but the decision was taken to import hides from overseas. It seems that importation is preferable from every point of view, as the imported hides are much cheaper and of better quality. The decision hasn't yet been taken to the King for his assent, but we can assume it's going to be ratified soon. It's what the situation demands, the reality we have to face up to!" he declared, and was about to rise from his seat.

"If the esteemed minister will permit me!" he exclaimed, holding out a restraining hand and the other replied:

"Oh, why the formal manners, as alien to you as they are to me – call me Nashdernach! I'm perfectly capable of preserving my dignity even when I'm addressed by name!"

"You're right," he smiled and added: "I have a suggestion regarding this question of the tanners on the Euphrates."

"You're suggesting we trust in Him?" he asked, a faint smile extending his fleshy lips and flickering in his oily eyes.

"That's the first step," he declared in all seriousness and continued: "It seems to me it should be possible to increase levels of production and attain acceptable quotas in terms of time, price and quality, and then importation from abroad would be superfluous, no longer an option."

"How will you do that?" – Nashdernach expressed interest, settling back in his chair.

"Conditions need to be changed, meaning – conditions of accommodation and conditions of work!" he replied, adding: "After two months, I estimate, the tanners on the Euphrates will be producing hides in the quantity required and of the quality required – and more.

Nashdernach studied him with a probing look, and came to a decision:

"You have two months!" He rose from his seat, approached one of his clerks and dictated a brief memorandum which he signed with the stylus that the clerk offered him, then returned to him, took from his finger a big ring bearing the King's seal, laid it on the table and said:

"This will be of use to you during these two months! The one who wears this ring is acting on behalf of the King, and every citizen of Babylon, soldier or civilian, must defer to him as if to the King himself and do everything to assist him in the performance of his task."

"I shall need a few armed men for an escort."

"Take a troop of twenty, commanded by..." Nashdernach pondered, and he suggested: "Or-Nego?"

"Or-Nego has more important things to do, but if he is free and agrees to go with you – you have my consent and approval. Don't forget – two months starting from today!"

Or-Nego agreed readily and personally chose the twenty soldiers who would accompany them. Two days later the deputation set out for the journey to the Euphrates, with Or-Nego in the lead.

A morning of searing heat descended on the land, while a boisterous breeze from the East dried the air and made breathing difficult. The horses whinnied, the soldiers were grim-faced and taciturn. At the Gate of Marduk they were stopped by sentries, but showing the ring bearing the King's seal was enough to have the gates opened, and men of the guard detachment stood to attention on either side of the door, their spears raised in salute. The same procedure was followed at the Shamash Gate, the fortified aperture in the outer wall. And here the Euphrates was revealed to them in all its glory: turbid, angry waves trying in vain to defy the ruthless onslaught of the east wind – waters heavier and more menacing than those of any other river in the world.

And perhaps – he mused inwardly, confronting the

strange spectacle of the river – it isn't always like this, the ancient river, the Euphrates. Perhaps it's a mood that is turning it ugly, the east wind is provoking it and it's powerless to retaliate – as if it were human...

They advanced in a narrow file on a narrow path, paved with stones dredged from the river. At a steady canter they covered a distance of four or five Chaldean parasangs, until they reached the foot of an arid hill, topped by a long, low ridge. Stepping lightly the horses climbed the slope of the hill and stopped on the skyline. Stretched out before them was the tanners' camp of the Euphrates.

At the moment they arrived on the ridge, a half-naked, fleshy overseer, with a long thick whip made from a buffalo's tail, was lashing a strange creature which at best could be described as a walking skeleton, and a lean skeleton at that – hunched and naked, with bones protruding through the transparent embroidery of the skin that was filthy and covered with sores; skull, ribcage and pelvis all clearly visible. The blow from the whip set the skeleton reeling, and it fell to the ground and lay still. The overseer raised the whip, poised to strike again at the body recumbent in the sand.

"Stop!" he shouted in a voice that cut the air, sharper and perhaps more painful than the brandished whip.

The overseer froze where he stood and cautiously turned his shaved head, set on a short, thick neck, towards the ridge.

The arm raised in an unequivocal gesture, the line of silent, armed soldiers – spoke for themselves. The overseer's hand fell limply to his side, denied the pleasure of further assault on his skeletal victim, who seized the opportunity to crawl like an insect out of the range of the whip, making his escape on four legs and then on two, tottering like a drunkard.

Accompanied by Or-Nego, the soldiers following behind, he cautiously descended the hill. The overseer stood his ground, in sullen silence.

He ordered one of the soldiers to confiscate the overseer's whip. He handed it over sheepishly, all his confidence destroyed, and stooped, as if waiting for a blow that did not come.

"Call the commander of the camp!" he bellowed in the ear of the flustered flogger, who disappeared into a maze of flimsy hovels – little more than booths made of reed-thatch, supported by poles of rough, unplaned wood.

As far as the eye could see the shore was littered with these hovels, like tilting mushrooms in the forest, and beneath them, as Gershon had described, scraps of straw matting were visible. At the riverside itself, in long lines of at least fifty to a line, were the naked tanners, scraping the hides spread out on the water, working listlessly, as if liable to fall down and die at any moment.

He had counted some thirty such lines, when a tall, corpulent man appeared before him, wearing the faded cloak of a soldier and carrying a curved sword in a shining brass scabbard. He was accompanied by a half-naked, stout individual in a grubby loincloth, with a ring of coarse gold hanging from one ear. His face was so flabby that his eye-sockets were reduced to narrow slits. The man seemed unruffled and confident in himself, but it was possible to detect behind the narrow slits an alert and inquisitive look. He held another of those lethal whips made from buffalo tails.

"By what authority?" – the man with the sword chose to open the proceedings in a tone of indignation and menace.

"By authority of the King and on his behalf!" he

declared, holding out his hand and displaying the ring.

"Oh!" – suddenly the man with the sword was all reverence: "All praise to His Majesty King Nebuchadnezzar, the valiant and the wise, conqueror of the world!" he cried in a fulsome, deliberate tone, and bowed ostentatiously, his overseer accomplice following suit.

"How can I be of assistance?" the camp commander inquired.

"You'll find out soon enough," he answered him. "Is there somewhere where we can talk?"

"Please be so good as to accompany me!" – the man with the sword repeated his obsequious bow and turned in the direction from which he had come, adding: "Distinguished guests from the Palace! An honourable visit such as this I haven't enjoyed since I was sent to this place, eighteen long, hard years! I'm used to getting petty officials, in a hurry. *Load up the hides!* or – *Is this all there is?* Or – *This isn't enough to pay for the beans that you eat!* And then it's – *If you don't meet acceptable targets this plant will be closed and the workers will all be sent underground to dig for copper. And you will have to face the King and invent good excuses for your failure!* That's it, year in, year out. The same words, the same haste, the same sacks of beans in exchange for treated hides, the same loads of fresh hides brought in for treatment. It's just the people who change. You know how it is – the ones who stay close to His Majesty the King, the valiant and the wise, conqueror of the world, climb the ladder of promotion, whereas with people like us," – he raised his arm in a gesture of sorrow and resentment – "it's a case of out-of-sight and out-of-mind!" Animal cunning, thinly veiled scorn, indignation and obsequiousness were blended in the voice of the chief officer of the tanners' camp.

Still on horseback they arrived at a large, tent-like pavilion, made of coarse cloth designed to repel the heat. Two of the camp attendants hastened to draw back the door-flaps, bowing low as they invited the guests to enter.

With an agile leap he dismounted from Orelian and handed the reins to one of the soldiers. Or-Nego did likewise and both of them went into the tent, leaving the soldiers to wait outside. Their hosts followed them, closing the door-flaps for the sake of privacy. The space enclosed within the tent was extensive indeed, crammed with tiny tables, a few chests, and stools and chairs of every conceivable description. In a corner, partly shielded by a thick curtain which had once been white, a bed was visible. Somehow, most of the stench of the camp had been excluded from this place, leaving behind only the mildest irritation to the nostrils.

A table was placed at their disposal and high-backed chairs, the most dignified ones that their obsequious hosts could find. They sat on one side of the table and the camp representatives on the other. Silence reigned in the shady interior of the tent.

The overseer's narrow eye-slits flashed with naïve curiosity. The mottled eyes of the tall and corpulent one with the faded military cloak twitched restlessly in their sockets, contemptuous perhaps, or arrogant, or simply trying to disguise the fear that had overwhelmed them.

"The King is far from satisfied with the standards of work and the goods produced in this place!" he began in a steady, even voice. "So, there are going to be changes in patterns of work and in methods of supervision, and in the duties of overseers and their superiors. It is all written down here, and signed personally by Nashdernach, senior counsellor to Nebuchadnezzar, the wise and the valiant

King, conqueror of the world!"

He took a scroll from the inner pocket of his cloak and handed it to the camp commander. The latter squinted at it, in blank incomprehension. He realised that the man could not read, and neither could the overseer sitting beside him.

"I shall read the scroll to you!" he said, and he untied the ribbon, opened the scroll, and began to read:

"From this day forward the following arrangements are to be implemented in the tanners' camp by the river Euphrates:

"First clause – the labourers are to work from daybreak until midday. At midday, they will return to their quarters and eat a nutritious meal to include, besides lentils, rice or beans – also eggs, olives and such other vegetables as are available.

"Second – after this meal the labourers are to rest in their quarters for one hour, after which they are to work until sunset, and no later.

"Third – at the conclusion of their day's work, the tanners will receive a second meal, to consist of bread, onion and cheese, figs and dates.

"Fourth – in their free time the tanners will build themselves substantial huts, using proper construction materials, each of these units to accommodate two to four workers, and no more.

"Fifth – each tanner is entitle to receive two shirts, one cloak and two pairs of shoes per year, plus six loincloths.

"Sixth – the overseers are not to beat or lash the workers under any circumstances and for any reason. From this day forward, all whips belonging to the overseers are to be confiscated.

"Seventh – on the first day of every month, tanners,

guards and overseers alike will receive payment from the royal treasury.

"And the final clause – any deviation from the provisions set out in this document, however slight, will be construed as an insult to His Majesty the King. A serious infringement will be regarded as treason."

He read through the document a second time and reminded his hosts that two further copies of it existed – one in the royal archive and one in the minister's office. He demanded to hear them repeat the full text of the scroll, sentence by sentence and clause by clause, then handed the scroll to the man with the sword, rose from his seat and commanded:

"Confiscate all the whips and bring them here!"

"We hear and obey," the two of them replied in unison, turning towards the door.

"You, wait a moment!" he called to the overseer with the slits for eyes.

"Sir?" he asked in a wheedling voice.

"Your whip!" – he pointed to the buffalo's tail wrapped around his arm. "On the table, now!"

"As you wish, Sir!" He left the whip on the table and turned to go.

"Do you think it's going to work?" Or-Nego asked, impressed and sceptical in equal measure.

"By His grace!" he answered him, with an upward glance.

Soon after this they left the tanners' camp behind their backs, every man of the escort troop carrying a dozen or so whips on the pommel of his saddle. Their hosts accompanied them to the slopes of the parched hill, where they bowed to them and prostrated themselves on the ground, and went on bowing and prostrating until they disappeared behind the ridge.

Or-Nego, his soldiers and he inhaled the fresh air with relief, as the stench faded away.

"My impression is that those scoundrels will hoodwink the workers and return to their evil ways," was Or-Nego's comment – "without whips admittedly, or perhaps that should be, without whips made from buffalo tails; and they won't give even a moment's thought to any kind of reform, to say nothing of the contents of the scroll, that they're supposed to have learned by heart!"

"Three days from now the first deliveries of food will arrive, consignments of nuts and almonds and eggs and fresh vegetables, and those consignments will remind them of our meeting and of the scroll that they have with them!"

"I think the consignments are more likely to inflame their primitive lust for profit," Or-Nego objected – "and they'll sell off the food and pocket the proceeds."

"We'll come back here in two weeks and see how the scheme has been implemented."

"That's the right idea," Or-Nego declared with the restrained enthusiasm that was his habitual tone – "we come back and check!"

They urged their horses on and quickly covered the ground. The hot wind had subsided. When they reached the gates the sentries did not delay them, but opened the gates as soon as they saw them approaching and stood to attention with spears raised in salute.

When they reached the forecourt of the royal palace, passing Or-Nego's spacious residence, the officer broke the silence, leaning towards him and saying:

"Adelain would be delighted if you would visit us!"

"Not this time, Or-Nego, begging her pardon and yours! I have much to do and Nashdernach is waiting for me."

Or-Nego was not offended by his refusal, and he appreciated this.

They parted company with an exchange of bows, agreeing to meet again two weeks hence for the return visit to the tanners' camp on the Euphrates.

If their first visit had astonished the supervisor of the camp and the overseer who was his acolyte, this time they were stunned into immobility, standing and gaping as the riders approached, like pillars of salt, or as if they had swallowed their tongues. The stench was as foul as ever, and the tanners were not noticeably more motivated than before, still standing in long silent lines in the turbid surf of the Euphrates, listlessly beating and scraping the hides. The overseers no longer brandished buffalo-tail whips, but used whatever implements came to hand – sticks, ropes or even stones with which they pelted their human targets, sometimes to encourage and sometimes as a release from boredom, a pleasurable pastime following the sumptuous meal that they had enjoyed at the expense of their workers.

There was no need for exchanges of words. The facts spoke for themselves. The man with the sword and his accomplice regained their wits and threw themselves down in the dust, even kissing the hooves of their horses, which whinnied and shied away from them. They wailed and wept, reeling off the names of wives and children and elderly parents who depended on them, and the supervisor ripped his faded cloak and beat his hairy chest and threw dust over his balding head, pulling out the whiskers of his greasy beard and howling incessantly. His assistant stripped stark naked and went on plastering himself with dust until he looked like a scarecrow.

They were both clapped into manacles and led to the tent where the previous encounter had taken place two weeks before.

Or-Nego and he took their places on the same high-backed chairs as before, the difference being that this time their interlocutors were grovelling tearfully at their feet. Two soldiers stood behind them, drawn swords in their hands.

He demanded that the guards of the camp and the overseers be summoned before him, and soon the tent was crowded with half-naked overseers and guards dressed in faded robes of indeterminate colour. He asked them if their superiors, the men now wallowing in the dust, had read them the King's edict, and the answers that he received were hesitant, mumbled and sometimes self-contradictory. Until one of the overseers came forward and said that their superiors had told them something about instructions from the King, and furthermore – there was among them a man who could read and write and he was asked to read them the contents of the scroll. His name was Harvud, and he was the scion of a distinguished family, fallen on hard times. He did as he was asked, reading the portentous words and even interpreting them for the benefit of the less educated among them. And then those two – and he pointed to the camp commander and his overseer acolyte – assaulted and abused Harvud and ripped the scroll to shreds, and threw the fragments on the ground and trampled them into the dust. And Harvud waited until the two of them had calmed down, and reminded them that according to the terms of the royal edict that they had just destroyed, they were guilty of treason and their lives were in danger. And they attacked him again and beat him with their fists, and not content with this they ordered that he be flogged. It was lucky for him that there was a shortage of whips in the camp, or he might not have survived the punishment.

"Where is this Harvud?" he wanted to know.

A lean young man, with flashing eyes and upright stance, wearing a faded but clean robe, stepped forward from among the group of guards and stood before him.

"You can read and write?" he asked him.

He nodded.

He handed him the copy of the scroll that he had brought with him and ordered him to read it aloud. In a ponderous but clearly audible voice he read out all the clauses one after the other and when he had finished, offered it back to him.

"Keep it!" he commanded, "And henceforward, you are to uphold it in the letter and in the spirit!" And in a solemn tone he added: "In the name of His Majesty the King I hereby appoint you the commanding officer of the camp of the tanners on the Euphrates!" From amid the massed ranks of the guards and the overseers a murmur of assent and deference was heard.

"And what's to become of us?" the former sword-bearer cried plaintively.

"You should lose your heads," he declared, the wailing of jackals accompanying his words – "for defying the King and disobeying his commandments! And yet – compassionate and merciful is His Majesty King Nebuchadnezzar, and since I have been appointed by the King's senior counsellor to do his will and judge in his name, I decree that you are to work as tanners for the remainder of your lives, and Harvud will supervise you and check the quality of your work, and if he has occasion to report the slightest infringement of the rules on your part, you will be led in chains before His Majesty and he will decide your fate!"

A nightmarish howl accompanied his last words, a kind of sound not easily identified as human, and evidently intended as an expression of gratitude for this show of leniency.

The supervisor's curved sword, in its brass scabbard, he handed over solemnly, before the eyes of the assembled company, to young Harvud, and there and then he had him swear faithful service to the King of Babylon and obedience to his laws and ordinances.

Once this oath had been sworn, they rose and left the camp.

About a month later, the first batch of hides worked by the tanners under the new dispensation was delivered, and it was more than satisfactory in both quantity and quality.

And when the day came, he accompanied Nashdernach and his three personal bodyguards on a further visit to the camp.

They arrived towards evening, when the tanners were sitting in rows on benches at tables, their faces bright and convivial. They were eating their second meal of the day, and all were wearing freshly laundered clothes. On seeing them they rose as one man to greet them, and even surprised them with an honorific anthem of their own composition, although it took three renditions for all the words to be deciphered:

There once was an angel who looked down on the earth, and he saw the suffering endured by the tanners on the river Euphrates. And the angel turned to the all-powerful God and told Him, weeping, my Lord and Father Almighty, God the all-powerful, I can no longer bear to look down on the earth at the dreadful plight of my brothers, human beings, the tanners by the Euphrates.

Send me and I shall do all I can to ease their pain, expel those who beat and chastise them, bring their agony to an end and succour to their souls. The all-powerful God was pleased by the words of his angel, by his heart, a true heart of gold, and his generous spirit. And He sent him on his way with a blessing and dressed him in human form and called him Belteshazzar, and appointed him to serve King Nebuchadnezzar, His Majesty!

And the angel in human form did not delay, and he went to Nashdernach, chief counsellor to the King, to complain at the conditions of the tanners. And Nashdernach arose, and put on his finger the ring of authority, and sent him down to the river, to the tanners working there. And Belteshazzar, the angel in human form, went down to that dark and evil place, and summoned the guards and gathered the slavedrivers, and told them of the King's command – that they should no longer chastise his brothers, nor make their lives a misery, nor torment them with abuse and arduous labour – but should give them clothing, put food in their mouths and a roof over their heads, and payment in due time. And they tried to dupe him, swearing many an oath to obey his commandments but with other intentions. And the angel in human form knew neither rest nor sleep until he had completed his mission, returning to his human brothers, and casting in chains all those who had persecuted them, the tanners on the Euphrates, and he appointed a new chief, one with a human heart, and he turned their misery into joy and their pain into delight!

"They even mentioned me in their song!" Nashdernach declared, fighting back the tears – "Quite unjustly, of course..."

"With absolute justice!" he retorted, adding: "Without your consent, nothing could have been done!"

"Not my consent but His!" Nashdernach corrected him, with a reverent glance heavenwards, continuing in the same vein: "So, we shall go on trusting in Him!"

"At all times and forever!" he concluded.

"And what became of those two scoundrels, the former commander and his sidekick, the fat flogger?" Nashdernach asked Harvud, who accompanied them part of the way.

"They tried working in the kitchen at first, but they were dismissed from there on account of their laziness."

"Who dismissed them?" he asked with interest.

"The cooks themselves, who used to be their accomplices in thieving and embezzlement."

"And what are they doing now?"

"Beating the most rancid hides that we can find. Surprisingly, they're not making a bad job of it!" Harvud expressed his sincere bemusement.

"You'll make true tanners of them yet!" was Nashdernach's jovial comment.

ON FIGS AND NUTS

One of those glorious evenings, rare in Babylon but familiar in the homeland, when the sky is a regal cloak of velvet and the first stars are the jewels in the crowns of angels, chanting "All Hail" to the God above – one such evening the slave informed him that a gentleman named Denur-Shag was asking to see him.

When Denur-Shag entered the room he rose to meet him; the two of them shook hands warmly and exchanged affectionate slaps on the shoulder, looking into one another's eyes with undisguised pleasure.

The teacher's sparse beard, once blond, was flecked with threads of grey.

"Old age creeping on!" cried Denur-Shag with that lively, vigorous voice of his, seeing the look in the other's eyes.

"Among our people grey hair is not a sign of old age!" he commented mildly.

"What does it betoken then?" Denur-Shag asked with interest, sitting down on one side of the high, polished table, with its cloth embroidered in blue and silver stripes – an impressive combination.

"Wisdom!" he replied, taking his place on the other side of the table.

"One who is endowed with wisdom is endowed with it from birth!" declared Denur-Shag with dignity, leaning back as far as the chair would allow him. "It's a gift of God," he went on to say, "and it doesn't depend on beard or hair of any style or any colour!"

"All the same," he riposted, a smile rising to his face

when he spotted a few oil-stains on the teacher's cloak, too big for him as usual – "as one grows older, so wisdom ripens and bears fruit!"

"Always assuming," Denur-Shag persisted – "that one was endowed with wisdom from birth in the first place!"

He made no further comment, and no attempt to challenge his guest's conviction.

It was then that the slave came in with a tray of inlaid silver bearing dried figs, almonds and nuts, a jug of honey-water and two clay cups.

"Is this your supper?" Denur-Shag asked curiously.

He nodded.

"An interesting meal, to be sure!" exclaimed Denur-Shag. "In content and in intention!" he added, and proceeded to explain: "The meal is modest but not frugal, nourishing but not fattening, mild but not bland! It is very possible, esteemed master, assistant and right-hand man of the King's chief counsellor as you are – that I have things to learn from you, especially where suppers are concerned, and I shall be your most avid disciple!"

"If there's no other subject that will make you my disciple..." he began playfully, but Denur-Shag interrupted him:

"There is!" he cried eagerly, with all the enthusiasm of a pupil who has just chanced upon the right answer to a question and cannot wait to reveal it to the teacher.

"And that is?"

"Faith!" exclaimed Denur-Shag, bringing his tiny, round fist down with a resounding thump on the elegant table-cloth, as if stating an incontrovertible fact.

"Faith is the gift of God," he declared earnestly, concluding: "And faith is the mother of all wisdom!"

"And have you received this gift?" – Denur-Shag's eyes flashed.

"It's a gift that is offered to every human being, and it's up to him to decide whether to accept it or spurn it."

"I assume that *you* have accepted it!"

"By the grace and the mercy of God!" he asserted, in a voice blending reverence and joyous freedom.

Denur-Shag took a shelled nut, put it to his mouth, added half a fig and while chewing, slowly and deliberately, closed his eyes with an air of contentment and remarked:

"The nut and the almond and the fig – they also originated from the Garden of Eden!" As there was no response to this he cleared his throat, held his mighty head high, shifted restlessly in his seat and finally broached the issue that was the real purpose of his visit:

"As you know, there are laws that are written and laws that are unwritten, and both kinds are of equal force, imposing obligations, usually heavy ones, on mortal creatures, while threatening penalties for those who infringe or fail to uphold these laws, whether written or unwritten."

Again Denur-Shag took a large almond, fresh and appetising, wrapped it in half a fig before putting it in his mouth, as if this were some superstitious ritual, chewing with the same deliberation as before, closing his eyes again and adding a hedonistic smacking of the lips.

He waited for the teacher to continue, unsure where all this was leading.

Denur-Shag swallowed his mouthful, and resumed:

"Remember that the glorious kingdom of Babylon does not look kindly upon celibacy, and by remaining a bachelor you are refusing to contribute in any way to the increase and the prosperity of the population. This is a law that is not to be infringed, and there are penalties attached to it..." Denur-Shag chuckled pleasantly, adding:

"This is a law that applies especially to those holding any kind of public office!"

"I haven't been approached about this yet."

"You will be!" Denur-Shag assured him, "And then you'll be in something of a predicament. You'll be made a generous offer that you simply can't refuse."

"Things don't seem to be as serious as all that!" he declared.

"I don't know what yardstick you use to judge the seriousness of things," Denur-Shag retorted, "but what I've just told you is what is going to happen, and is bound to happen – and happen soon!" And seeing the questioning look in his eyes he explained: "If you don't take the initiative yourself, it will be taken by your friends or those who consider themselves your friends. And you'll get a proposal that you can't reject and you can't ignore."

"I've already turned down one such proposal and I refused to discuss it, but in such a way as to leave no hard feelings behind."

"I can well believe it!" Denur-Shag concurred, adding: "But the next offer that you receive – and it's coming soon – is one that you can't afford to refuse or reject under any circumstances whatsoever."

"And who is the man whose offer, whatever it may be, I can't refuse or reject?" he demanded to know, sounding almost indignant.

"His Majesty the King!"

He weighed these words, astounded to the roots of his soul, and finally responded:

"Are my personal affairs discussed at such a high level?"

"In a tightly regulated state, like Babylon, citizens have no privacy and no personal affairs. The citizens of the kingdom of Babylon are loyal to their King and seek his approval, and they worship and revere him above any god or image of a god, and they hide nothing from him. In fact, they consider themselves honoured to keep no secrets from him. At any rate, that's the theory, and it explains why the citizens of Babylon are the most smug people on the earth! And if it is ever revealed that any subject, through negligence or forgetfulness, to say nothing of malice, has concealed any detail of his private life, this will arouse the justified anger of the King, and his fate will not be a good one, not by any means"

Changing the subject abruptly he asked:

"Aren't you going to join me in this agreeable meal?"

"I'm accustomed to praying before I eat."

"Go ahead then!" the balding, middle-aged man urged him genially.

"May the food that comes from Your hand sustain our hearts and purify us on our way to You! Amen and Amen!" – and immediately after the blessing he took a nut from the tray, wrapped it in half a fig and put it into his mouth, chewing steadily.

"You've been named as a candidate for several marriages," Denur-Shag went on to say. "The charming daughter of one of the King's senior officers has been mentioned, but if that idea doesn't appeal to you for reasons best known to yourself, then you will be offered one of thirty-seven beautiful princesses, daughters of the King himself, and whichever she is you cannot reject her without causing offence to her father, the King. You know perfectly well that such a refusal would be seen as a crude and premeditated insult to the honour of the Crown, and you know the penalty for that..." Denur-Shag drew his finger across his throat, a meaningful gesture.

"How can it be?" – he expressed his sincere bemusement – "How is it that so much priority is being given to such a peripheral, essentially pointless issue, as my future wedding?"

"In the royal palace, there is endless, unremitting activity," Denur-Shag sighed as he split the kernel of a walnut into two equal parts, with intense concentration. "A living, vibrant body is the palace of His Majesty King Nebuchadnezzar, and his courtiers never sleep, never take a moment's rest. They are pushing forward the affairs of state, and advancing their own interests and the interests of others, in the best possible way of course, according to their acute perceptions and clarity of thought. It may well be that somebody is anxious on your behalf, concerned at your bachelor status and afraid lest you fall into the embrace of the wrong woman, and is preparing for you, secretly and in a spirit of true friendship and fellowship worthy of the name – your future bride. Something which you would never regret, and which you might even find impossible to regret, and most important of all, as has already been made clear to you – something which you cannot under any circumstances reject or refuse. But if you have other ideas," Denur-Shag reverted to his equable tone of voice, assessing him with a quick glance and then turning away before continuing: "Move quickly and establish facts on the ground, anticipate, put the remedy in place before trouble strikes! And as far as my knowledge extends, and if my memory is not misleading me," the guest looked up and glanced at his host with an air of innocence – "this expression 'putting the remedy before the trouble' is a good old-fashioned Hebrew phrase, or I should say, it isn't a part of the new, 'progressive' language, or 'Jewish Hebrew' as it is currently called."

A warm glow filled his heart. He gazed at Denur-Shag, who had gone back to the choice nuts and the almonds and the figs, the lines of his face tensed as he studiously ignored his radiant look, expressing warmth, friendship and gratitude.

"It happens occasionally that someone has the opportunity to act as an envoy of Providence!" commented Denur-Shag, uncomfortable with the tide of gratitude flowing in his direction.

"Not everyone is endowed with that special grace, to be the redeeming envoy of Providence!" he retorted.

"You can be sure that these special people aren't balding teachers, who have to deal with artisans of all descriptions as well as ignorant dolts!" said Denur-Shag evasively, returning his attention to the almonds and nuts. He carefully poured himself a cup of honey-water, and drank it all down in one long gulp.

"These people are called true friends, and they are sometimes rated more highly than the ministering angels themselves!"

"Such concepts apply only to people of truly outstanding faith!" Denur-Shag protested, "And I can't claim the honour or the privilege of counting myself among them!"

"Not everyone who calls himself a believer is a believer, and not everyone who excludes himself from the category of believers is lacking in faith."

"Who then is the true believer?" Denur-Shag asked with genuine interest, the look in his eyes pure and childlike – and childishly innocent.

"He who loves God with all his heart and all his might, and his neighbour – as himself!"

"Just as I feared! Such people are prodigies!"

"They never see themselves as prodigies!"

"They truly don't see themselves as prodigies, or are they just pretending they don't see themselves that way?"

"They really and truly don't see themselves that way!" he insisted.

"In that case…" Denur-Shag hesitated "…in that case I suppose I could apply for membership of that unexceptional family of believers. And by the way, if you're interested in Judah, where things appear to be going from bad to worse and nothing is as it should be – your fellow exile, whose Chaldean name is Abed-Nego and whose Hebrew name is Azariah, is putting together some kind of expedition, heading for Jerusalem to recruit skilled craftsmen. He has been given the necessary permits, and I advise you to talk to him at the first opportunity!"

He was distressed to hear of the state of affairs in his homeland – "going from bad to worse", evidently, and "nothing as it should be".

"The surprising thing," the guest remarked as if reading his thoughts, "is that a land such as your homeland, where one would suppose there are many people of faith, which appears from outside to be a place reserved exclusively for people of outstanding faith – is on the verge of catastrophe, and there is nothing anyone can do to prevent that catastrophe!"

"As I told you, not everyone who seems to be a believer or is called a believer or calls himself a believer – is a believer. People lie to themselves, and degeneracy sets in, and collapse is not far behind, with destruction closing the circle. Our great prophet, Isaiah, described it thus:

Then the Lord said: Because the women of Zion hold themselves high and walk with necks outstretched and wanton glances, moving with mincing gait and jingling feet, the Lord will give the women of Zion bald heads, the Lord will strip the hair from their foreheads. In that day the Lord will take away all finery: anklets, discs, crescents, pendants, bangles, coronets, head-bands, armlets, necklaces, lockets, charms, signets, nose-rings, fine dresses, mantles, cloaks, flounced skirts, scarves of gauze, kerchiefs of linen, turbans and flowing veils. So instead of perfume you shall have the stench of decay, and a rope in place of a girdle, baldness instead of hair elegantly coiled, a loin-cloth of sacking instead of a mantle, and burning instead of beauty, and your men shall fall by the sword and your warriors in battle."

Denur-Shag listened solemnly. When the recitation was over, he had his say:

"These words of the holy man of God – a vivid description of a state of affairs that leads always to failure and destruction! If your people had only the sense to grasp this, like that people that once dwelt in Nineveh, that put on sackcloth and ashes and the Lord revoked the doom that He had called down upon it– these disasters would not have befallen it. The same applies to all nations on the face of the earth, at all times and in all places, from time immemorial to the end of all the generations – those who cannot stop themselves in time, will be forever lost!" Denur-Shag declared, his brow wrinkled and sorrow in his eyes.

"The truth is always simple, and he who does not try to flee from it and does not reject it out of hand – no disaster in the world can befall him! And the contrary applies – he who ignores the explicit truth, his doom is sealed! As the doom of your people has been sealed in our times, and as the doom of the Chaldean people shall be sealed, likewise the doom of every other people and nation and race – if in the days to come they try to ignore the truth!"

"You are a prophet!" he exclaimed with warmth.

"Perish the thought, Beltezhazzar!" Denur-Shag protested, lifting up both hands before him as if to defend himself. "I am no prophet nor the son of a prophet, just a man endowed with a modicum of healthy intelligence!"

He rose from his seat, stretching his limbs.

"We have babbled on too long!" he sighed, gathering up the tails of his tattered gown, "And perhaps we have steered in directions that were not the most appropriate, or should I say – not the most practical. Still, we have not committed any sin, perpetrated any dastardly crime, broken any law, written or unwritten – nor have we neglected the issues of the day!" He raised his arm and held up a finger as a warning signal, then lowered his arm and spoke again as if simply making casual conversation:

"There is a certain energetic and exceedingly resourceful trader, who is doing great and wonderful things in the service of the King. One of the exiles of course – Chaldeans have never been renowned for their commercial acumen, only for what they call 'valour' – which translates as slavish devotion to instinctive violence. This exile, who is of the same age as you and arrived with you in Babylon and so it seems, is also a former pupil of mine, has access to every corner of the palace of King Nebuchadnezzar, His Majesty, the valiant and the wise. And he knows how to whisper, he's a master of the whispering art, as you might put it in your new-fangled style of Hebrew, but there's nothing entertaining, no novelty or fascination in the gossip that he peddles. It is highly probable that all this urgency to push you up the ladder of Chaldean propriety, to draw attention to your prolonged celibacy, and even to choose for you a well-connected bride, a Chaldean through and through – all this originates from the whispering of that trader. And you," he turned to him as if remembering the essence and dispensing with the inconsequential – "be well, my pupil hitherto, my master and my teacher henceforward!"

With a smooth, yet imperious movement, Denur-Shag raised a silencing finger to his pursed lips, and he restrained himself and did not respond. They repeated their exchange of firm handshakes and cordial shoulder-slapping, and the slave escorted the guest to the main door and saw him on his way.

BETWEEN THE WALLS

He asked after Azariah at his lodging. A servant told him he had gone to visit the parents of his betrothed, Havatzelet, of the family of Joseph Hannagid, who lived in one of the houses between the walls, beneath the carved lion, the last one on the north-eastern wall.

He left the residential apartments and before setting out in the direction of this house, sent word to Nashdernach that he expected to be absent from the palace for the rest of the day.

The climate was pleasant, with the sun tending westward and a light breeze blowing. He was in no hurry, and was glad to inhale the fresh air of the open spaces.

His time was divided, usually, between sitting in the office of the King's chief adviser and his quarters in the vicinity of that office. Sometimes he also dealt with official business in his home, and sometimes – until a late hour of the night. Because of his seclusion from the sun, involuntary seclusion as it was, and prolonged confinement within enclosed spaces, his cheeks were turning pale. Noting this, Nashdernach used to urge him to leave the office for recreation, despite the pressure of work, and if only for a short time, to mingle with people and breathe the outside air. "Conversation with simple folk," Nashdernach was fond of saying, "is a thousand times more refreshing and instructive than all the dry scrolls and tablets that are gathering dust in the royal library!" It was true, he often spent his few free moments in that library.

The open air cheered his spirits and he strode the broad royal highway at a brisk pace, skipping occasionally and feeling that his feet would gladly have sprouted wings and carried him far away, somewhere over the horizon, towards that bright iridescence, into the very enchanted heart of the light.

The road stretched the full length of the north-western wall and it was straight, gleaming, and teeming with people in a hurry, with horses and carts, with cattle and oxen uttering their restrained, resigned lowing, white foam dripping from their mouths. At the side of the road he caught sight of a man with grey hair and beard, staring blankly at a cart of which one of the two wheels had come off the axle and rolled away into the dust, while the she-ass was sprawled on the ground and the load, sacks of carobs for cattle-fodder, remained on the cart. The man stood beside the stricken vehicle, baffled and helpless.

He hurried towards him, bent down and tried to lift the cart and free the she-ass from the yoke. And then he realised just how heavy the cart was, realised too that the animal was showing no inclination towards moving, and all this time the owner of the cart was standing aside, staring at him in bemusement, as if he had lost all his senses. A crowd began to gather around, composed mainly of women, old folk and children, as most of the men were working at this time in the fields and the factories, and all of those present looked on with astonishment, clicking tongues and offering advice, and pointing out what had caused the cart to capsize – a paving-stone that had not been bedded in properly with the others; the carter should have paid more attention and steered his beast away from the obstacle, instead of bringing down all this trouble on his greying and balding head.

When he asked one of the youths to come forward and hold the shaft for him, and addressed the same request to an older man standing amid the spectators, both backed away hastily and disappeared into the crowd.

Again he gripped the shaft, exerting all his strength, and suddenly the she-ass came back to life and rose to stand on her feet, pulling the cart up with her, and before it could collapse again he supported its weight and shouted to the carter to fetch the wheel that was lying at his feet. The old man was jolted out of his stupor and he picked up the wheel and fitted it on the axle, and with a joint effort they heaved it into place. Once the cart was standing upright on both its wheels, he found the peg that held the errant wheel and secured it, hammering it home with a stone.

The old man hugged and embraced him, and showered him with thanks and benedictions and compliments, and invited him to come to his house between the walls, to be a guest beneath his roof and dine with him and his family.

He freed himself from the old man's grateful embrace, reminded him mildly that "all praises are due to God", and was about to turn and disappear into the crowd, when his ear caught something in the old man's exuberant and barely coherent litany of thanks – the reference to a house "between the walls".

"Is that where you live, between the walls?" he asked.

"Yes indeed, most generous of masters!" the old man replied, gratified by this sympathetic display of interest. "And I shall be delighted, as will all the members of my family be delighted, if my lord will honour us with a visit and sit down to dine with us..."

"At all events," he said smiling as he brushed dust from his cloak, "I shall accompany you to your house, and it may well be that we dine together yet, as I am on my way to visit one of the families living between the walls, under the last of the lion carvings."

"That is the place!" cried the old man, his eyes sparkling. "It must be the will of God, that I met you on the way and I can guide you to those houses between the walls," – and he turned and asked him in a more practical tone: "And the family that my lord is visiting, what is the name?"

"Joseph Hannagid," he answered him.

"He is my brother!" exclaimed the old man, raising his arms and waving them as an expression of astonishment. "Is he expecting you?"

"Not at all," he answered him.

"So why do you need to see him?" the old man asked, sounding disappointed.

"A friend of mine, named Abed-Nego, is betrothed to your brother's daughter, Havatzelet."

"Aha!" the old man expressed pleasurable surprise, drumming his fingers on his temples. "A-ha!" he repeated with emphasis and went on to say, "In my homeland of Judah they say that a lucky man such as yourself must be a saint because... because..." – the old man racked his brains, trying to dredge up the proverb he wanted.

"The one he is going to, comes to meet him!" – he completed it for him.

The old man, about to urge on his she-ass, turned to him and gave him a long look. His eyes were bright, tending towards green, glassy. Finally he asked:

"Is my lord a Jew?"

"He is."

"One of those boys who came with the betrothed of my niece, Havatzelet?"

"One of those boys," he confirmed.

"And your clothes tell me that you hold a senior post in

the court of the King of the Chaldeans!"

"I wouldn't call it a senior post," he answered him with a smile, and suddenly felt a strange pang of resentment, for no good reason that he could think of. "I work in the office of one of the ministers, that's all. Like Azariah!" he concluded as if talking to himself.

"Like Azariah!" the other repeated like an echo.

The she-ass waited patiently for her master to pay her some attention, and he did so eventually, gripping the halter and tugging at it roughly with a cry of "Let's go!"

"My name is Raphael," the old man introduced himself and went on to say: "Today I have earned the privilege of performing a sacred service, helping a righteous man to find his way. What is my lord's name?"

"Belteshazzar."

"The Jewish name, I mean!" he insisted drily.

"Daniel."

"I think I have heard of you, and of your activities. Activities which are strange indeed!" – the old man snorted and added: "Or so rumour has it..."

The old man lowered his head, with an air of gravity, tugged at the halter with an effort and without turning to look at him, spoke again:

"I have saved my esteemed lord much toil and travail. It isn't easy to find the way to our house between the walls. The Chaldeans ignore us and would prefer to forget that we exist. To them, we are strange creatures, and they miss no opportunity to report us to the authorities, over the most trivial of matters. And they are quick to investigate, arresting innocent people and dragging them through the courts, and they are not content with warnings or with lenient fines, as is the way of the world, but they demand gold shekels, and the Chaldean shekel," the old man explained, "is worth twelve gold shekels from

Jerusalem. And all this – for some footling misdemeanour!"

"And what are the crimes that the Chaldeans accuse you of?" – he listened intently to the old man's words.

"From disrespect or contempt, as they call it, towards some pompous official or other – to sedition and incitement to rebellion. And this of course we vehemently deny, with all the force that we can muster, and still we are dragged from court to court, paying lavish bribes until the charges are dropped. For sedition and incitement to rebellion there is only one punishment – death!" the old man concluded.

"Why pay bribes, when it's all down to slander?" he asked innocently.

"My lord has the demeanour of a dignified gentleman, and he has a wise look about him, and even his high forehead tells of intelligence – and yet his question is naïve, if he will excuse my uncouth tongue," – and without waiting for a response, the old man continued: "Venomous tongues and bloodshed have always existed and will exist until the coming of the Lord's Anointed. Until then – we must pay bribes, if we don't want to give the Chaldeans the pleasure of chopping off the heads of pious Jews!"

"I do not share your opinion!" he retorted with a touch of asperity, meant to ensure that his words would be heard, and indeed – the old man paid close attention, listening tensely.

"You have to trust in God and turn to Him, and lay your entreaty before Him and cleave to Him firmly and believe in Him – then everything will be settled properly, and peaceably, without bribes and lies and deception!"

"You speak with great eloquence, Sir!" the balding old man required, a bitter kind of smile passing like a shadow over his tanned, deeply wrinkled features. "This God of ours, Himself and in person, neglected us and abandoned us on account of our iniquities, and hid His face from us, till the uncircumcised and the Gentile, who knew him not, triumphed over His holy people and did with it as they pleased!"

"He did not neglect us nor abandon us – it is we who neglected and abandoned Him, and did what was evil in His eyes, and closed our ears lest we hear the word of His holy prophets!"

"I see, esteemed Sir, that you know a great deal, but in my humble opinion, all of your knowledge is flawed, flawed fundamentally! We have to fight the pagan and the Gentile, we have to defend Jerusalem the Holy City, destroy the Chaldean conquerors and put them to the sword, subdue them and annihilate them, leave no memory or vestige of them! And if God is truly with us and we are, as He says, His chosen people – then let this God of ours stand at the head of our armies and rout our foes, and bring a swift end upon our enemies."

The two men exchanged glances. The old man's eyes flared and burned with dry fire, zealous and vengeful; his eyes shone with a light that was all invincible strength.

For a brief moment, the old man looked away, yanking at the halter of the she-ass with quite unnecessary force. The unfortunate creature uttered a whinny of helplessness, or of weariness, or of both.

A portion of the route passed by in silence, and suddenly the old man turned to face him and said:

"Now I remember who you are, esteemed Sir, and the illustrious deeds that you have performed! At first I couldn't believe what I was hearing – the very notion that a man of intelligence, with Judah for a homeland and Jerusalem for a home town, could do the things that you have done! I refused to believe. But now, having heard your voice and listened to your words, I believe it absolutely! Was it not you who took pity on the race of the tanners, most of whom are pagan Chaldeans and only a minority are exiles, and you treated them with kindness, and brought them from death to life, and gave them food to eat and clothes to wear, so they might flourish and prosper, the better to conquer and enslave other peoples, as they have done with us, the chosen people of God... And we have heard of your compassionate heart and how you reduced the quota of rice demanded in tribute from an impoverished region, and were it not for this reduction they would have rebelled against King Nebuchadnezzar and shaken his power, and this would have helped us, the Jews, in our struggle against the Chaldean conqueror! Is it not incredible," the old man cried, his voice hoarse and strained – "an intelligent Jewish youth, strengthening the hand of the Chaldeans against his own people? Do you realise esteemed Sir what this means, does my lord even know *who he is*?"

He restrained and suppressed his swelling rage, keeping his temper, and answered the old man quietly:

"One who trusts in God, and trusts absolutely!"

The old man's wrath was seething, beyond any control. He turned on him and it seemed he was about to attack him with his fists, but then he tripped on an irregular paving-stone, stumbled and fell headlong in the roadway.

He leaned over him and tried to help him up. The old man pushed away his outstretched hands, but finally, seeing he could not possibly stand up unaided, he allowed himself to be helped, with an expression of revulsion and distaste, and once back on his feet he said:

"You are a sorcerer Sir, a sorcerer and a prig and..." – the word stuck in his throat and would not emerge from his dry mouth.

The old man's glassy eyes were livid with disgust. He gave him a baleful look, and without another word spoken, he gripped the halter of his she-ass once more, leading her with surprising tenderness, and continued on his way.

He was left standing, waiting for the old man to move on and disappear from view, but he stopped the cart, turned back and said in a low voice:

"I very much hope that his honour will not disgrace me, but will come with me as was agreed between us, before I spoke out so foolishly. When all is said and done, a man of my age is apt to be foolish! Please show me a little tolerance, and forgive and have mercy, and do not add further grief to my grief!"

Without another word spoken, he joined him.

Towards evening, when the sun had disappeared but not yet withdrawn its light, they turned northwards from the internal gate of Marduk and stood before the tall outer wall, at its eastern end, and here he realised the old man had been right when he spoke of doing him a favour, since he would never have imagined that below the last of the reliefs there was an aperture almost invisible to the eye, low down but just wide enough to squeeze through, and from this point a short dust path led down to a dense cluster of low buildings made of rough stone, standing on the narrow patch of ground with an air of brooding defiance and proud alienation.

The old man led him to one of the narrow entrances to an extensive building and said to him:

"This is where my brother lives, the family of Joseph Hannagid, that you are seeking! And forgive me if I have offended or insulted you, but Judah my homeland and

Jerusalem its capital are very dear to my heart!"

"They are dear to the heart of every Jew," he responded calmly.

"No two hearts are alike!" declared old Raphael and he disappeared behind the cluster of silent houses.

He knocked on the door. An attractive girl opened it and asked what he wanted.

"I'm looking for my friend, Azariah!"

"Oh!" – and with a gentle, graceful movement the girl held the door wide open and said:

"He's here, and I'm sure he'll be glad to see you!" It was both question and statement. "Who are you Sir, and how shall I announce you?"

"Daniel," he said.

She ushered him into a dingy hallway, asked him to wait for a moment, went inside the house and called: "Az-ar-iah!"

He heard his friend's cheerful voice:

"Here I am!"

The girl called out again:

"A distinguished gentleman, looks like a scholar, his name is Daniel... I asked him to wait for you in the lobby."

Before she had finished the sentence Azariah was there before him, holding out a warm and firm hand to shake his, then drawing him into a long, low room, lit by a broad window.

In the room sat a middle-aged man, his face lean and an intense look in his eyes, with an air of confidence about him, the confidence of one who is well aware of his own worth.

"This is Saul, my future father-in-law," Azariah introduced him.

They bowed to one another in the Chaldean fashion.

"And this is Daniel, my friend from childhood. His Chaldean name is Belteshazzar," Azariah concluded.

"*That* Belteshazzar?" asked the man, who was sitting on the end of a broad bench which also served as a bed, made of unplaned wood and still smelling faintly of pine, strewn with mats as a substitute for a mattress.

"That Belteshazzar!" Azariah confirmed with a sigh, and invited his friend into one of the several side-chambers opening off the main room.

He entered the little side-chamber with its narrow, curtained window and prevalent gentle gloom, and sat down on the one chair. Azariah sat on the bed, made of the same wood as the other but rather more comfortably upholstered, with straw mattress, blankets and thick embroidered quilts, warm and woolly.

At the end of the room he noticed a narrow table covered with a cloth, bright blue in colour with fringes embroidered in white.

"What brings you here?" asked Azariah.

"That delegation setting out for Judah – when is it due to leave?"

"The day after tomorrow."

"I have a favour to ask of you!"

"I shall be happy to do it!" – Azariah gave him a clear answer, from the heart, and he was glad of this and felt more at ease.

"I want to ask Nejeen to come down to Babylon and marry me. I have written a few words..." He drew a tiny scroll from the pocket of his cloak, tightly coiled and carefully wrapped.

"I'm asking you to approach the leader of the delegation and talk to him – if, that is, you trust him. By the way, do I know him?" he asked.

"I rather think you do," Azariah replied, wrinkling his

brow into a frown of ironical concentration. "After all," he continued smoothly, "at this very moment you are handing over a scroll to the leader of the delegation in person, as large as life! As to whether he can be trusted or not – that's a tough question to answer!"

They fell into one another's arms and broke into peals of limpid laughter that was all purity and irresistible youthful energy.

"So you are the one who is going?" he asked, detaching himself from his friend's embrace, and gazing at him with deep affection.

"I am the one!" Azariah replied.

"So," he sighed with relief, "you can tell her about the situation here, and pass on my greetings to my mother and my sisters and the baby, who hasn't been a baby for some time now..."

"You can rely on the leader of the delegation to say what he has to say and pass on what he has to pass on! Incidentally – how did you find me here? To this very day I have difficulty myself finding that strange doorway leading to the space between the walls... You've met my fiancée – so what do you think of her?" he asked.

"I think she's delightful!" he declared, adding: "As to your other question, about finding that strange doorway giving access to the Jewish quarter, and the quarter itself is just as strange – I doubt I'd have found it at all if I hadn't been assisted by a benefactor, called Raphael..."

"Saul's brother!" cried Azariah.

"That's him. He was my guide."

Azariah grew serious and seemed to withdraw into himself. Then he looked up and asked:

"And he didn't recognise you, didn't raise all kinds of rumours that have been going around here, in this strange community as you have described it?"

"He most certainly did, and at length!" he declared, laughing. "These Jews are zealots, but not zealous for their God, rather for their hatred!"

"They are strange, but not lacking in courage."

"That which drives and spurs on the zealot is not courage but pride," he declared and concluded – "and it is a dangerous thing, for him and for those who surround him."

"They have strange ideas," Azariah commented, with some hesitation.

"They mean to rebel against the King of Babylon?"

"To incite to rebellion."

"Incite whom?"

"The King of Judah, of course!" Azariah replied, adding: "Except that, so it seems, he doesn't need any encouragement. One way or another – they are in close touch with the homeland and they know everything that is going on there, to the minutest detail."

"What of the prophet Jeremiah?" he asked with some anxiety.

"King Zedekiah is scheming against him, but not in the same way that Jehoiakim used to do it. On the one hand, he draws him close and on the other – he incites his ministers to persecute him and put him in chains. Zedekiah is a man of troubled mind, and it seems he realises his revolt will not succeed and he will have to answer before his God and yet, he is forever making plans. He summons the prophet Jeremiah secretly, asks to hear the will of God, and the prophet tells him, and he disregards it. He lacks strength of character, and in the end he will bring down disaster upon his people, upon himself and upon his household!"

"And the family of Joseph Hannagid – whose side are they on?" he asked.

"They're inclined to support the zealots."

"And you?" he asked.

"Sometimes – I can't help but admire their courage, even though there is no faith there and as you have said – arrogance and conceit are at the root of it. In the early days I tried to talk them round, and when I realised no one was listening, I took a vow of silence on all these matters. The others have done the same. Mishael's future in-laws, on the other hand, are siding with Jeremiah, and for this reason they have been told to leave their house. They are outcasts here, and ostracised by the majority," Azariah explained.

"And have you been asked to take messages to certain people in Jerusalem, and carry messages back?"

"I've been asked," Azariah replied, giving him a measured look and adding: "I refused."

"How was your refusal accepted?"

"They had no choice but to accept it. Anyway, the important thing is that Havatzelet is standing by me, and it seems she's looking forward to leaving her parents' house."

"When will you be married?"

"On my return from Judah. Mishael and Hananiah too. Three weddings in one and perhaps" – he suddenly remembered and asked – "will there be four?"

"Perhaps," he replied, and Azariah concluded:

"We have here among us the righteous scion of a priestly family, and he is the one who shall marry us."

Havatzelet served milk in clay pitchers and dishes of honey. They said their blessings, drank the milk and tasted the honey. He rose to take his leave.

"We'll go together," said Azariah. "This isn't an easy place to get out of!"

"If you'd rather stay here, I can find my own way."

"No, it's time to go. I shall say goodbye to my in-laws, prospective in-laws I should say, and then I'll be with you." True to his word, Azariah disappeared briefly and returned to him.

Havatzelet accompanied them to the door of the house, wishing them well and replying to their blessings. She watched Azariah go with eyes full of longing, and he turned back to bid her one more farewell, from faraway, with a raised hand. And then the two of them walked following the narrow dust track with its slight upward incline, suddenly finding themselves at the end of the outer wall, facing the gate of Marduk.

THE DELEGATION SETS OUT

The next day he reported to Nashdernach and asked to confer with him privately. Nashdernach gave him a keen look with his tiny eyes, as if trying to work out what was bothering him, and without further ado he ushered him into a side-office, telling the clerks that they were not to be disturbed.

Nashdernach took his seat at a broad and heavy and highly polished table, on one side of it a selection of styli and on the other – scrolls of parchment, some blank and others covered with the cuneiform letters of the Chaldean script.

"Won't you sit down?" – Nashdernach pointed to a roughly hewn wooden chair, unpadded but comfortable enough.

He sat, and there was a moment of silence.

"I hope," the King's senior adviser began in his nasal, sometimes abrasive voice, "you haven't found another far-flung province where the inhabitants are clamouring for a tax rebate – or have you heard a rumour that the blacksmiths are unhappy with their working conditions?" Nashdernach spoke with mock-seriousness, and while speaking he picked up one of the scrolls and glanced at the contents, before hurriedly rolling it up and putting it back in its place.

"Neither of those is the case," he replied calmly, in all earnestness.

Nashdernach raised a short and bushy eyebrow, in token of surprise and bemusement, and he was indeed curious to know what Belteshazzar, his clerk, was about to say.

"It is my intention to marry."

"Aha!" The expression on his superior's fleshy face softened, as a smile broadened his lips and twinkled in his oily little eyes. "A most welcome statement! And what is more – a timely one!" he said emphatically, and proceeded to explain: "In an audience that I had with His Majesty the King, there was talk of you. When the King mentions your name, it is as if a smile lights up his stern face, and that is an exceedingly rare thing! 'The victorious rider' he calls you, and 'that clever lad from Judah.' And he has expressed his complete satisfaction over the episode of the rice levy, and the story of the tanners on the Euphrates gave him so much pleasure he actually clicked his tongue as a sign of approval, and all are agreed that such a thing has never happened before, at any rate not since he was crowned, and ascended the throne of the glorious kings of Babylon. And he, as I say, asked about you, and was particularly keen to know whether you are married or a bachelor, whether you have any commitment in the matter of marriage. And I had no choice but to admit to His Majesty that I had no precise knowledge of this and I would prefer not to speculate, however close to the truth such speculation might be, and I undertook to give him a full answer by the end of the week, or by the end of the day if the matter was considered urgent. And the King reassured me, saying the matter was not urgent, but all the same he wanted to know the position and would be pleased to receive my answer within three days. He went on to say that he considered this a most unsatisfactory state of affairs – a court official and his chief adviser not knowing the marital status of one of his senior clerks. I offered His Majesty fulsome apologies and begged for his indulgence, and he was kind enough to grant it."

He bowed to Nashdernach, a gesture directed not so much towards him as towards the King; the chief adviser appreciated this, and nodded with an air of complete satisfaction.

"As I informed you just a moment ago," the younger man responded, choosing his words carefully and speaking with absolute candour, "I am committed to marriage. There is a girl living in Judah who is destined to be my wife."

"And you have waited until this moment to tell anyone about this commitment of yours, myself included?"

"I suppose so," he admitted, adding: "I didn't realise it was a matter of such importance. In any case, I have asked the man leading the delegation to Jerusalem to find my future bride and bring her back with him – assuming, of course, that she hasn't had a change of heart. And not long ago she sent me a gift..."

With a dismissive gesture Nashdernach prevented him completing the sentence.

"If the girl has had a change of heart," he retorted with some warmth, "you stand to gain more than you lose! The King of Babylon, in person, is said to be arranging the most illustrious of marriages for you! As for bringing this girl to Babylon," he added in a changed tone of voice, "that is definitely the right thing to do! Incidentally, can you show me the gift that you mentioned, if indeed you have it with you?"

"It is with me wherever I go!" he replied, and drew out from under his robe the seven-branched candlestick, hanging on a slender silver chain.

Nashdernach rose, rounded the table, took the pendant in his little hand, probed it and turned it over, put it down finally, returned to his seat and exclaimed:

"That's a national symbol! Admittedly, Babylon isn't in the business of humiliating the Jews, and it hasn't forbidden them to cling to the national symbols that nourish their pride, although sometimes it seems that the Jews misinterpret the tolerance of His Majesty's government! Our great King has dealt with them generously and with justice, and has demanded no tax that is beyond their means, nor put one of his sons on the throne of Judah, letting Zedekiah rule instead, that young and not very promising man who has been appointed by the laws of Judah to sit on that throne! And Nebuchadnezzar, His Majesty, King of Babylon, the valiant and the wise, required one thing only, that the young Jewish king swear allegiance to him. And Zedekiah swore him a threefold oath, by his God, by the sacred scriptures that are said to be your life-blood, and by holy Jerusalem. He swore willingly and now..."

"What now?" he asked, a crease of concern showing on his smooth, open forehead.

"As I said before, you have done well in seeking to bring your betrothed out of Judah at this time, in these days," Nashdernach continued, ignoring the interjection. "Furthermore, I'm absolutely convinced that she has not had a change of heart!"

"How have you come to that conclusion?" he wanted to know.

"The gift that she sent you, and the very fact that you carry it with you wherever you go. There exists between you a deep bond that will not easily be broken. No, it will not be broken!" he declared confidently. "The girl will come here and will be your wife, and there's every reason to expect she will make an exemplary wife, and you will have joy in her and she will have joy in you. And so that she will be brought to Babylon in the style befitting her –

befitting you, in fact, as senior clerk to the chief of the King's advisers, I shall order that a special wagon be added to the convoy, luxuriously appointed in the manner suitable for ladies of noble birth. I assume she is of distinguished lineage, is she not?"

"She is," he answered him, reluctantly for some reason.

"How do you know her?" Nashdernach went on to ask, and he realised that his interlocutor was trying to fill in the gaps in his knowledge about him, and this on account of the King's reprimand.

He answered him willingly:

"Our families were closely acquainted. Her father, like my own revered father, served King Jehoiakim. My father was killed in battle, one standing against many," – he thought it worth pointing out – "and her father disappeared. No one knows what became of him."

Nashdernach was satisfied. He could tell that his senior assistant was doing his best to help him, filling in the gaps that had led to the reprimand, and he gave him a warm look of gratitude and appreciation.

"Don't forget," he reminded him, "to check that the wagon I just mentioned has been added to the convoy. I shall give the order today. What's her name?" he asked.

"Nejeen of the house of Gamliel," he answered him.

"Nejeen of the house of Gamliel!" he echoed, slowly and pensively, as he perused the little parchment scroll that had been filled during the course of the conversation with dense cuneiform symbols – letters forming words and words forming three short sentences, peremptory in tone and relating to the special "luxury" wagon that was to be sent with the delegation.

"A most agreeable name!" He looked up and scanned him with inquisitive eyes. "The damsel Nejeen of the house of Gamliel!" he repeated in a tone of pleasure and respect. "She adds a degree of urgency to the entire mission!"

"And what is the reason for this urgency, if I may ask?" he inquired earnestly, his voice sincere and imbued with a strength of purpose that could not be easily resisted.

In reply, Nashdernach told him that matters were complicated, and deeply worrying:

"Something strange is happening in Judah, your homeland! Zedekiah, the young king, who sits on his throne with the backing of the Chaldeans, and with the consent of their King, seems to be devoid of any intelligence or any of the qualities appropriate to a monarch. He associates himself with a coterie of young men who are... how to describe them... let me think for a moment... frivolous one might say, or 'vain and reckless' in the language of your Scriptures. And even if he himself is not vain and reckless, if we turn once more to the wisdom literature of the Hebrews and one of your most beautiful hymns: *Blessed is the man who does not take his seat among the scornful* – the meaning is that a man, even one who is not scornful himself, may be tempted to associate himself with the scornful, and thus lose his last opportunity to avoid falling into this sinful state..." Nashdernach tried to smile, without success, and added: "I'm sure you are familiar with the rest of this glorious psalm!"

He nodded, feeling his heart shrinking within him.

"And this King Zedekiah has been induced, or persuaded, against his better judgment – if indeed he has anything of the kind – to appoint worthless characters such as these to be his ministers and advisers. And here you have a fine example of the magnanimity of our King, His Majesty, and his generosity and tolerance. He does not interfere with the internal affairs of Judah. He is content with a small and symbolic tribute, and the choice of ministers and advisers he leaves in the hands of the King, who rules with his consent and has sworn him an oath of allegiance. So Zedekiah proceeds to make his appointments, invariably the wrong ones, while our King, His Majesty, looks on from the sidelines, showing great patience and waiting to see how things develop.

"And something else you should know, my lad," Nashdernach continued, suddenly adopting an affectionate mode of address; his voice was warm, and rising in his eyes was a kind of distant sadness, musings of the heart drawn up from the depths of the soul. "This King of ours, His Majesty, whom I so admire – is the most God-fearing man alive! He will not take a single step without consulting God. He is the total opposite of the boy, Zedekiah, who sits on the throne of the kingdom of Judah, which had a glorious past and roots running deep, and used to be ruled by men whose way was lit by the fear of God! And the voice of God addresses Zedekiah directly and explicitly, morning and evening, warning of the disaster that he is inviting upon his people and upon himself, and calling on him to abandon his perversities. And he, this boy, closes his ears and refuses to listen, as did his predecessor, Jehoiakim!"

"Where does it come from, the voice of God that addresses him directly and explicitly?" he asked in a wavering tone, knowing that Nashdernach spoke the truth. And Nashdernach answered him willingly and at once:

"From the lips of Jeremiah the prophet."

His head slumped. It was as if whips had struck him down. Nashdernach realised that he had touched a sensitive point, and was silent.

After a lengthy pause, the Chaldean spoke again:

"Better perhaps not to inquire too deeply!"

"Not at all!" He looked up at once, his voice steadier now. "I'm eager to know all the details, if indeed you have details to give me."

"Indeed I have," Nashdernach sighed and added: "As with every sensible government, Babylon too has eyes and ears in the lands it has conquered, and in those it is yet to conquer. It's a disreputable business but – a practical necessity!"

"This 'business' as you call it doesn't say much for the faith of those involved."

"You're absolutely right!" Nashdernach agreed with him, adding: "This is a secret service, doing its work, disagreeable work, in the best possible way. From the point of view of faith, even wars are forbidden. *Not by force and not by power, says your God, but by my spirit.* Do you agree?"

"In all respects!" he stressed.

"Except that in the case of Judah there is no need for these 'eyes' and 'ears' operating secretly," the other continued. "Everything is done there in the light of day, in public. Perhaps Zedekiah knows that in the end all will be known, and hiding it is just a waste of effort."

"What is he doing now?" he asked.

"Fishing for support."

"Fishing where?"

"In Egypt."

He lowered his head again. This recurrent error on the part of kings of Judah and Israel. Egypt – the "broken reed".

"And preparations for revolt?" he asked, wanting to know for how long Nejeen would be safe.

"In the early stages. Let us wait – and hope!"

Nashdernach sighed again.

"And pray!" the other added, thoughtfully.

At the order of the King's chief adviser, a special wagon was added to the convoy setting out for Judah, well upholstered and designed to withstand the rigours of the journey, however long it might be.

Taking the advice of Nashdernach he came and inspected the wagon: inside and out, shafts, suspension, upholstery, canopy, wheels, axles. All was to his satisfaction.

"By the decree of Nashdernach, chief adviser to the King, the delegation is not to depart until Belteshazzar, his senior aide, has authorised it!" Azariah proclaimed with joyful enthusiasm and handed him the papyrus sheet for his signature.

He took a pen and signed in red ink, under the few words stating that the extra wagon had been checked and found fit for travel – his Jewish name in full and alongside it the Chaldean name that he was growing accustomed to, Belteshazzar.

"I shall keep this certificate!" cried Azariah with youthful ebullience. "In my mind there isn't the shadow of a doubt that seeing this signature of yours will set her heart a-flutter and fill it with joy!"

The delegation set out on its way.

THE MAN WITH THE DAGGER

One Sabbath he met with Hananiah and Mishael.

"We are on our way to visit the Jewish community, down there between the walls, and if you feel like joining us – you'll be very welcome!" Mishael invited him.

"What we are really doing is visiting our fiancées and their families!" Hananiah explained with a gentle smile. Mishael added:

"From what we hear, it seems you too will soon be in need of the priestly services of that community, just like us! Anyway, it will do you no harm to become acquainted with these Jews, most of whom trace their ancestry from genealogical scrolls that they have in their possession; a few are of priestly or levitical descent, and there is also a family descended from the Tribe of Benjamin. And the Jews have strange stories to tell about themselves and their community."

"Such as, for example?" he asked with amused interest.

"Such as, for example," Mishael proceeded to elaborate, in an entirely earnest tone of voice, "the story that their forefathers settled in the place before the outer wall was built, and this was many generations ago, in the time of King Solomon, and they came here in obedience to his explicit decree, or so they claim, these strange Jews! And those genealogical scrolls of theirs leave no room for doubt."

"And why did King Solomon command their forefathers to leave their native land and their patrimony and abandon their homes, and pitch their tents in foreign parts?" he asked, still in jesting mood.

"They have an explanation for this," Hananiah interjected with a grim look on his face, "and they whisper it among themselves like a secret that must not under any circumstances reach 'Gentile ears' or the 'house of the Gentiles' – as they are fond of repeating. According to their account, a mission was entrusted to them – to be the vanguard of the army of the greatest of all the kings of Judah, and in their opinion – greatest of all kings of the universe, the wisest of all men. They were to settle in foreign lands and when the time came, go out to meet his army, coming to take Babylon by storm, Babylon the wicked city, as they call it, as is the will and the commandment of God, and to destroy the homes of sinners and set them ablaze and above all, to tear down utterly the 'temples of Moloch' – their name for all the deities of Babylon – and smash his abominable idols and obliterate the lascivious wall-paintings and prove before all the nations of the world their right to be called the true heirs of Abraham their father, who did the same thing in his time and smashed the idols in the house of his pagan father."

"And how do they reconcile themselves to the fact that the armies of King Solomon did not come here, as they expected and as they hoped and, if their account is to be believed, as was promised to them by none other than King Solomon himself?"

Mishael was quick to answer:

"They don't reconcile themselves to it at all. Nor could it be said that they ignore it – they are aware of it, but they don't consider it rationally."

"So what do they do?" he asked, the humorous note fading from his voice.

"They wait. They go on waiting, from day to day, month to month, year to year, decade to decade, generation to generation, century to century. They wait in the belief, firm as iron, that the event will come about, and everything that has been spoken of and is awaited with yearning will be fulfilled, and when the army of Jewish liberation approaches, all the Jews will rise as one man and slaughter the pagans, and put them to the sword, and destroy, and smash, and ruin, and set ablaze, and they will go forth clean and purified to meet the holy army, and greet the King who stands at its head, and join forces with him, and they will deal ruthlessly with all the peoples who remain, leaving no vestige of them, no survivors and – in defiance of the edicts of Scripture and the precepts of the Torah – they will show no mercy to women, to the old or the young."

"There are some," Hananiah interposed, "who hold that there is a duty to show mercy to domestic beasts, that the beast is not infected by the pagan sin of its master, but the majority dismiss this argument with contempt, declaring that not even the beast is to be spared. And all of this passes from father to son and from teacher to pupil, as a great secret and a holy commandment, and this small community does everything in its power to stay confined within its walls, enclosed and shut off and separated, shunning involvement with the peoples around it, or as they put it, avoiding 'contamination' and preserving their 'purity' – and waiting with peerless, incomparable patience for the coming of salvation."

They left the royal palace and made their way on foot. The warmth was pleasant, with rays of sunshine sparkling in the clear air. It was easy to breathe air such as this.

"This climate is reminiscent of the homeland," Mishael commented.

"Except for the summer," he answered him and

explained: "The summer here is arid and oppressive, and were it not for the Euphrates, Babylon would be nothing but a desert country."

Their gait was brisk and vigorous and yet – light and surprisingly steady, in a fashion not typical of men of their age.

"And how do you fit into this legend?" he asked as they walked.

"The beliefs and hopes of these Jews?" Hananiah answered with a question.

He nodded.

"Sometimes they are amusing!" Mishael laughed lightly. "Sometimes – they leave behind an unpleasant taste."

"How so?"

"It's because this zealotry is dark on the one hand and on the other..." Mishael deliberated, turning to him without slackening his pace and measuring him with a quizzical look, before concluding the sentence, with an air of absolute seriousness: "On the other hand, it arouses reverence and respect!"

"You're saying these people arouse reverence and respect? How?" he persisted.

"With their fanatical devotion to an idea," Hananiah interjected, "however grotesque and demented and mortally dangerous that idea may be."

"Do they appeal to God and seek His help?" he asked.

"There is a family of priests among them, so I suppose it is theoretically possible," Hananiah surmised

"To the best of my knowledge," Azariah commented, "they don't feel the need for any such appeal. They have unshakeable trust in themselves, and that is what turns their heads."

"Their belief in their mission is strong," Hananiah

added.

"Their belief in God too?" he persisted.

Neither Hananiah nor Mishael could give him a clear answer.

"Sometimes," Mishael resumed, "they look demented, and sometimes – as mild as babies! The family of Deborah, my future bride, isn't among the zealots. Her father is a dedicated campaigner for peace and a man of innocent faith, and all the talk of insurrections and revolt and bloodshed and destruction, and royal missions to which they're supposedly committed – elicit from him nothing more than a tolerant smile. And my belief is that if only he could, Baruch, my future father-in-law, would leave this strange community behind and move to somewhere that isn't hemmed in by walls all around."

"Why doesn't he do that?"

"Because he has children who are all dependent on him, and his income is meagre," Mishael explained. He has a field and a few milch-cows, and hives some distance away – and that's all. And he's not renowned for his courage. He works his field and milks his cows and extracts his honey, and sells his produce in the market by the temple of Marduk. When he has cash in his hand, then he's in high spirits and he's a pleasant fellow to talk to, and when business is poor his heart is heavy and at such times he may turn to drink, quaffing the potent Chaldean liquor that is brewed from all kinds of toxic herbs, and he sits at home listless and morose, saying nothing. I have happened to be in his company in these disagreeable moments, and despite my best efforts to hold a conversation with him, if only for a moment, I've failed utterly."

"Simeon, the father of Hannah my future bride," Hananiah interjected, "is one of the fanatics. Unlike

Baruch, whom Mishael mentioned just now, he isn't prone to changes of mood – he has a stern look on his face at all times, and you would think he'd been gloomy since the day of his birth. He says little, and there's no way of knowing what is going on behind that wrinkled brow, or buried deep in the recesses of his frozen heart. And yet, he showed some signs of pleasure when giving consent to the betrothal of his middle daughter, Hannah."

The morning sun was still high in the sky when the three of them turned aside from the broad, paved, royal highway, teeming with men and beasts, carts and wagons – and plunged into the dark passageway leading to the north-eastern wall. Soon afterwards they received an enthusiastic welcome at the house of Deborah, Mishael's betrothed, where Havatzelet and Hannah, future wives of Azariah and Hananiah, were also waiting for them. The three maidens were brightly dressed in freshly laundered festive costumes, coloured pink, blue and purple and trimmed with silver lace. Baruch, Deborah's father, pronounced the blessings, and his broad, round features shone with the light of exuberant high spirits.

"He must be trading at a profit!" Mishael whispered in his ear, smiling broadly, and sure enough, Baruch was quick to confirm his future son-in-law's hypothesis:

"Yesterday the Lord held out to me His generous hand, and bestowed upon me a share of those favours of His that gladden the heart. Everything that I took to the market of Marduk was sold in no time at all, and I made a handsome profit!"

"Damn him to Hell!" – a sour-tempered man entered the room, tall of build and heavy of movement, wearing a woollen shirt, coarsely sewn and coloured black, and breeches of the same colour. He identified him at once as

Simeon, prospective father-in-law of Hananiah. "Curse the name and the memory of all pagan idols!" the newcomer stressed, accompanying his words with a grinding of teeth, and they realised it was Marduk he was referring to. Tucked into his broad black belt was a long-bladed dagger.

"For my part, I shall never mention his name again!" Baruch hastened to soothe these passions, adding: "All the honey and the fresh milk that I brought to that market," – he was careful this time not to give it a name – "was snapped up, pounced on, and in such a short space of time! God has indeed shown me His manifold mercies and not withheld His favours from me. Sit down my lords, let this table be your table, and my house your house. Let your hearts not be sad, and dispel gloom from your faces!"

"Is that a dig at me?" Simeon's rusty voice rasped over the heads of the assembled company.

"No, not at all! Such a thought never occurred to me!" Baruch tried to give his voice an emphatic edge. The angry frown on the brow of the questioner eased a little, as the host added: "I was referring to myself, and to anyone else who might be listening."

They moved to take their seats at a long table covered with white cloths, and by the time they arrived there the refreshments had already been served. He asked Mishael where the other members of the family were, and he in turn consulted Deborah.

"They have gone out," she replied, "to stroll in the fields outside the walls. We stayed because we knew you were coming, you and Hananiah. And your friend too, who is most welcome here!"

The table was laden with good things: milk in clay pitchers, red wine, pats of butter and cheese on broad fig leaves, dried figs, dates dried and moist, home-baked hallah bread and fresh honey, its sweet aroma still intact, and served in cups. Baruch recited the grace beginning "He who has given us life" and Simeon grunted something which was presumably meant to be an "Amen", and hosts and guests alike took plates from the pile at the end of the table and filled them with whatever they fancied.

The young ladies made an effort to restrain themselves and not share in the gluttonous frenzy that had gripped the menfolk, but to no avail, and it was not long before they were gobbling with equal gusto and seizing everything that their eyes coveted.

He was hardly aware of the first mouthful. Walking in the fresh air had sharpened his appetite, and the hallah bread still held the fragrance of the fields. He remembered the hallah offered to him in the low, shady houses outside the walls of Jerusalem. Friendly people, of simple ways and warm hospitality, somewhere in the distant homeland, had begged him to take the produce of their hands and bless the living God. He recovered his wits, and took no further share in the collective frenzy. His movements were measured, his eating sober. One after the other, Hananiah and Mishael followed his example.

The diners rose, and the girls began clearing the table while the men made their way to the main living room of the house and from there to a small lobby, the exit to the outside world. A light push and the heavy door swung open before them, revealing the spectacle he had least expected to see: a broad, cultivated field, extending to the ridge of a low hill, enfolding it all around and forming a close horizon. Above their heads stretched a blue sky, mottled with feathery clouds whiter than snow.

"We're outside the wall!" Hananiah enlightened him, seeing his bemusement.

"This field belongs to the community," Mishael added,

"all of it!"

"To a few families," he corrected him mildly.

Somewhere, at the far end of the field, the silver ribbon of a flowing stream could be seen, and on one of its banks – a group of women and children. The women saw them and blessed them with raised hands, and they returned the greeting.

To their right, stood a stooping fig tree, with a thick trunk and dense foliage rustling in the light breeze, clearly inclining towards them as if offering shelter. They came and sat down beneath it.

"This is my portion!" he told them calmly, drawing lines in the air to indicate a modest area of land. "The territory that used to belong to my father," he explained, "was of considerable size – but it was divided! I have six brothers, and each received an equal share, as was the explicit will of my esteemed father. It was also a fundamental contravention of the rules laid down in the Holy Torah!" he added in a tone of mild indignation. "After all, I am the firstborn, and according to the Law..." he sighed and left the sentence unfinished.

Three men appeared from behind them, advancing quietly and joining them. He recognised one of them – Saul, Azariah's future father-in-law. All three wore brown cloaks, bound at the waist with black leather belts.

"This is Nehemiah!" Simeon introduced a portly, broad-shouldered man – "And he is of priestly lineage!" he added with an air of superior satisfaction. "This is Gideon, one of Baruch's brothers, and beside him is Saul. His daughter, Havatzelet, is betrothed to your friend, Azariah!"

"When is this wedding due to take place?" Gideon asked.

"When the time is right," the priestly Nehemiah sighed,

as the newcomers shook the hands of the guests and exchanged greetings.

"And that time is drawing near!" Simeon's rasping voice was heard again, as he tried to imbue his words with mystery and dark significance.

"What do you mean by that?" he asked.

"As the prophet has seen fit to tell us – the end of wicked Babylon is at hand. From that time on, all will be fire and destruction and mayhem – so the sooner this marriage takes place the better!"

No one responded to the impassioned words of the man with the dagger. He felt ill at ease, and turned to the priestly Nehemiah in search of corroboration.

"Is it all true, what he has said? You, as a priest and the son of a priest, are empowered to confirm or deny this."

"It is true, the statement is accurate!" retorted Nehemiah earnestly, a thick edge to his voice. He added, in a tone of stern authority: "The Lord will deal severely with all those who have not believed in Him, and who have perverted their ways and bowed down to idols and images, and have not repented in time – and that time is not far away!"

"We shall all be called upon then to do the Lord's work, and cleanse the land of pagans and Gentiles, who have derided the Holy Name of the Lord, and afflicted and scorned His people!" Saul concluded with eyes downcast.

"This will be the great day of the judgment of the Lord, the mighty and awesome warrior, the day of anger and of wrath, the day of fire and pillars of smoke, the day of death and vengeance, such as the world has never seen and the like of which it will never see again!" Simeon declared with grim intensity, lightly fingering the hilt of his dagger as he spoke.

Something in the depths of his soul was chilled with

dread. Had it not been said of these people, that they have eyes to see and see not, ears to hear and hear not? And without the mercy of Heaven – where are they going?

"What is the sign portending this time?" he asked.

Simeon hastened to forestall the priestly Nehemiah, answering him:

"Zedekiah, the anointed of the Lord, who sits on the throne of David, who knows the times and knows what is to be – he will show us the sign for which we are waiting, and we shall put an end to Babylon the wicked, as is the commandment of our holy God, and set on fire all the temples of Moloch!

"And you boys," – Simeon rounded on them, his voice raised and with an unmistakable note of menace, "sitting at your ease in the palace of the pagan king and serving him, will have to decide – to go on pandering to the Chaldeans or to return to your God and cleave to Him and go forth to exact vengeance for His people, the holy nation. No one shall escape the wrath of God, as it is written: *If you soar like an eagle and make your nest among the stars, from there I shall bring you down!*"

He rose to his feet.

"I think it's time to leave!" he said, addressing his companions.

Without another word spoken, the two of them stood and joined him. Baruch accompanied them part of the way, and tried to reassure them, in a hesitant voice:

"Not everyone agrees with Simeon, not everyone will listen to him!"

He nodded thoughtfully.

As they left the passage, Nehemiah caught up with them, panting from the effort of running, stopped them with his hand, and turning to him he said:

"As you know, marriage is only one of the great

commandments of the holy law of Moses! And as I am sure you have heard, the more generous the fee paid by the groom to the priest – the finer the wedding!" He winked conspiratorially, a strange smile twisting his thick lips, and stood his ground, watching them go. And when they had walked some distance and Hananiah looked back, Nehemiah the priest raised his arm and waved to them in valediction.

BELTESHAZZAR

He awoke with a strange sensation of weight and oppression. His heart was thumping and he was short of breath – *as if I have been plagued by a nightmare*, he thought – but he could not remember if he had dreamed at all. *It's a passing sensation!* he concluded, but still he could not overcome the feeling of suffocation. He tried to calm himself but knew that something was happening or was about to happen, and someone had been hurt or was about to be hurt.

He knelt at the head of his bed and joined his hands in prayer:

"If I have found favour in Your eyes and grace in Your presence, my Father in Heaven, my God, have mercy on those people who have departed from You and have rejected You, and whom disaster threatens!"

His consciousness was cleared and cleansed, and the sense of oppression eased before disappearing altogether. Tears welled in his eyes, tears of gratitude.

Without rousing the slave responsible for the household, he put on a gown and went to the bathhouse; after refreshing himself in cold water he felt almost inclined to burst into song. The cook was aware that his master was awake and he set about preparing his breakfast. When he entered the dining room, he found the table already laden with fresh and warm milk, honey, eggs, toasted bread, cheese and vegetables.

He arrived early in the office, and to his surprise, did not find it empty – Nashdernach, himself and in person, was pacing back and forth, the length and breadth of the office, in a state of obvious agitation, with twitchy fingers clasped behind his back. He did not sense his arrival.

He stood motionless. The first thought that occurred to him was that the trouble he had anticipated had come about and disaster had struck. Was Nashdernach the victim?

"Belteshazzar!" The Chaldean was startled to see him, and in the effort to cover the alarm apparent in his exclamation, hurriedly asked: "Do you always arrive so early?"

"No," he replied. "This morning I woke earlier than usual, with a sensation of weight and oppression, and I turned to my God and prayed, and the oppression disappeared as if it had never been."

"I wish I had somewhere to turn to!" Nashdernach sighed, and he saw that his face was pale and his eyes sunken.

"Except that, so it seems..." his supervisor hesitated, and added, as if going off at a tangent: "We Chaldeans were born under a very strange constellation, a gloomy and oppressive one! Saturn has, quite simply, stamped his seal upon us, or perhaps – it's just in our nature!" And while continuing to pace back and forth, from one end of the office to the other, he went on to say: "There's no denying it, trouble has come upon us, and disaster is set to strike some of the most eminent officials of the government, strike them mortally!"

"You too?" he asked, the composure of his voice shattered.

"No! Certainly not me. I'm not possessed of the qualities that the people I mentioned are endowed with, or are supposed to be endowed with, those upon whom this terrible blow has fallen. Lend an ear, Belteshazzar, and listen! Our King, His Majesty, the wise and the valiant, conqueror of the world – has dreamed a dream!" And seeing the mystified look in his face he hastily explained: "And this is the entire cause of the trouble and of the looming disaster. The King dreamed a dream," he repeated emphatically, "and his heart pounded, and he rose from his bed, and ordered the immediate summoning of all the soothsayers and magicians, the sorcerers, diviners and astrologers. And all those who were summoned came at once, consumed by panic and shaking with fear, and they stood dumbfounded in a semicircle at the foot of the high throne of the King. And the King, seated on his throne in all his pomp and majesty, addressed his flustered courtiers and made of them – to say the very least – a most unusual demand. It could be described as a demand the like of which has never been heard before. And included in this assemblage of soothsayers and magicians and sorcerers and astrologers was my brother-in-law, a genial fellow and a family man, who has no truck with the world of diviners and magicians and their dubious profession and their delving into mysteries, in any respect whatsoever – other than through the fact that his father was a talented soothsayer, a veritable wizard, as was his grandfather, and they, the father and grandfather, served the Kings of Babylon faithfully and were guests at their table and lived lives of comfort and ease. And my brother-in-law, in accordance with the enlightened laws of Babylon, inherited their appointment, along with all the trappings that belong to it.

"And since this dream that our wise and valiant King, His Majesty, so graciously dreamed, my brother-in-law, a peace-loving man of simple pleasures, has lived in the shadow of the deadliest danger!"

"The King demanded of all those soothsayers and

magicians – that they interpret his dream?" he asked.

"Yes!" Nashdernach replied, and he stopped, turned and stood facing him, no longer fidgeting nervously with his fingers behind his back. "Precisely so! He demanded that they interpret his dream! But the problem is that not one of the King's eminent soothsayers, not one of his magicians, never mind all the rest," – Nashdernach raised both arms in a gesture of utter helplessness, as if pleading for the mercy of Heaven – "has the faintest idea what he is supposed to be interpreting!"

"The dream, surely!"

"The dream, yes, to be sure. Just as you say. To interpret the dream, explain it, solve it – that's the inimitable skill of these people! Tell them of a vision in which all the characters participating are split into two halves, and there are many of them, and the situations in which they are embroiled are strange and inexplicable, and they, these cunning readers of mysteries, will turn to you with broad smiles on their smug faces, bow to you and say: 'You are going to hear good news from relations and family, and bad news from one who is half a friend.' And if the news described as 'good' fails to satisfy you, your melancholia is directed at those who trouble you. And if the bad news changes its skin and becomes good – it is because you have sacrificed a bull-calf to the god and your sin is forgiven; and if you haven't yet sacrificed a calf, nor even so much as a dove to one or other of the deities – hurry up and do it, they will tell you – before it is too late!

"And the whole business is clear as the light of day, a matter of simple routine, except in this strange instance involving the King, our wise and valiant King!" – and Nashdernach thumped on one of the tables with his round little fist. "They are all intent on not sparing themselves hard work and travail in the effort to demonstrate their skill in the arts of interpretation, and even, within a short space of time, to attain a remarkable degree of unanimity, in their customary style, the only problem being – to the bewilderment and grief of all – there is nothing to interpret and nothing to explain!" Again Nashdernach raised both arms towards the ceiling."

"The dream!" he reminded him.

"Of course, the dream!" he repeated in a hollow voice. "This extraordinary royal dream... This time the King is not content with interpretation and explanation; the demand is a different one, involving a prelude to conventional interpretation and solution!" And Nashdernach resumed his tour of the office, his fingers clasped behind his back.

"So what is His Majesty's pleasure?" he asked, intrigued.

The minister turned sharply and came hurrying towards him, staring at him with a look of despair and giving full voice to his woes:

"First and foremost he wants to be told what was the dream that he dreamed! Yes, absolutely!" – Nashdernach paused for emphasis. "Interpretation and explanation can wait. First and foremost he wants the dream revealed to him, the dream that he dreamed himself, in person, no one else. So, the King's spirit is troubled twice over: first on account of the dream itself and second – because this unique and special dream has fled from his memory! This, then, is the royal demand – that he be told what he dreamed! And as is his way, the King concludes his edict with the customary royal formula: 'If you do not reveal to me what I dreamed, and interpret the dream that I have forgotten – your blood be upon your heads!' Meaning, your blood will be spilled at the hands of the royal executioner. And the word of His Majesty the King is not spoken idly. This morning I was told of the execution of the chief of the sorcerers, and there will be more to come!"

And without a pause, Nashdernach continued, breathing heavily: "They are trying, the soothsayers and the magicians and the sorcerers and all the rest, to play for time, for they have no other way of resisting the cruel decree and forestalling the sword that is brandished above their necks. But the King can read their minds and he knows what they are thinking and he is incensed at them, and there is a rumour going about among the courtiers that he intends to wipe out his entire staff of seers and wizards, most of whom obtained their posts through family connections rather than through skill and expertise.

"And because there is no solution and no escape, some of those subtle sages are trying to point the finger at you, the Jewish exiles in the service of the King, you and your three companions, Shadrach, Meshach and Abed-Nego, as those who used spells and secret knowledge to make the King forget, and should now face the consequences of their actions! And there are others who oppose this malicious proposition, but who will gain the upper hand – it is too early to say!"

The keen look that he gave his interlocutor showed him that Nashdernach was among the opponents of the malicious proposition.

He looked down and made no response, and Nashdernach went on to say:

"And in the meantime my mild-mannered brother-in-law is so terrified he has taken to his bed, and his body temperature is fluctuating wildly, his teeth chattering and his hands shaking, and he has neither saviour nor redeemer.

"Lord of the world, Belteshazzar!" cried Nashdernach in bitter despair, "Can you not appeal to your God, pray to Him, lay your entreaties before Him – plead for an end to the killing, and the repeal of that cruel decree?"

"With your permission, I shall sit for a moment!" he said and sat down at the table, hands clasping his temples.

Nashdernach stopped, quietly pulled up a chair and sat on it reversed, a cavalry officer's pose. His tense look followed every one of his movements, and in the gloom of his oily little eyes there rose the pale glimmer of a distant hope.

He laid his hands on the surface of the table, looked up and said:

"That mild-mannered brother-in-law of yours was in the wrong, pretending to be a magician or an astrologer and accepting payment that wasn't his by right, and the same judgment applies to all his colleagues, including those who are now making every effort to incriminate the innocent as a way of saving their own skin. I shall try to meet the challenge, and contend with the evil. For three days you shall not see me, and when those three days have passed, I hope I shall have an answer for you."

"And what is the purpose of those three days?" asked Nashdernach.

"Fasting and prayer" he replied and left the room.

He called upon Mishael and Hananiah and they, knowing what was afoot in the royal court, and having heard of the proposal to lay the blame upon them and sacrifice them as scapegoats, were troubled and fearful, not knowing how to behave and what to do. He addressed them and asked them too to fast and pray, so that the good God might see their oppression and also take pity on the soothsayers and astrologers of Babylon, and save them all from the hands of the executioner.

He shut himself away in his lodgings, and ordered his slaves not to disturb him and to admit no guests or visitors. All official business was to be referred to Nashdernach, his superior. And so he prayed and fasted, with pleas drawn from the depths of his grieving heart:

"The people have sinned, sinned in pretending to be what they are not and eating bread for free, bread that is not theirs!

"My God, my holy Father in Heaven, my lord and teacher and master! You are love and you are all forgiveness and mercy, and they – they who do not know how to repent, let them be saved, by your grace, from the hands of the executioner, and their families spared from grief and penury and from the torments of fear. Give them the joy of Your pure love which whitens every sin, and ease their suffering, and bring them out of darkness into a great light!"

Indeed, his heart told him that more members of the royal household – wizards, astrologers and magicians – were bound to pay for their deception with their lives, their unfortunate families despoiled of their property and evicted from their homes. And this thought tormented and saddened him until he cried out in his prayers and in the depths of his grief, not rising from his knees day or night. He could no longer feel the limbs of his body, and it seemed to him it was not he but some other person, not known to him, who was kneeling there, clasping numb and frozen hands and praying without cease.

And suddenly he was visited by that familiar sensation, a feeling of cautious relief arising in the heart and spreading through every part of his body. And for the first time since embarking on his fast, he was aware of his limbs, emerging painfully from their torpor, and this in itself was a comfort.

He crawled to his bed, and with strenuous efforts that seemed to last hundreds of years, managed to climb into it. And then, as his body began to relax and to regain its vigour, he saw the dream that the King had dreamed, that troubled his heart but was forgotten when he awoke.

He called to his slave, and was surprised by the sound of his own voice, which was thin and barely audible. He had to muster his strength and cry out again to make himself heard, but to no avail. Nobody heard him and nobody came. An oil-lamp made of clay stood on the tiny table beside his bed and he pushed at it, knocking it to the floor. The lamp shattered, making a sound loud enough to reach the ears of his slave, who came running. He tapped on the door, and hearing the faint voice of his master, opened it.

The tanned face of the slave was alarmed, as were his bulging eyes, twitching in their sockets.

"Enter!" he cried, relieved to find that his voice was becoming clearer. The slave entered hurriedly and stood before him. Seeing the fragments of clay on the floor, he stooped and started picking them up.

"Leave those!" he commanded and added: "Go to Nashdernach at once, run to him! Tell him that the problem is solved! Run!"

No further urging was required. The slave was aware of the situation and of the exceptional circumstances involved: his master's prolonged fast, his lean appearance, the breaking of the lamp as an alarm signal, and the strange words about solutions and urgency – all of these gave him wings, and he ran out of the building, passing the sumptuous residences of the senior counsellors and reaching Nashdernach's house. He knocked on the great door, and panting heavily succeeded in transferring his panic to the footman, who ran up the stairs to alert his master, at that time in his night-shirt.

"Imp-p-p-portant message from Beltesh-esh-esh-azzar – s-s-something's s-s-solved, s-s-solved!" was the garbled message delivered by the stammering footman, but Nashdernach immediately understood what he was being told, and he changed his clothes and without another word spoken set out in pursuit of the messenger-slave. Despite his age – at least two decades older than the slave – he overtook him and arrived first at Daniel's bedside.

"So?" he asked him, breathlessly.

"The killing can stop!" he told him, his voice still thin and grating. "There is a solution! Go to Arioch, the chief executioner, and tell him I am ready and prepared to stand before the King tomorrow…"

"The Heavens be praised!" Nashdernach interrupted him with his high-pitched exclamation and added: "The solution has come just in time! Arioch, the chief executioner, wants your life and the lives of your companions, since the rumour going about the palace is that you are sorcerers, casting magical spells to destroy the sages of Babylon, and the King has decreed that your fate will be the same as that of the astrologers, and if you fail to tell him the dream that he has dreamed – you will be taken to the scaffold! And I asked Arioch to wait until first light, giving you time to fast and pray to your God, the all-powerful God, and he could expect a miracle that would stop the killing! This day alone," Nashdernach continued, "three more sages have been beheaded, and Babylon is plunged into grief over the bitter fate of its sorcerers and magicians, wizards and astrologers!"

Nashdernach shook his hand firmly and warmly, and

retraced his steps at the same hectic pace, making his way to the house of Arioch, chief executioner to the King,

He dressed and sent his slave to summon his friends. When they arrived and stood before him, tense and nervous, he was quick to reassure them:

"The name of the Lord be praised from everlasting and to everlasting, to whom is all wisdom and might! He is the Lord of all and the One who changes the times, and all things own his sway and He it is who deposes kings and appoints kings, giving wisdom to the wise and understanding to the judicious, knowing things that are hidden from the eyes of mortals, and He is the one and the only light, the living light!"

And here he went down on his knees and his two companions did likewise, and he joined his hands and raised them, and went on to say:

"To You, my God and my Father, be thanks and praise, seeing that through your bountiful grace and your manifold mercies, and Your love that embraces the whole world, that conquers all – You have given us wisdom and strength and have revealed to us what we asked of You, the solution to the King's riddle and the dream that he dreamed, the dream on account of which many have died, and we too were in mortal danger, and You, in Your might and Your mercy, will save us from death in this foreign land, the land of our exile!"

He rose from his knees and his two companions followed his example, and they were light-hearted and in good spirits, praising God and jesting among themselves about the unwarranted terror that had gripped them. And meanwhile the kitchen slave informed them that, as the fasting was now over, a meal had been prepared and would shortly be served, and would the gentlemen be so kind as to take their seats at the table. He thanked his scullion warmly, and invited his friends to break bread with him.

Later that night he was visited by Arioch, the chief executioner.

He told Arioch: "You need slay no more of the sages of Babylon! Take me to the King tomorrow and I shall show him his dream!"

The following day Arioch was waiting for him in the avenue leading to the palace and the royal residence, and he was impatient, because the King's edict was still in force and if the solution failed to satisfy the King, then a grim fate was in store for him, his life in jeopardy.

Armed guardsmen opened the great door of the royal council chamber before them. At the end of the room stood the high throne of the King, three steps of cast gold leading to it, and the throne itself fashioned from gold and ivory, and Nebuchadnezzar seated there in all his regal splendour.

A broad strip of purple carpet stretched from the throne to the entrance, and on either side of the carpet troopers of the royal guard were drawn up, standing in motionless ranks face to face, wearing blue tabards embroidered in gold with the three recumbent lions that were the emblem of the royal household. Around their waists the guardsmen wore black belts with gold buckles, and each carried a gold shield in his left hand, and a broad-bladed drawn sword in his right. On their heads were gleaming helmets, likewise of gold.

So they entered, and Arioch hastened to lie full-length on the ground, and he did the same. Then they stood up and paced towards the King who sat on his throne awaiting them, until they reached the stool at his feet.

They prostrated themselves once more before the King, and did not rise until so commanded.

For the second time he looked into the bronzed features of King Nebuchadnezzar, reminiscent in their composure and their ferocity of the face of a lion, crouching in his lair, confident of his power and ready at any moment to spring upon his prey.

The King wore blue breeches embroidered with gold, a white shirt also with gold trimmings, a broad white belt set with pearls and other precious stones, and a straight-bladed sword hanging from it in a gold scabbard, the hilt inlaid with silver and ivory.

"Speak!" the King commanded, his voice calm, clear and resonant, the voice of dominion and authority, not to be defied.

He bowed to him once more, and began:

The secret of which the King is asking – sages, wizards, astrologers and magicians could not explain to him. But there is a God in Heaven who reveals secrets, and He is telling King Nebuchadnezzar what is to be hereafter...

Your Majesty, thoughts came into your mind as you were in your bed, as you sought to know what is to be hereafter, and the Revealer of secrets showed what is to be. By the grace that has been bestowed on me, the secret has been revealed to me, so that I may stand before your Majesty and inform you of the solution, and you shall know the thoughts of your heart.

You looked, Your Majesty, and you saw before you a great and wondrous image. The head of the image – pure gold, the chest and arms – silver, the belly and thighs – brass. Legs of iron and the feet – partly of iron and partly of clay. As you looked on, a stone was hewn from a mountain, and not by any hand, and it struck the feet of the image, that were of iron and clay, and destroyed them and pounded them to dust. And then all was shattered together – the clay and the iron, the brass, the silver and the gold, and they became like chaff from the summer threshing-floor, and the wind bore them away, and no one know whither, and the stone that struck the image became a great and high mountain and filled all the earth. This is the dream, he concluded, his voice miraculously clear and limpid, like the voice of an angel, and the meaning of it I shall explain to my lord the King:

Your Majesty, you are the King, and the King of Kings, to whom God in Heaven has given the kingdom, the might and the valour and the glory, and wherever men dwell, and wherever there are beasts of the field and birds of the air, he has given you dominion over them. You are the golden head. After you, will come another kingdom inferior to yours, and another, a third kingdom of brass that shall rule the whole earth. And the fourth kingdom shall be strong as iron, for iron crushes everything, and as iron shatters and crushes, so it shall shatter and crush. And as for the feet that you saw and the toes, partly of clay and partly of iron, they will be a kingdom divided in itself, and it shall have something in it of the strength and fortitude of iron, while the other part will be brittle. As for the iron that you saw mixed with clay, when this is joined by the intermingling of the seed of mankind, there shall be no cleaving together, for iron does not cleave to clay. And in the days of those kings, the God of Heaven will set up a kingdom that shall never be destroyed, and no other people shall prevail over it, but it will shatter and crush all those kingdoms and it will last forever. And the stone that you saw, hewn from a mountain not by any hand, and shattering the iron, the brass, the clay, the silver and the gold – the great God has made known to the King what is to be hereafter. The dream is true, and its interpretation to be trusted.

Hearing his words, the King rose from his throne and descended the three gold steps, deeply moved, and he bowed to him and prostrated himself on the ground before him, and rising he clapped his hands and commanded the slave who appeared at once to bring offerings to Daniel and to anoint his feet with incense. Then he turned and addressed him, shaken to the very roots of his soul, his voice quaking:

"Truly, your God is the God of Gods and the Lord of kings, and of the kings of kings, and a revealer of secrets, even of this great secret!"

And the King sent word that the chief steward of the royal household be summoned, and he appeared in full ceremonial regalia, his clerk and slave following closely behind him, with a phial of ink in his belt, stylus and pen in his sleeve, and parchment scrolls in his pocket. And the King commanded that around the neck of Daniel the Jew, the revered Belteshazzar, there should be hung a gold necklace, with a pendant bearing the royal cipher, a sign and a symbol not to be ignored, and henceforward Belteshazzar was to be deputy to the King and all were to acknowledge his sway. He was to be the first and the chief of ministers, with authority over every official, clerk and counsellor within the palace and outside it. And the King ordered that he be allotted suitable remuneration, and given a house in the royal compound, and provided with as many slaves and maidservants as he wished for, and according to the King's own specific proclamation, all the soothsayers and wizards and magicians and diviners and astrologers in Babylon were to defer to him, to Belteshazzar, who would deal with them as he saw fit, with powers of life and death to be wielded entirely at his own discretion.

And Daniel bowed at the feet of the King,

Nebuchadnezzar the valiant and the wise, conqueror of the world, and prostrated himself before him, and then rose to his feet and thanked him profusely for the honour done to him and for the recognition accorded to his God, the God of Gods. And he added that he had a favour to ask, and the King replied:

"Speak, and it shall be done!"

He reminded the King that he had companions who were scholarly and knowledgeable, God-fearing and God-loving, and loyal subjects of the King, and he asked that they be appointed his deputy ministers in all respects.

"So be it!" the King replied, beckoning to the chief steward of the royal household, and he hastily ordered the slave who accompanied him to record on parchment all of the King's edicts and stipulations, which would then be given to the copyists to transcribe in the proper manner; thus the King's will would be done in the great city of Babylon and throughout the Chaldean nation, and in every race and principality and state and country that the King ruled by right of conquest.

And so it was.

I AM YOUR SERVANT

He was given charge of a department adjacent to the royal council chamber, composed of five separate offices, and on the instructions of the King himself, he was assigned the largest of these offices, opening directly into the council chamber. His door was guarded by two sentries, men of the elite royal household corps. Three of the offices were allocated to Mishael, Hananiah and Azariah and one was left unoccupied. He was minded to offer this for the general use of the other ministers, but then an idea occurred to him and he decided to try to implement it.

One evening he knocked on the door of Denur-Shag's lodging, after dismissing the pair of bodyguards accompanying him.

The old slave opened the door cautiously, and the moment he saw him, he fell at his feet, prostrating himself before him.

"Get up, please! Please get up! There's no need for this!" There was a note of annoyance in his voice, which only added to the confusion of the slave, who now tried to scramble up from the floor and found the effort beyond him. He stepped forward and took the slave's arm , helping him to stand upright.

"My Lord," the slave mumbled, the pupils of his eyes dilated in abject fear, "my Lord and deputy King! Let this not be held to my discredit, may I rather gain grace and favour in Your Worship's eyes..." his voice trailed away.

"Calm yourself, my good man!" he addressed him

mildly, adding in the same tone, "if Denur-Shag is at home, please be so kind as to inform him of my arrival, and ask if he is prepared to receive me!"

"Of course, my gracious Master, it shall be done at once!" In the slave's big eyes bewilderment was taking the place of fear, though without dispelling it completely. The words of the chief minister, the King's all-powerful deputy, were incomprehensible to him. Had he really heard it, with his own ears – this Belteshazzar, wearing the gold pendant with the royal cipher about his neck, wielding the power of life and death at will – asking permission of his humble master, the diminutive schoolteacher in the shabby cloak, to be received in his home? It made no sense to him at all.

Limping slightly the slave hurried into the house, and finding his master engrossed in one of his almanacs, he informed him in a quaking voice of the strange visit and the even stranger request.

And he answered him off-handedly:

"Tell him to come in!" – showing no sign of excitement or urgency, not rising from his seat or diverting his attention from the almanac.

The slave returned to the visitor, bowed down as low as he could without collapsing on the floor, and repeated his master's words:

"Tell him to come in!"

He entered the narrow, low and familiar house of Denur-Shag. The latter rose to meet him, with a firm handshake expressive of warmth and fellowship, and a look of satisfaction that he was unable to conceal.

"Be blessed, my friend, and may you continue to go from strength!" he cried, adding: "That gold necklace that hangs round your neck is many times heavier than its actual weight! Sometimes – you will have to defend it, defend it at the risk of your own life, and sometimes – hide behind it, and if you fail to conduct yourself properly this necklace will become for you that thick and knotted rope of notorious repute!" Denur-Shag returned to his seat and fell silent. The other began by saying:

"I came to ask you to participate in matters to which you are not indifferent!"

Without responding to this, Denur-Shag invited him to sit and called to his slave; when the latter opened the door a crack and peered through it, he asked him to fetch red, kosher wine, dates, goat's cheese and bread. The slave disappeared, to return moments later with everything that had been requested.

"How does he manage to get all these things?" he asked, intrigued.

"He's a very resourceful man," the host replied. "He knows what is where, and so he doesn't waste his time running around and looking for things, to the advantage of his master and his guests, and most of all – to his own!"

They both laughed, and then, with emphatic solemnity, Denur-Shag poured some of the clear liquid, the colour of the sunset or the ripe cherry, into two thick glass goblets, not of the finest quality, set one of them before him, raised the other in his hand and pronounced the blessing:

"May your all-powerful God be with you always!"

He replied with a brief blessing, giving thanks for food and wine, then picked up his goblet and drank from it, as did Denur-Shag, and put it down beside the long-necked earthenware bottle. And then he looked at his former teacher and asked him: "Well?"

Denur-Shag lowered his eyes, staring quizzically at the table for a while, before slicing the bread and transferring the soft cheese into clay dishes. Finally he looked up and said:

"There is no service that isn't the service of God. Even someone who has strayed far from Him and denies Him, in the final analysis is serving Him, even if this is not what he wants. Obviously, the correct and praiseworthy thing to do is serve God willingly, with love, and everyone with a brain should be asking himself if he is really doing this, and to what extent, and how. Your compatriots have the saying, *The voice of the people is the voice of God*, meaning, in my humble opinion, that anyone who serves the people, any people, faithfully and not with a view to profit, is serving God. And 'not with a view to profit' can be interpreted in certain cases to mean 'not in the bright light of publicity'. And service such as this is perhaps the one and only thing capable of bringing deep satisfaction, true satisfaction, and for this reason it is preferable that I don't accept an appointment in your office or more precisely – one of the offices allocated to you, as it has already been whispered in my ear that one of them is vacant." Denur-Shag grinned and added: "But I know for a fact that it wasn't for this that you approached me, even though as far as I'm concerned, it's all the same.

"If I thought that was where I belonged, I wouldn't have spurned your proposal without first delving into your motives – the overt and the covert ones! However," he continued, pushing his goblet towards him, "it's obvious to me that my place isn't there, and official posts and government offices are not for me, and moreover it's reasonable to assume that you know this, but to avoid the mistake of appearing heavy-handed, you came to me to hear me say it. Am I right?"

"You are right," he admitted to him, and to himself. The motive behind this visit – it was becoming clear to him – had been nothing other than the need to pay his former teacher the honour due to him, and somehow express his appreciation and his gratitude.

"Nevertheless," Denur-Shag went on to say with an air of clear satisfaction, "you won't be getting rid of me as easily as that! I shall stand by you, if the need arises – even if it isn't what you want. But I won't be on the sunny side of the street! I'll be lurking in the shadows, out of sight – and there I shall be at your service!"

They both resumed their sipping of the light wine, its delicate sweetness turning in the void of the mouth to distant flashes of song and fields of flowers.

Denur-Shag bit into his slice of bread, chewing steadily and with an air of undiluted pleasure, swallowed and continued:

"Your sudden rise to eminence has come as a shock to Babylon. Babylonians are by nature excitable, with a propensity towards the sensational, but the excuse for indulging their emotions that you've given them is in a class all of its own, virtually unique.

"It's reasonable to suppose that the coming days will have more surprises in store for us," Denur-Shag went on to say, speaking with unaccustomed gravity. "From the moment that Jews come to power in any country, that country will be blessed with chronic turbulence, enjoying ups and downs, miracles and wonders. Yes, it's a specific trait of your race, the Jewish race. They do very well serving as deputy to some king or other, or senior adviser to a governor, or treasury minister to a potentate. It's a different story when they take power into their own hands, and become the kings and the governors themselves. That's when everything falls apart, when the wheels come off the chariot! That's because the Jews were never meant to *do* things; their job has always been to have ideas, which others implement. Since the dawn of antiquity they were assigned the role of serving God, and

He, God, is their only king, governor and leader and ruler. So anyone who sets out to imitate God, becoming king, conqueror or ruler, will ultimately encounter devastating defeat, and bring disaster upon his people and himself, is it not so?" he asked and he answered him:

"The role of imitating God was claimed by the power opposing him, the one who tempted mankind saying: *"You shall be as God"*

"If imitation isn't an option, what else is there?" asked Denur-Shag.

"Revelation," he declared, "meaning, the discovery of God in your own heart, and waking up to know yourself an inseparable part of Him."

"Outstanding!" enthused Denur-Shag, thumping the table top with his fist and setting all the utensils jangling.

Denur-Shag looked down again, pondering, and finally looked up and said:

"One way or the other, I have not a shadow of a doubt that the golden age of Babylon, as you predicted to the King, is close at hand and will soon be reaching its zenith, and why is this?" He was not expecting an answer and when none came, he went on to say – "Because Babylon, in these days of ours, is administered entirely by Jews! With the exception of the King himself. No one can compare with the Jews when it comes to conveying the blessing of God – to others, not to themselves. This is their fate as a race and a nation and a people until the coming of the last days, when God Himself shall rule His chosen people in His own kingdom, the Kingdom of Heaven!"

Again they sipped the kosher wine which Denur-Shag had thoughtfully provided, concluding their meal with the bread, freshly baked in the royal bakery and still smelling fragrant, accompanied by thin slivers of cheese.

"This Babylon, of today, is enjoying the festival that it

owes to you, and is celebrating the saving of the lives of those wretched magicians, with the display of excessive exuberance and reverence – worshipping you in song and in dance and in procession – that is so typical. Tomorrow, according to the same norms and traditions – you will be envied and reviled, and those naïve and wretched magicians will look at you with jealousy and malice, and some will kindle virulent hatred of you, of which you will be only too well aware, and then perhaps, by God's grace, I can help you, standing in the shadows as I shall be!

"This is perhaps the role that God has enjoined upon me, and although I make no solemn vows or pledges, I shall fulfil this role of mine to the best of my ability, in other words – above and beyond what is to be expected and perhaps even – above and beyond what is tolerable and desirable." He raised his goblet, taking small and frequent sips until it was emptied, then putting the empty goblet before him, he spoke again:

"It has also come to my ears that you have succumbed to the Chaldean tradition that is linked to the superstitious belief that a bachelor is unfit to serve the State, and you are soon to marry. And of your future wife, it is said she is some fairy-tale Jewish princess."

"It is true, she is related to the royal household, but she is no princess," he replied.

"According to what is said in your writings, your God gave Adam the prospect of ascending and approaching Him, by creating him in His image and His likeness but not in His spirit, and He set the woman before him as a challenge. And if your first father, who you say is the father of every race and nation, had withstood the challenge of the woman as he should and not been tripped up by her – he would have earned the privilege of discovering the spirit of his creator in his heart and thereby knowing himself. Instead of this – he slipped and fell and showed the flesh to be as it is today – corruptible matter."

"It follows then that the penitent will regain his prospects, and he is the one who will find the spirit of his Creator in his heart," he completed his host's peroration.

"And how can man repent, and approach his Creator, and repair what he has spoiled, and know divine love?"

"By following the divine way that says: You shall love the Lord your God with all your heart and with all your might and with all your soul, and your neighbour as yourself!"

He stood up from his seat and bade Denur-Shag an amicable farewell. The host accompanied him to the door of the house and said to him as they parted company:

"Don't forget, my Lord and deputy to the King – I am your servant!"

WITHOUT MAKING A SOUND

His hands were spread on the top of the broad, oblong table, constructed of polished oak in its natural colour and heaped with rolled parchment scrolls and clay tablets, some separate and others strung together, alongside a selection of high quality styli and pens, and red and blue ink in phials of ivory.

Before he could begin the routine of the day, he heard a knock at the door, the light knock of his office slave.

"Enter!" he cried and the latter, a bright young lad from the northern isles, with a film of soft downy hair on his cheeks, dressed in blue livery, his Chaldean name Oshrich – opened the door and stood on the threshold.

Oshrich bowed to him, stepped inside, closed the door behind him, bowed again and on straightening up said: "A lady named Adelain is asking to see you, Sir!"

For some reason this announcement struck fear into his heart. He suppressed it and turning to Oshrich said: "I shall receive her in a little while!"

"You will call me, Sir?"

"I will call!"

As soon as Oshrich had left, he fell to his knees, raised his hands, palms together, and looking up at the sky, through the broad window behind his chair, began:

"Purify me I pray, my Father in Heaven, my God, guide me I pray, my Father in Heaven, my God. You are in me, my Father in Heaven, my God, and I in you, for ever and ever!"

The light of joy filled his heart, streaming in the void of his spacious, sumptuous office.

"For ever and ever I shall give thanks to You my Father in Heaven, my God! I thank You for the abundant grace that You have awarded me, and would that I were only worthy of it!"

He rose to his feet, took his seat at the table, clapped his hands once, twice, and the door opened. Oshrich stood on the threshold, bowing.

Rising to his full height he glanced at him, and for a long moment froze where he stood, motionless, his eyes reflecting utter astonishment, bordering on panic and veering towards reverence. Without realising what he was doing, the slave bowed down before him once again, prostrating himself at his master's feet as at the feet of a deity: his master's face was aglow with ethereal light.

"Be so good," he addressed him with an unfamiliar, musical lilt to his voice – "as to call the lady Adelain and ask her to come here!"

"As you wish Sir, so it shall be done!" Oshrich replied, his voice too seeming to deviate from its normal tone of restraint, and his face flickering with either a strange delight or with reverent fear.

Adelain entered. On her trim body a white dress, white as the virgin snow on the mountain tops. The dress was gathered at the waist in a broad leather belt of a deep velvet colour, its buckle silver studded with sapphires, and on her head was a turban the colour of her dress, fastened with a pearl brooch.

She turned upon him her big, deep, subdued eyes, and stood there tongue-tied and nervous, until a strange kind of merriment, excluding all else, took over her entire being.

"Good day to you, Adelain!" he greeted her, his voice vibrant, as if laden with confidence and hopeful tidings.

She did not return his greeting, preferring instead to

express something of the intensity of the feelings that were making her heart flutter.

"Your face is radiant!"

"That's just the sun," he said with a modest smile, "the light of the sun on my face!"

"It isn't the light of the sun! You are a wonderful sight!" she insisted, the musical lilt of his voice now audible in hers, and her eyes absorbing and reflecting the purity in his eyes.

"How happy I am to be in your presence, to hear your voice, to be refreshed by the pure light that shines from your eyes!"

"Please be seated!" He pointed to the chair opposite his in an attempt to stem the flow of adulation, of compliments that were not to his taste, and he asked:

"What brings you here?"

"My desire to be, if only for a moment, close to you!" she declared sincerely, without hesitation, with none of the awkwardness that would be expected of a young woman in such circumstances.

Her candour took him aback. The thought crept into his mind that she was beautiful, and that her quivering voice could set hearts ablaze.

"I won't disturb you at all!" she declared, adding by way of explanation: "I shall sit by myself behind your back, without making a sound. You won't know I'm here!" she concluded, and without waiting for consent or rejection, she found a stool that had been left in a corner and saying not another word, sat herself down behind his back, not too close to him.

He had to admit that she was right; he was not aware of her presence. Even her breathing, which was not quiet, no longer reached his ears.

"You must do as you please!" he said without turning

to face her. He unfolded a yellowing parchment scroll and settled down to read it.

Soon after Adelain's arrival, he called Oshrich and handed him a scroll to be passed on to one of his aides. And the slave was incapable of maintaining his composure or curbing his astonishment at the spectacle revealed to him: a young woman blessed with quite exceptional beauty, of distinguished family, judging by her attire – sitting on a low stool, tucked away in a corner of the office behind his master's back, and doing nothing and not making a sound, like a spare item of furniture, doing neither service nor disservice.

The bemusement reflected in the face of his slave made no impression on him, not because of the latter's clumsy attempts to hid it, but because he had completely forgotten Adelain's presence.

She sat without making a movement, as if she were not a body at all but a vapour, dispersing into the void and becoming a part of it. Furthermore, the matters he was supposed to be dealing with were urgent and demanded concentration and focus, and he spared himself no effort in working through each problem, understanding the implications and mastering the details and arriving at solutions, however abstruse and elusive the issues might be.

An hour passed, perhaps more than an hour. Again, Oshrich knocked on the door, entered and announced:

"The minister Nashdernach, chief of the King's advisers, requests an audience with you, Sir!"

"Show him in!" he cried.

Oshrich opened the door wide and stood back, bowing and making way for Nashdernach to pass by him.

The newcomer delivered his greetings and took a seat facing him, a friendly gesture.

"Did you know," he began, with a kind of tension in his voice that he was making an effort to conceal – and then Nashdernach noticed the young woman, sitting in silence on a low stool, in a corner, behind the other's back.

The chief of the King's advisers stared at her with his tiny, oily eyes, which were open wide, as wide as the eyes of a man who arrives at his workplace as usual and finds his father, long since dead and buried, sitting there grinning at him.

Nashdernach was struck dumb, unable to avert his gaze from the figure in white, sitting in silence as if detached from the world.

It was only then that the other remembered Adelain and the fact that she was sitting behind him. He turned, and the astonishment in his eyes changed rapidly into something that could be interpreted as a query, such as – *Well, what now?*

Without a word, without any acknowledgement whatsoever of the two men, Adelain rose and left his office.

Nashdernach lowered his gaze and sat for a while in silence. Finally he looked up and said, a twinkle in his oily little eyes:

"If I am not mistaken, she is the daughter of our valiant and illustrious commander, Or-Nego."

"She is indeed."

"This is a strange state of affairs. Women are strange, and that lady – she's in a class all of her own!" he asserted, going on to say: "I once heard of a woman, a relative of mine in fact, who loved a wise and handsome man, loved him with a love as strong as death, in the words of your scriptures. And his heart went out to her, and he asked her to marry him and be his wife – and she refused. Her love was so strong, she said, that it needed no physical contact. As simple as that! Have you ever heard of such a thing?" he asked.

"No," he answered him, adding, "but I understand your relative's attitude. Love is not dependent on the physical body, and distance and time do not exist where love is concerned."

"Anyway," Nashdernach resumed with a sigh, "that's how it was with my relative! The case caused something of a stir at the time, which is how I came to hear of it. She married no one and remained a virgin. A beautiful woman by all accounts. He on the contrary, married a wife and was divorced, and married again – and was divorced again. In the end he lived with a mistress. He didn't understand my relative's love and he used to complain that it wasn't love at all, but cruelty for its own sake. I don't know if the pair of them are still alive. To tell the truth, I just don't understand this kind of love," – Nashdernach expressed his bemusement with a shrug of the shoulders, "I mean, if she loves the man and she's going to be true to him, why not marry him and put him out of his misery? Is she afraid that this weird love of hers, or higher love if you prefer – let's not quibble over definitions – is she afraid that this higher love is going to be spoiled by physical intimacy?"

"The higher, the true love is eternal, and nothing can prevail over it, and it certainly won't be spoiled by any kind of contact," he replied.

"Why then, did this loving woman refuse to marry her lover?" Nashdernach persisted.

"I suppose that your relative reckoned marriage was liable to be harmful to him, and he wouldn't be prepared to do without physical intimacy, despite his repeated protestations to the contrary. And the proof of this – he separated from the wives in whom he sought this intimacy."

"Oh!" Nashdernach lowered his greying head, as if thinking through the implications, and then summing up for his own benefit:

"So she sacrifices herself on the altar of her higher love." And looking up again and fixing his little eyes on him he continued:

"As for *this* young woman, young and utterly delightful as she is – I reckon that the very fact of her visit to you and the time spent in your office, will do irreparable harm to her honour as a maiden and her good name as a woman, and she will no longer be eligible to marry according to the law, unless *you* marry her. And you're waiting for your princess from Judah! So things are becoming a little complicated, and this lady inspires admiration and compassion, and heart-ache as well. I suppose you could take her as a mistress? I'm sure she would agree to anything if it meant being close to you."

"I could never agree to that!" he protested.

"Your future wife would object?" asked Nashdernach, in a toneless voice.

"She wouldn't express any objection, but deep down she'd feel damaged. But even leaving that aside, the idea doesn't appeal to me."

"Why is that?" Nashdernach persisted.

"Because I don't believe in polygamy, and in my heart I know that polygamy is contrary to the will of God."

"Your forefathers married many wives, and to this very day the practice is tolerated among your compatriots!"

"The murder of animals and the consumption of their carcases are also practices condoned by the Torah, but this is a late version of it, a compromising version. It isn't the consummate worship of God, doing the true will of

God."

"And is there to be no compassion for this young woman, no easing of her grief?"

"There is help for her," he declared, "but she has to consent to it."

"And how is she to do that?"

"By strengthening her faith in God, and loving Him with all her heart and mind."

"Aha!" exclaimed Nashdernach, his tone acknowledging that a valid and persuasive point had been made. And then he took a thick scroll from his pocket, laid it on the table, opened it and said:

"Now for the business in hand. We need to discuss the status of soldiers who are permanently disabled as a result of injuries sustained in war."

NEJEEN

With the onset of spring a wind from the east descends upon Babylon, gusting strongly day and night without respite, bearing on its wings grey dust from the roads and sand from the desert. People try to protect themselves from it by sealing the shutters of their homes and veiling their faces.

One such morning, when the east wind was beginning to subside, and the sky was peering through gaps in the swirling clouds of dust, he rose from his bed with a feeling of light-heartedness and merriment, bathed and dressed and went out to the broad veranda of his house, all awash with flowers, a rich tapestry of colours. He sat on a chair beside the oblong table, covered by a blue cloth with silver trim.

He knew the source of his exhilaration: *she* was coming.

How would she look? And what of the future relations between them? And the joy in his heart swelled and grew ever stronger, until it was no longer to be easily controlled or suppressed.

"My Father in Heaven, my God, what is the nature of this joy that fills my heart and thrills every fibre of my being? Is this joy pure? Are You the source of it? Does it have another source?"

"No my son! This joy arises and emanates from the fountains of my light, and it will not divert you from the way! Delight in it and bless it!"

The household slave was trying to attract his attention as he paced back and forth among the vases on the veranda, moving them this way and that, and when he finally succeeded and he looked back at him with a questioning glance, he bowed to him and informed him that Denur-Shag was asking permission to enter.

He broke off from his meditations and asked the slave to hurry and admit Denur-Shag to the house.

A few moments later, his former teacher was standing before him, trying to dissuade him from rising to meet him and to shake his hand.

"You shouldn't deprive us of the pleasure of prostrating ourselves before a person of exceptional authority!" he commented, adding in typical style: "Not that the exceptional is something that I care for particularly, but where persons of authority are concerned, it is the routine that repels – and I'm talking about smells here. Authority trapped in a frame of routine gives off a familiar smell, quite pungent and very similar, if not identical, to the smell that assails your nostrils in the vicinity of a slaughterhouse. In agriculture, for example, routine works wonders, and it's a boon to the farmer, to the land and to all of humanity, and its smell is clean. However, the routine that I like best of all is the routine of family life, paved as it is with petty disasters and delights."

He signalled to the slave, and he brought in figs, nuts and dates, an Egyptian jug made of the finest glass and containing honey-water, and matching goblets. The foodstuffs were served on small dishes that were smooth inside and out, gleaming white in colour and hand-painted in blue with images of trees, people and flowers – real works of art. Denur-Shag picked up one of the dishes, turned it over in his hand and studied it from every angle, finally declaring:

"Sent to you direct from the royal warehouse, I assume."

He confirmed this with a nod.

"I don't suppose that in the whole of Babylon there are exquisite objects such as these to be found, except in the possession of the King himself and now – in your possession too. I may be mistaken, and perhaps that clever trader who has the strange-sounding Hebrew name of Adoniah, and the equally strange Chaldean name of Adeshech, is among the few who own articles like these. As I'm sure you know, they are made by those faraway people with the slanting eyes, who weave silk fabrics made from caterpillars, or more accurately – from the cocoons of caterpillars, which, if allowed to live, would turn into winged butterflies of breath-taking beauty. Our faraway brothers are harsh in their treatment of these unfortunate caterpillars, stripping them of their cocoons and leaving them to die, naked and helpless, in excruciating pain. Such is the typical behaviour of mankind, and yet according to your sacred writings the first man was appointed to 'give names' to all living creatures, from the butterfly to the elephant, meaning – that man is supposed to defend them, and delight in them and love them, so that they will love him in return, and gladly provide him with wool and milk and with impressive displays of colour and movement.

"But here mankind has failed and has betrayed God's trust, and instead of 'giving names', mankind is deleting names from the list of living things, and is exploiting those that remain and tormenting them and preying on them. Was this your God's intention when He created mankind?"

"God is love," he responded evenly, while pouring honey-water into the goblets of fine Egyptian glass, "and love does not impose itself on the object of its love, love bestows freedom. Man is liable to make the wrong use of the freedom that he has been granted."

"I wouldn't say he was 'liable' to do that," Denur-Shag objected, taking the full goblet that was handed to him and raising it in a gesture of benediction, then taking a small sip from it. "Man has done it – and is still doing it, and is bringing down on his head all the disasters of the world."

Denur-Shag took a shelled nut, chewed it in his mouth for a while and before swallowing it said:

"Yesterday, at a late hour of the night, I had a visit from someone who is reckoned to be a relative of mine – by marriage," he saw fit to stress, and added for further clarification: "This is the family of my rustic wife, one of the most 'extended' in the kingdom. It has so many members that no one knows the precise number, but all of the people of that village, to the very last one of them, have close family ties between them and as you might say – they take responsibility for one another.

"And ever since I had the good fortune to marry a daughter of the village of these agreeable people – it's only logical and natural that, according to the rigid rules of that mutual responsibility, I should be acknowledged as a member of the tribe and of the family unit, and guaranteed their full support. To their credit I may say, they expect nothing from me in return.

"This relative, it turns out, joined some delegation or other and went away to Judah some months ago, and now he's glad to be back in Babylon. He had a specific job as a runner – carrying messages, letters, news and items of small value between members of the delegation, and between members of the delegation and outsiders. Exploiting his role as a harbinger, and using the expertise and the wealth of experience gained through this unconventional profession, he decided to precede the delegation, moving ahead like the vanguard of an army on the march, and he came to me yesterday, in the late hours of the night. And the boy didn't want to go to bed and rest from the rigours of the journey, perhaps because of the rigid rules of the mutual responsibility code – or perhaps he just wanted to share some of the impressions stamped on his peasant mind.

"Anyway, he sat down with me, this distant relative of mine, and while partaking of the modest repast which I served to him, he proceeded to tell me his story. And the story was a long one, extending into the dawn and even beyond, and it couldn't be described as interesting and pleasant to listen to either. This peasant boy is far removed from anything that could be called eloquence, and not much of a story teller, but that clan code demanded of him whatever it demanded, and I had to sit and listen closely because of my obligations under that ancient code – a fascinating object of study for anyone researching into ancient laws and customs, written and unwritten."

Denur-Shag returned to his drink, drained his goblet and without saying a word, took the bottle and refilled it.

He himself had not yet touched his drink, instead listening intently to the words of his guest.

"Are you bored?" Denur-Shag asked, taking a ripe date between two fingers and putting it to his mouth, without looking at him, as if ignoring his very presence and as if talking to himself.

And sure enough, the questioner did not wait for an answer, but went on to say:

"These words were by way of a preamble. And for some reason it seems to me – and 'seems' is just a sterile, evasive expression – it would be more accurate to say 'I'm sure', yes 'I'm sure' without any hesitation or prevarication, that the next part of the story will be of great interest to you. You can visualise it, and see the whole episode unfolding before your mind's eye!

"Well then," – Denur-Shag took another sip of his drink, "my relative told me that in the convoy travelling with the delegation there was a special wagon, with padding and upholstery, closed most of the time, and occupied by a wondrous Jewish princess. Wondrous, that is, in her beauty and also in her demeanour. My rustic relative referred specifically to an exceptional kind of behaviour, quite unfamiliar to him, something testifying to noble lineage or, as he tried to express it with his inferior eloquence, something showing that this lady was 'born to be a queen' – a common and hackneyed expression, but like so many such expressions, both succinct and accurate!

"And while on the subject of the exceptional behaviour of this Jewish princess, the one 'born to be a queen', my rustic relative told me that at one of their overnight halts, on the way back from Jerusalem, not far from Tyre, bandits got into the camp, tied up the two sentries who were supposed to be guarding the horses, and they were about to cut off their heads and steal the horses, leaving the convoy without any effective means of transport, stuck in the middle of nowhere, hopeless and helpless – when all of a sudden the Jewish princess appeared. She confronted the bandits, all five of them, and ordered them to untie the captives and set them free, to leave their booty behind and to go back to their haunts the same way that they had come. And this is the point: she didn't urge them, didn't plead with them, didn't cry or try to appeal to their compassion – no, she *ordered* them, in the clear voice of a born leader and commander. That is the testimony of the captives themselves, they saw her and heard her, and they were amazed by the glorious vision and by the regal sound of her voice. And no less impressed, so it seems, were the bandits themselves. Those five tough men obeyed her and even bowed to her, they released their captives, mounted their horses and rode away, leaving their booty behind, and disappeared into the darkness, as this was the third watch of the night. And the sentries who had been freed and had escaped with their lives did not know themselves for joy and even tried to offer some gift to the princess, but she flatly rejected any attempt to reward her, and when asked how she realised what was happening, unlike all the other members of the delegation who didn't wake or hear anything, and how she had mastered her fear – the Jewish princess explained that her wagon was parked close to the horses' enclosure, and with her sharp ear she heard the nervous whinnying of the horses and went to see what was afoot. As for fear, her comment was – anyone who trusts in God is exempted from fear. And as a direct result of this statement, referring as it did to the God of the princess, a number of Chaldeans converted there and then, following the lead of the two sentries who owed their lives to this God." Denur-Shag concluded his account and there was a long silence. Eventually he continued:

"This, in my humble opinion, is the least boring part of my story. According to my estimation, at this moment the delegation is crossing, or has just crossed, the bridge over the Euphrates, and it is due to arrive at the royal palace shortly after midday. If you want to meet the delegation in appropriate style, you have two hours in hand. As for me, I have no intention of staying around here and joining the reception committee, but before we part company, I shall tell you the third and final part of this story – yes, the story does have a third part!"

Denur-Shag leaned back in his chair and continued

calmly:

"It turns out that my relative's visit to foreign parts, meaning Jerusalem, the sacred capital of Judah, had a profound effect on him. It wasn't just the emotional strain of distance from his native village, it was a traumatic spiritual experience that he had, by his own admission – the first such upheaval he has ever known.

"The youth told me of a man, the like of whom he had never seen before nor met before, not even in the great metropolis of Babylon. He had never dreamed that such a person even existed. A long, long beard, not neatly trimmed and plaited in the Chaldean style, but wild and unkempt, as is the hair of his head, and he wears a simple robe, a rope for a belt at his waist, and he walks about barefoot. Nothing remarkable so far – it could be that the man has eccentric tastes, or he could be short of cash. What astonished my relative was seeing the eyes of this man, eyes unlike any others he had known. One glance was enough to convince him this was the only pair of eyes in the world, the only eyes that could truly see. These eyes do not glitter or sparkle, but there is light in their depths, flaring up at intervals like a burning torch and at intervals subsiding, sometimes gleaming as bright as the sun. And yet these eyes are not troubled, on the contrary they are serene, with a serenity that is detached from all things, and that is why it is so potent, inspiring fear on the one hand and on the other, boundless admiration and exaltation of spirit.

"Anyway, this man walks the streets of Jerusalem, and speaks out in a clear and resolute voice, untainted by arrogance, and he turns to the people who follow him, and there are many who follow him, and he addresses them sometimes with stern words of reproof and sometimes with words of consolation and encouragement. And he always emphasises that it is not he who speaks but God, your God, speaking through him. And his words are an awesome warning – if the Jews do not learn to manage their affairs properly and proceed in the ways of reason – Jerusalem will be ruined and set ablaze. More than this – he demands there must be no revolt against the King of Babylon whom He, God that is, your God, calls 'my servant' – meaning, the one who does His will. And the reaction to this man, whose name by the way is Jeremiah, the priest from Anathoth, is entirely predictable. People respond to his conduct and the message that he brings in the traditional and time-honoured fashion: beating him with their fists and spitting in his face, waving sticks at him and pelting him with stones, yelling with the righteous anger of all patriots, 'Death to the traitor!' and leaving him to lie, barely conscious or not conscious at all, slumped at the roadside or in a corner of the marketplace. And there are indeed some who try to shield him from his assailants, but they are very few, and most of them old men, and their way of defending him is to stage public debates which, as you know, do more harm than good.

"Returning to that innocent youth, to whom I am tied by that reciprocal family code, attention should be drawn to something else that he said, an uncouth remark but vivid and significant for all that:

"He told me he had met a number of Egyptians, leaders among their own people, who disguise themselves as traders and simple folk and try to look like Jews in every respect, but their diction gives them away, as does their clothing. They are not used to the Jewish mantle, but to robes that flap in the wind, and when they try to move about in the tight confines of the mantle, it looks ridiculous and it betrays their origins. These Egyptians come and go in the court of King Zedekiah and this, like everything in the third and final part of my story, should engender surprise and raise questions and above all, strike fear into the heart. For it seems, and Jeremiah, the priest from Anathoth, confirms this wholeheartedly – darkness is descending on Jerusalem and a bloodbath is in store for Judah. And there is one question that is always asked before something happens that is supposed to happen – is this bloodbath inevitable?"

"No," he replied, "this bloodbath is not inevitable. There is no such thing as an inevitable bloodbath. As for the means of preventing it, it is the same as for any bloodshed anywhere in the world, past, present or future. Only one method is effective, no other."

"And that is?" Denur-Shag pressed him.

"Adherence to values."

"And what does that mean, 'adherence to values'?" Denur-Shag wanted to know.

"Devotion to the truth and the truthful."

"In other words, if people respect the truth in all things, in thought, in word and in deed – that is enough to avert a massacre?"

"It is enough!"

"Perhaps an exiled Jew, one who is in favour with King Nebuchadnezzar, could talk with those Jews who remain in their homeland, drinking their good wine and eating their sweet figs – and persuade them to mend their ways."

"If Jeremiah from Anathoth, through whom God speaks, failed in his mission – could an exiled Jew do any better?"

Denur-Shag pondered for a while, ignoring what remained of the refreshments, and thinking something through, weighing it inwardly at some length and finally asking in a faint voice:

"Why are the Jews such a stiff-necked people?"

He answered him calmly, although with a hint of bitterness in his voice:

"Because of the arrogance with which they are infected. They see themselves as standing above all other peoples and races and nations, and as long as they cannot cure themselves of this infection – disaster awaits them."

"But you are not like that," Denur-Shag protested, "nor are those three friends of yours!"

"Because our faith is the true faith," he explained.

"And the faith of your compatriots is not true faith?"

"Where there is arrogance, there is no room for true faith."

"And what is to be done to combat this fatal arrogance?"

"True faith is the only answer."

Denur-Shag rose heavily from his seat, shook his outstretched hand in silence and for a moment looked like a very old man, bowed under the weight of his years, defeated by life.

"Where are you rushing off to?" he addressed him kindly, still holding his hand and wishing he could give him some encouragement, however fleeting.

Denur-Shag looked up at him, and the expression of his face changed; the dejection dissolved, and a faint but steady light was ignited in the depths of his eyes.

"The Jewish princess is due to arrive at any moment! Anyone wanting to greet her had better hurry and make the necessary arrangement. And something else I shall tell you – there is hope for the Jewish people, and I wish there were just a small portion of it for the Chaldean people!"

"In what do you see this hope?" he asked.

"In that Jeremiah, the man of Anathoth, and in you and in those who are like you! Be well."

WITHOUT ANY CONNECTING THREAD

He could not believe what his eyes were seeing and his ears hearing. Nevertheless, it seemed to him there could be no sight more natural, more anchored in reality than this, no sound more familiar and responsive to his expectations than the voice he heard. On the one hand – it was as if the world had turned upside down and the new, without any connecting thread to what had gone before, was revealed to him in all the glory of its youth, while on the other – it seemed nothing had changed or was even capable of changing; the past being the present, and the present never deviating in the slightest degree from what used to be.

She stood before him, straight-backed, her long face pale, her forehead clear, a little arched, so pure it might never have been polluted by a deviant thought, or a less than exalted notion. And her eyes...yes, in her eyes there had been a change though it was barely perceptible. More precisely – the nature of the change was perceptible but not its extent. The luminous depths, familiar from days gone by, no longer knew any limit but flowed freely, from one eternity to another. The dark blue, that transported anyone seeing it beyond the furthest Heaven, was darker still, sometimes turning to the young violet of dusk.

The eyes resembled twin pools, deep, calm and smooth, drawing serenity and steadfast assurance from an unflagging source, and in the clarity of this source there was an astonishing wealth of tenderness, nobility and compassion.

It was Azariah who accompanied her to the threshold

of his house, and after a firm handshake said awkwardly:

"I shall return later," and turned away.

The two of them shook hands and for a moment it seemed their hands would never be parted; then they parted them and gazed into one another's eyes with a look that was sincere, radiant, proud.

He began to speak, surprised at the sound of his calm, controlled voice:

"I very much hope that Babylon will be to your taste. It isn't Judah and it isn't Jerusalem!" he said, and heard her voice for the first time in eight years:

"God is everywhere!" – and her limpid voice was like a hymn of praise, of which he too was a part.

He repeated after her with a kind of joyful submission:

"God is everywhere!"

"I bring blessings and greetings from your mother, from your sisters and brother..."

"The baby!" he cried eagerly.

She smiled, and the high-ceilinged reception hall was swamped with light.

"He's eight years old!" she reminded him and added: "They asked me to tell you that they're proud of you."

"Why should they be proud of me?" he asked.

"Among other things," she answered him, "for interpreting the dream of the King of Babylon. Your mother says you are following in the path of our forefathers, who were commanded by God to make His will known to Jews and Gentiles alike."

"She's exaggerating!" he protested, in an attempt to dampen something of the admiration in her voice, which was indeed restrained but clearly perceptible. "What's your opinion?" he asked.

"What she says is the truth!" she replied simply, in her old style. "My mother's proud of you too," she added, "as are many of the citizens of Jerusalem..." Her voice quavered and her eyes fell.

"And there are also some who are not proud but angry," he suggested, and she confirmed it.

"There are indeed." Her voice was steady again.

He suggested they go to the veranda, and she followed him.

He sat down at the table as he had sat a little while before with Denur-Shag, noting inwardly that the strange, unfamiliar sensation of shining light, grace and quiet pleasure was taking over his entire being.

When the slave had served refreshments and a jug of warm honey-water, he resumed:

"I have heard about Jeremiah the prophet – how they are conspiring against him and humiliating him, how he has been beaten and persecuted!"

"It is true," she said, and suddenly the soft radiance of her eyes captivated him and he was all exaltation. He remembered the words of Adoniah, that one glimpse of her would be enough to persuade the worst of felons to mend his ways and repent.

My Father in Heaven, my God – he spoke to his heart, which was quivering with a rapture such as he had never known – *Am I worthy of this grace?*

And he heard her voice, offering strength and solace:

"Jeremiah the prophet has heard about you, too. When my uncle, my mother's brother, told him I was going down to Babylon to marry you, he took the trouble to come to us and he sat in our house three days and two nights, most of the time shut away in a room with the door locked, not saying a word and barely eating. Until finally he turned to me and said:

'Convey the blessing of God to your future husband and my blessing too, and tell him to be joyful and be glad, because his mission is ordained by God, a source of wonder and delight, and all the humble among my people will rejoice in him!' And seeing the look of astonishment on my face, the prophet added: 'Despite the contempt, and the ingratitude, the beatings and the abuse, the banishment and imprisonment to which the envoy of God is subjected, there shines in his heart the eternal joy of the awareness of God and the knowledge of Him! The reward of the envoy of God – is God Himself!'"

"That is indeed the truth!" he declared warmly, pouring out some of the honey-water for her and for himself, and taking only a tiny morsel of the bread. She asked him why he was abstaining from the lavish spread that was laid out on the table and he explained that earlier that morning he had been visited by a dear friend, the one who informed him of the imminent return of the delegation and her arrival – and they had broken their fast together.

"He wanted to cheer you up," she remarked casually, like him taking a small piece of bread and drinking thirstily from the liquid – light and refreshing and still retaining its warmth.

"He wouldn't miss an opportunity to gladden the heart of his friend!" he agreed, and smiled at her, a deep smile that she took in without raising her eyes, and her pale cheeks flushed slightly.

"Do you remember the bears?" he asked.

"I remember," she replied, looking up and calmly meeting his gaze. "Do you remember how many cubs there were?"

"Three!" he smiled again.

"And the colour of their fur?" she went on to ask, her voice light and vibrant with youth, as well as a sense of good-natured mischief.

He racked his brains, thought it over, seeing in his mind's eye the cubs and their mother... all standing there before him as if alive, and he even inhaled the peculiar balm of the air in the Jerusalem hills, but the colour of the fur of the cubs had vanished from his eyes.

"No," he looked up, admitting defeat. "I can't even remember if there was any difference between them. Do you?"

"One of them was very light, almost yellow, his brother was dark brown, and the youngest of all had tufts of brown fur on a lighter background." She laughed a full-throated, resonant laugh, pleasing to the ear, melodious as the laughter of a child.

They sat in silence, and the longer the silence lasted, so they felt the pleasure bridging the gap between them, redolent with faith and strong in its unflagging purity.

"How do you like the idea of bringing the marriage ceremony forward?" he asked, his tone calm and harmonious.

She answered him in the same tone:

"As you wish!"

"Would you like to see the house?" he asked.

"Gladly!"

He showed her round the two-storey house placed at his disposal, with its sixteen rooms and two halls, a large hall on the ground floor and a smaller one above. And then he showed her the seven-roomed apartment set aside for her, and introduced her two Chaldean chambermaids who greeted her with a bow. A spacious bed chamber linked her rooms to his.

"Do you approve of the arrangement of rooms?" he asked finally, as they sat facing one another in the parlour that was now hers.

"Very much so!" she answered him sincerely, and

added: "Whatever pleases you, pleases me sevenfold. As it has been for as long as I remember!"

"I could say the same thing of myself," he smiled, and his smile again brought a flush to her cheeks: "Whatever pleases you, pleases me sevenfold!" He bowed lightly to underline his words.

"Your friend Azariah was very helpful to me, so please thank him in my name!"

"I'll thank him in my own name too! Azariah is a loyal friend and a devoted companion."

"We heard the rumour that you asked the King to appoint him a minister, and your other friends too, Mishael and Hananiah. In my humble opinion you did the best thing possible, and I have no doubt it will bear fruit."

"We work together, and by the grace and the mercy of God, we're trying to bring some relief to the peoples that Babylon has subjugated."

"That's what the prophet Jeremiah was saying – that your mission is a divine one and you could achieve a great deal – so he said, and you would also be tested by temptation, but God would always be with you to save you from death. Those were his explicit words and he went on to say you should be strong and take courage, as your words and your deeds will be the property of all generations of mankind yet to come, and there will be many who love you and more who hate you, and those who hate you are those who hate God and defy Him, and those who love you – are lovers of God who do His will."

"If only God will give the strength to cope with all of them!" he said, adding: "It is written in the Scriptures, *I am not jealous*, meaning that he who has earned the privilege of loving Him, the Blessed One, yearns for nothing else other than Him. All that he seeks, he seeks through Him, and all that he does, he does for the greater glory of His name, and all that he loves, he loves through Him and for His sake."

"May His name be forever blessed!" she pronounced the benediction in a remarkably even voice and raised to him her open, candid gaze, dismissing hypocrisy and banishing evil thought or malicious intent.

Again he was swept by that tide of pure delight and exuberance of spirit. He remembered Adoniah and asked her:

"Not long ago you sent me greetings through Adoniah, one of the exiles, who serves the King as a trader and a go-between."

"I remember him well," she replied. "A young man with all kinds of ideas running around in his head, not the kind of ideas likely to bring him closer to God. I entrusted to him a gift and a message for you."

He unbuttoned his shirt and showed her the seven-branched candlestick, hanging about his neck.

For a moment her eyes glowed with satisfaction, and then she went on to say:

"He told me certain things, some of which I was interested to hear."

"Such as?" he asked.

"Such as the horse race that both of you, it seems, took part in. At first he said he was crowned the winner, then he changed his story and said he almost won, and finally he admitted it was all lies and the winner was none other than you. Naturally I was pleased to hear this and I was proud as well. And then the man launched into a recital of gossip that I barely paid attention to, until he seemed to lose the thread and cut his speech short, stopping altogether and even apologising. Then he gave me some conflicting versions of his life story, saying how miserable he'd been, with no one to talk to or confide in, and then he declared with a kind of arrogance, to say nothing of pretentiousness, that the work he was doing was on behalf of the King of Babylon, and he was doing it well, and this role of his had opened up all kinds of opportunities for him, and he was seeing the world and gaining experience and most important of all – enjoying himself. Still, I see he did his task faithfully, and gave you what he was asked to give you!"

"He almost forgot!" he said lightly, with a chuckle.

"To tell you the truth," she replied – "I wouldn't have been surprised if he had forgotten. He looked so preoccupied."

"With what?" he asked.

"With himself!" was the clear and simple answer.

He took his leave of her, and told her chambermaids to prepare her a hot bath; they assured him it was already done. He watched the porters bringing in her belongings and for the third time that day, for no immediately obvious reason, he felt overwhelmed by glee and exuberance of spirit, and were it possible, at that moment he would have embraced the whole universe and given it all that was in him, and more.

Azariah he met the next morning, and he confirmed the rumours coming out of Judah, concerning Zedekiah and his rebellious intentions.

And Azariah went on to tell of the profound impression made by the interpretation of the King of Babylon's dream, and of people on the streets of Jerusalem saying: "See, a true prophet has arisen for us, and the Lord has visited His people and has sent His prophet to deliver us from the hands of strangers and from the yoke of the Chaldeans." And in the same breath, with the praise and the approbation, come the rage and the resentment – people of Jerusalem and Judah asking one another why is he, Daniel the Jew, fraternising with the Chaldean King, "the wicked King" as they call him, or "the heathen" and other such derogatory epithets. Why, they say, is this chosen son of our holy nation, our proud race that is set apart from all others, working in the service of an alien king, rather than serving us and our Jewish king? And to the question – how is this to be done, the startling answer is:

"He must threaten that King with ruin and destruction, if he does not lift his yoke from our necks!"

If they hear the answer to the other question – that it's his duty to preach the word of God before the King and before anyone else to whom God sends him, and this message that they want to convey to the King of Babylon is not from God! – they are incensed, those milling crowds of Jews, and they insist that every word spoken by a man such as this is the word of the living God, and if he has any interest in delivering his people from the Chaldean yoke, then he will not hesitate or prevaricate, but hasten to the enemy's lair and say what he has to say, and the tyrant will take fright, and he will restore the freedom of Jerusalem, and cancel his taxes, and never again dare to raise his hand against Judah. "Such are the words of the ignorant populace," Azariah concluded his account.

He did not reply to Azariah for better or for worse, but instead raised the subject of the weddings and asked him to discuss it with Mishael and Hananiah and let him know which day was acceptable to them for the raising of the canopy. With Azariah's approval, he would consult with Nehemiah, the priest of the community, to decide the order of service, and moreover he would choose a site and invite guests.

Azariah left his office and two days later returned to

him with two dates that were acceptable to all three of them. He picked one of them and preparations for the wedding ceremonies, due to take place three weeks hence, began in earnest.

FOUR WEDDINGS

Long before the appointed time the Jews, members of the old community of Babylon, began streaming towards the maidan behind the wall, where the four wedding ceremonies were to take place. They left behind their daily labours, their curiosity urging them to come and feast their eyes on that prophet in whom the spirit of the Lord moved, who not only interpreted the dream of the dreadful King, as they called Nebuchadnezzar among themselves, but also saw in his mind's eye the same dream, an apparently impossible feat which had never been matched, which was beyond the ability of diviners and soothsayers the whole world over. It was certainly the grace of God that was revealed through this Jewish youth, known as Daniel in his homeland and here, in Babylon, as Belteshazzar, and the pagan King had the wisdom to acknowledge the miracle and to glorify Daniel, promoting him above all his other clerks and appointing him his viceroy, like the righteous Joseph in his time, to whom Pharaoh gave charge of the whole land of Egypt, wielding the power of life and death as he saw fit.

The wide open space, green and luxuriant, was crammed with bearded folk, wearing robes of all fabrics and colours known to man – ranging from the coarse and the dark, tending towards black or brown at best, the symbol of the meaner members of society – to the royal blue and the gleaming purple of fine linens and silks, embellished with all kinds of ornaments, from nuggets of silver and gold to precious stones of all kinds and colours. Almost all wore on their heads turbans of the same fabric as their robes, and broad sashes around their waists. Most wore shoes of leather or cloth, but a minority from among the less well-to-do proposed to attend the weddings barefoot, somewhat to the annoyance of their well-shod counterparts:

"They should be ashamed of themselves! If they had asked, we would have given them shoes as an act of charity. The truth is they're just lazy, it's in their blood, and it's a disgrace!"

And there were those who heard the indignant words of the complainers and declared explicitly that it was not up to the barefooted to come and ask for charity from the elders and the burghers of the community; the elders and the burghers of the community were supposed to know how poverty-stricken these people were, and supply them with whatever they needed. In any case, the bare feet of the barefooted was not necessarily evidence of laziness, but pointed, among other things, to the stinginess of the gentry, occasionally employing these barefooted workers and paying them virtually nothing.

One way or the other, they were all here, men, women and children, and everywhere there was jubilation, bridging the gaps between social classes and blurring divisions, the old and the new, the severe and the trivial.

Faces shone with cheerful radiance and even Simeon, father of Hanna, the destined bride of Hananiah, smiled into the rising sun and greeted his neighbour Baruch, Deborah's father, with a light bow and a firm shake, and a blessing of "So, to life!" that was almost free of any kind of resentment.

Also among the guests were Gabriel and Uziel, wearing the brown robes of minor officials. Adoniah had sent a message, regretting that he was unable to attend and exchange handshakes and good wishes with his old friends, as he had been sent on an urgent mission to the lands of the East, to repair trade links that had been disrupted by a series of obstacles and misunderstandings.

Nashdernach was present as the King's official representative. The four grooms for their part had invited Denur-Shag, and he arrived in a carriage drawn by six magnificent horses, hired at his own expense from the royal mews.

"At last, I shall see a Jewish wedding!" he exclaimed in typically jovial style, and tried to jump down from the carriage, and were it not for the grooms, who were standing there in line waiting to greet him, and who stepped forward and caught him just in time, he would have fallen flat on his face, treading on the tails of his elegant cloak, too big for him – as always.

Denur-Shag laughed heartily and after expressing warm words of gratitude he turned to them and said:

"I was testing your alertness! From now on it will be up to you to do everything you can, and more, to keep your wits sharp! This is one of the relatively few blessings that marriage confers on a healthy young man – it forces him to stay alert, and he has to learn how to put the remedy before the injury!"

Or-Nego was among the guests too, and with him Adelain. They met before the ceremony began. Or-Nego was wearing his parade uniform of blue shirt and white satin breeches, both embroidered in gold. On his broad blue sash, also with gold embroidery, hung a thin-bladed sword with gold hilt and a pommel of silver encrusted with pearls. The buckle of his sash showed a gold engraving of the three royal recumbent lions. His shoes were as white as his breeches.

Adelain wore a pink robe, hemmed in white. On the buckle of her sash was the engraving of a fig-tree on a background of cast gold. When he asked her what it represented she told him:

"It's the emblem of novice-priestesses in the shrine of Bel!" and gave him a long look. Behind the enforced gaiety, there was a deep sense of despair.

The two young women studied one another briefly, shook hands and exchanged greetings which sounded sincere. Then they were separated by the press of the crowd.

At his suggestion all four of them wore the same costume – white shirt and breeches, broad purple sash, white turban and shoes, all trimmed in gold. Belt and shoe-buckles were gold, the collars of the shirts embroidered in gold and on every turban was a blue jewel on a gold background. The brides on the other hand were dressed in various colours – blue, purple, white and violet, with matching belts studded with jewels of varying quality, size and colour.

The gigantic canopy was set up in the heart of the maidan, on a low stage, a slender wooden pole at each of its four corners supporting an awning of blue. In accordance with the custom of the place all the men, young and old, wrapped themselves in white and blue shawls, and the women covered their heads with kerchiefs. At the edge of the maidan stood the four couples, in line, while Nehemiah, resplendent in his priestly robes, took his place at the head of the procession and set off towards the canopy, as a young man walked at his right hand swinging the incense burner and the crowd made way for them. And the priest began in a guttural voice *"Blessed is the man"* – and the congregation gave the response, chanting with him *"who does not sit among the scornful"*. And the couples advanced steadily towards the canopy and reached it to the swelling strains of the chorus, mounted the low stage and entered beneath the canopy.

The priest recited the nuptial contracts in that same guttural, well-lubricated voice, accustomed to recitation, and after the contracts came the blessings, and after each blessing the packed assembly replied "Amen!" as one man, and when the blessings were done the priest cried out in an awesome voice:

"If I forget you Jerusalem, may my right hand forget!" and he raised his arm aloft, and all the mighty crowd replied in the same tone and with the same gesture – *"If I forget you Jerusalem, may my right hand forget!"* – until the air itself was shaken by the force of the vibration, and then all at once there was silence, and the priest repeated his energetic gesture and cried:

"Next year in Jerusalem!"

And the crowd repeated the same words with the same gesture as before and in the same awesome tone:

"Next year in Jerusalem!"

And when the moment came, and each groom sanctified his bride with the words "You are sanctified to me," the congregation ripped the void apart with cries of "Sanctified! Sanctified! Sanctified!"

And before the happy couples left the canopy, Nashdernach was invited to stand and to speak, to bless those who had just been united in the name of the King and of his Council.

The oration was brief, but was marked by a degree of vehemence which was clearly felt and which struck fear into the hearts of some members of his audience and embarrassed others, while there were some who were simply enraged by what they heard him say.

After congratulating the newly-weds in the traditional manner, and passing on to them the best wishes of the

King and of the Court, and his own, and announcing the gifts that the King in his generosity was giving to them – lavish sums of money – he spoke briefly in praise of the community of Babylon, which according to him, had always demonstrated commitment and their loyalty to the Crown. And here he made the comment that as among the Babylonians themselves, among the Jews of Babylon too there existed a small and insignificant minority, promoting seditious ideas and trying to spread them among the members of the community at large. This effort was clearly doomed to failure, he assured them; after all, was there any group more fortunate than the Jews of Babylon, any benefiting more than they from the affluence and the freedom and the equality that the wise and valiant monarch, His Majesty King Nebuchadnezzar, had conferred upon all the nations and people under his sway, and he was confident that the decisive majority of the Jews of Babylon would take control of that insignificant minority and restore it to the ways of understanding and healthy reason, lest it invite disaster upon itself and upon the whole community.

Nashdernach concluded his clear and unequivocal speech with the exclamation:

"All praise to the King, the valiant and the wise, conqueror of the world, Nebuchadnezzar, His Majesty!" and he added to this "Long live the King!" The response to this was not the deafening chorus that might have been expected, but something more muted – and far from unanimous. Children and old men and some of the women took up the cry at full volume, as did a minority of the men. Among adult males some muttered the words reluctantly, others were silent, and tried to disguise their silence by turning to right and left and talking with their friends, others were ostentatiously silent, grim-faced and defiant.

Or-Nego pronounced a blessing too. He extolled the unique qualities of the Jewish people, a people distinct from all other races and nations, for better and decidedly not for worse, an asset of lasting value to the Chaldean kingdom in particular and to all races and nations in general. And here Or-Nego saw fit to stress that he had come to this conclusion through his close contact with the four bridegrooms and in particular with Belteshazzar, their leader, and to this very day – he went to say in his powerful, well-modulated voice, he was experiencing anew and reliving still the deep impressions made on him by that direct and dramatic first encounter. And he thanked God repeatedly for the privilege he had gained, and he was sure beyond any doubt, there was no people closer to God than the Jewish people, closer to the living God, and the salvation of the world and of all humanity depended on this people. And here his oration was interrupted by loud cries of "Hurrah!" and "Bravo!", accompanied by hand-clapping and foot-stamping, roars and whistles. And when the crowd had been hushed by the elders and dignitaries of the community, and the silence was broken only by a distant whistle or a faint cry of "Hurrah!", Or-Nego concluded his speech with the statement that all he really wanted to do was thank the grooms and their brides and the congregation for the honour of being allowed to attend the ceremony, and pass on special wishes for health and happiness from his daughter to Belteshazzar and his lovely wife.

Or-Nego stepped down from the stage, and the crowd resumed its chorus of cheering, hand-clapping and foot-stamping, which continued for a long time after he had disappeared from sight. Next to leave the stage were Nehemiah the priest and the newly-married couples.

Refreshments were served, and the foodstuffs were many and varied. Mostly meat dishes and all in abundance, with the wine flowing freely.

Denur-Shag approached him, a full goblet of wine in his hand and asked him:

"What's the meaning of those incantations, *If I forget you Jerusalem, may my right hand forget!* and *Next year in Jerusalem?*"

He admitted to Denur-Shag that he was no less puzzled himself. But then Baruch, Mishael's father-in-law, who was standing close by and overheard what was said, turned to them and explained:

"Those incantations have been part of the ritual of the Jews of Babylon since the community was founded, hundreds of years ago. They express the desire that will never fade for the return to Zion. And this will be fulfilled one day, and the Jews and all Israel shall return to their homes and dwell in Jerusalem the Holy, and worship God there until the end of all generations."

"Indeed, indeed!" Denur-Shag muttered, in genuine amazement, and commented: "Your people is indeed a stiff-necked people, but one with a vision! It seems that in the end this vision will be realised, even above and beyond what is hoped for!"

"So be it!" Baruch replied, and turned and disappeared into the crowd.

Oshrich, his office slave, who was now employed in his household as well, approached him and after offering warm congratulations, told him that some of the worthies of the community were asking his master to spare them a little of his time. They were sure he would not disappoint them, and they were waiting for him at the house of Simeon, Hananiah's father-in-law.

He did not deny their request, and leaving Nejeen in the company of her fellow-brides, he went with Oshrich to Simeon's house.

In a large and gloomy room sat about a dozen elderly men, wearing festive garb and prayer-shawls, who rose as soon as he entered and blessed him and wished him well. He was offered a seat, and when he had sat down, the hosts returned to their seats.

For a moment there was silence.

Simeon cleared his throat and began:

"We are very proud to welcome among us the King's viceroy, the wearer of the gold chain. We are grateful for the honour that he has conferred upon us and we congratulate him on his recent marriage, wishing every happiness to him and to his spouse!" And without any apparent connection to what had gone before he added: "The business of seeing the dream that the King saw and interpreting it, cannot but remind us of the saintly Joseph, who interpreted the dream of Pharaoh, King of Egypt, and rose to high office and when the time came – helped his brothers and his kinsmen and delivered them from the scourge of hunger."

And at this point somebody called out from the corner:

"The case of the saintly Joseph is not the same as the case of Daniel the man of God – a difference in favour of the latter!"

"What do you mean, Benjamin?" demanded Simeon, his thick brows knotting in menace.

Benjamin smiled awkwardly – a middle-aged man with light complexion and soft brown eyes, hair and beard in neat ringlets, clad in a robe of deep blue girded by a grey belt, and over his robe, like all the others present in the room, wearing a white shawl with gold embroidery:

"I mean," he replied, "that the saintly Joseph was

required only to interpret the dream, whereas this man of ours, whom we are delighted to be entertaining in our midst, was required to reveal exactly what it was that the King dreamed, as the King himself had forgotten it, and only after revealing it – to interpret it. An important distinction!" the speaker added in an attempt to regain some of the self-confidence that Simeon's scowl had shaken.

"Both of them alike have served as glorious instruments in the hands of our God, Blessed be He, creator of Heaven and Earth!" Simeon declared, as if asking not to be interrupted again, or distracted from the main issue

Benjamin clearly had something to add, perhaps even points that he wanted to score over Simeon, but he kept his silence and seemed to shrink into his corner.

Simeon turned to him and asked him:

"Does your opinion differ from mine?"

"Not at all!"

"You are both glorious instruments in the hands of God?"

"And I am the lesser!"

Something resembling a smile twisted Simeon's heavy, dead lips.

"Do you hear that, Benjamin?" – he spoke without turning towards the one the words were directed at, and he pursed his lips again. The momentary spark that had shone in his dark eyes disappeared as it had never been.

"As I was saying," Simeon continued, "we are proud of you because you are a compatriot of ours, although few of us have had the good fortune to see the holy landscape of our homeland and to breathe its enchanted air. Still, it lives in our hearts and its fire will forever burn there, unquenched – until the time comes for our return thither, as it written *And the children shall return to their borders!* And we have no doubt that you will do everything in your power to ease our long time of waiting, marred as it is by suffering and abuse – and to shorten it as far as is possible, and hasten and bring forward that wondrous hour, the hour of our return to Zion!"

"It is not for me to hasten or bring forward the return of anyone to anywhere," he declared. "It is God who knows these things and God who decides them!"

"And what does God know, and what is he going to decide?" asked a man sitting close by, his voice low and barely audible, his garments suggesting that he was not among the elite of the community.

"It is God who knows when you will be worthy to return to your homeland and to your patrimony, and He it is who will decide the time," he replied.

The men stiffened. Someone shouted:

"Do you not think us worthy to return to Zion?"

"That is not for me to judge," was his answer. "God will decide."

"And we are sitting here at His command!" cried Benjamin, who had evidently mastered his confusion and regained his confidence, and he added: "So at least our fathers taught us!" The one sitting beside Benjamim leaned forward, with an emphatic movement, turned to him and said:

"We are here to safeguard the border of the holy kingdom of Judah, as was promised in our Scriptures. Surely that border is – the Euphrates!"

And at this point Simeon raised his voice, addressing him directly and saying:

"And it is your duty to assist us in this."

"In what?" he asked calmly, his eyes keen.

"In the destruction of the wicked kingdom!" shouted

somebody amid the gathering, somebody he did not recognise.

He did not respond.

Silence fell in the room that was decorated with flowers, polished weapons and tapestries hanging on thick walls freshly daubed with lime – and yet in spite of this was sombre and chilly.

"I have heard much about your family," Simeon resumed his speech in a conciliatory tone, "from your friends and from many of the exiles who praise your father – a hero who fell honourably and died a martyr's death defending Jerusalem the Holy City! His memory be blessed!"

The gathering repeated after him in uncoordinated voices:

"His memory be blessed!" – and as they did so, rose fractionally from their seats.

"Yours, anyway, is the sacred obligation, as the loyal son of a valiant father and as a God-fearing man – to take revenge on his killers! As it is written in our Law, the Law of Moses – *an eye for an eye, a tooth for a tooth!* We shall all be with you and support you, and offer you all the help that you need and do as you command us to do, just so long as the death of your father, so much admired by all of us, does not go unavenged!"

All eyes were turned towards him, in tense anticipation, and in a kind of impossible innocence – with darkness at its core.

"It is written, *For I am merciful and I shall not bear grudges, forever!*" he replied, his voice reverberating in the stress-filled void.

After a long moment Simeon regained some composure and cried:

"You mean you're not interested in avenging your

father's death?" – the tone of his voice resembled the snarl of a wild beast, ready to pounce and prey on whatever comes its way.

The one sitting beside Simeon echoed his protest:

"Will you refuse to take the field against the killers of your revered father, to fight them, strike a victorious blow and even die with honour – anything rather than do the bidding of one who ordered your father's murder?"

And Benjamin interjected:

"No Jew forgoes the honour that is due to him, and if it is decreed that he shall fall in battle, like his father, then fall he shall – there is no escape for him!"

And he replied:

"I do the bidding of no man and obey the will of no man, but of God alone! And because I obey His holy will, Blessed be He, I can stand against any man, be he a King of great renown, be they my brothers and compatriots, who are too blind to see!"

"And what is God commanding you now?" asked Simeon, clearly enraged.

"That which He commanded through the prophet Jeremiah!"

"Jeremiah is a traitor! A false prophet is Jeremiah!" Some of the men rose from their seats and waved clenched fists at him, their eyes shooting sparks.

"Jeremiah is the prophet of God, and all his words are the truth, the word of the living God!" – he cried in a clear, ringing voice, filled with unshakable, impregnable conviction.

"He who says that the Chaldeans shall defeat our holy people, this nation that the Lord chose from all the nations!" Benjamin intervened again from his corner.

"Jeremiah says," he insisted, "that if our people will not repent and mend its ways in time, nor cleave to the Lord, the loving Lord, nor uphold His holy Law that it swore to uphold – then it shall be trampled beneath the feet of its enemies."

"You too are an accomplice of this traitor!" cried the man who sat beside Benjamin, waving his fist menacingly.

"Jeremiah is the living voice of God, and anyone that does not obey him is defying and opposing God!" he declared.

Benjamin's neighbour stood up from his place, pushing his chair back noisily, apparently intending to attack him with his fists, and three others seemed ready to support him. Simeon hurried to his protection, shielding him and sending those who had risen back to their places. Then he turned to him and said:

"You have no intention, then, of taking up the sword to avenge the death of your revered father?"

And he replied:

"So long as I do the will of God, and hear His voice, I shall know for sure that my father is honoured and blessed in me!"

"It is the fault of people like you that our honour has been defiled, our people are oppressed and our enemies rejoice in our undoing!" raged Simeon.

"It is the fault of people who close their eyes from seeing and stop their ears from hearing the word of the living God, and call His prophet a 'traitor' – that calamity will come and disaster fall on our heads, and Judah will be ravaged and its people exiled from its land and dispersed among all the nations, to the ends of the earth!"

He turned and left the room, leaving its occupants stunned and stricken dumb.

JAHANUR

When it was that the King gave orders for the building of a gigantic statue in the valley of Dura, no one knew. It may be that it followed soon after those tempestuous days during which a dream was dreamed and forgotten, and the magicians and astrologers of Babylon were summoned to reveal and interpret it before the King, and when they failed Daniel came forward, the Jewish exile also known as Belteshazzar, and he revealed the dream and interpreted it, and earned high renown.

It may have been in the wake of these events that the King set to thinking and made his decision, and ordered the construction of this gigantic statue, sixty cubits in height, to stand in the heart of the valley of Dura and be a landmark visible from far away.

The building work proceeded, and Daniel paid no attention to it, nor did his friends, Mishael, Hananiah and Azariah. In their capacity as ministers they used to meet regularly to discuss matters of state, deciding which issues should have priority and precedence over others, which proposals should be dropped and which referred to the King for his approval. The business of the statue was never mentioned in their conversations, nor did it occur to them to imagine how fateful this statue would prove to be, how it would determine the course of their lives for the future.

One day Nashdernach came to his office, sat down facing him, cleared his throat and finally began:

"If I understand it correctly, the God that you worship

is not one of those who are represented by images of clay or wood or iron or gold."

"That is correct," he answered him.

"And you are not permitted to bow down to any image, embodying any element of the divine, even of your own God?"

"Correct again!" he smiled.

"Even if the King himself commands you, and you know with absolute certainty that anyone disobeying the King's command shall surely die?"

"Even if the King himself commands me, and I know with absolute certainty that anyone disobeying the King's command shall surely die!" – he repeated Nashdernach's words with clear and earnest conviction, leaving no room to doubt his sincere intentions.

Nashdernach smiled awkwardly, rose from his seat, shook his hand warmly and left his office.

About a week later Nashdernach came once again to his office, and sitting down to face him in his customary fashion, told him:

"The King is asking to see you!"

He rose from his seat and followed Nashdernach, and the two of them entered the same hall in which he had revealed to the distraught King the dream that he had forgotten, and delivered a clear and succinct interpretation of it.

They passed between ranks of guardsmen standing to attention with swords drawn, bowed and prostrated themselves at the feet of the King, and when he had greeted them, rose and stood upright before him.

There was something of a gleam in the stern face of the King, in those bronzed features that did not know the meaning of fear, that struck terror into all those who saw them and set their heart-beat racing.

"My wish," said the King, addressing him, "is that you go to the mountainous northern region and to the town of Jahanur. You are to stay there a month, residing in the royal summer palace. Inspect the town and discover all that there is to know about it, and report to me on the number of inhabitants, their sources of livelihood, and how firm is their loyalty to the Crown!"

And Nebuchadnezzar turned to Nashdernach and said to him:

"For this month you are to take his place and do his work according to his instructions, everything to be put in writing and sealed by your hand!"

The two men bowed and prostrated themselves once again before the King, and saying in unison "His Majesty's will be done!" they withdrew, faces towards the throne and backs to the door.

On their return to his office, there was a certain awkwardness between them, for no apparent reason. He was entirely confident that Nashdernach was incapable of doing anything contrary to reason and integrity, and he was inclined to believe this was all down to caprice on the part of the King. Or perhaps this was the King's roundabout way of sending him to the hills for a period of rest and recuperation, although he had never complained of feeling overworked; on the contrary, he had fulfilled his duties conscientiously and gladly. Or was it the King's intention to treat him and his new bride to a honeymoon... But this explanation too failed to satisfy him.

"The whole of this business," Nashdernach said suddenly, "was arranged at my specific request!"

This admission by Nashdernach was utterly unexpected, and he gave him a startled look, though still without the slightest hint of suspicion or resentment, even in the depths of his heart. He waited for Nashdernach to clarify this remark and he did not have to wait long.

"About ten days from now the image that stands in the Dura valley will be dedicated, and the citizens of Babylon will be summoned by royal command to come and bow down to it, and anyone who does not come forward and bow to the image – will be thrown into the furnace! You will be among those summoned, and if you go to this place and refuse to bow to the image, in obedience to your God but in defiance of the King – you shall be thrown into the furnace. This is not what the King wants, nor is it what I want, your faithful servant! When the issue was explained to the King, just as I have explained it to you, he thought it over and came to his decision. As for that summer resort," Nashdernach continued with a cheerful smile – "there's no place that can match its beauty anywhere in the kingdom! It stands on a low hill surrounded by groves of pines with their sweet-smelling resin, and there are ancient vines in plenty, figs and olives and nuts and almonds, and bubbling streams. The inhabitants are hospitable, and the air is clear and invigorating!"

"And what is to become of my three friends, Shadrach, Meshach and Abed-Nego?" he asked, more interested in their fate than in lyrical descriptions of Jahanur.

"To the best of my knowledge," Nashdernach replied, "they are not required to be present at the dedication of the image, unlike you – the King's viceroy! And the solution that the King has devised for you is eloquent testimony – equivalent to that of a thousand witnesses – to the high regard and the warm favour in which he holds you. And this very day the leader of the council of Jahanur will be notified post-haste of your forthcoming visit and its purpose, and they are to prepare all the information that you require. I shall stay here, in your place, and do everything I can to expedite your projects in the best way possible, so you need have no concern on that account!"

He shook Nashdernach's hand firmly, and had to work hard to resist the impulse to embrace him – a mutual impulse as it was. They shook hands again, and slapped one another's shoulder, and when they parted, each noticed that the other's eyes were moist.

Before three days had elapsed, the convoy heading for Jahanur set out from the royal palace. One wagon sufficed for their possessions and they themselves rode in a light chariot, drawn by a pair of white horses.

As they approached the precinct of the shrines of the idols, they were halted by a procession of girls in white dresses, tallow candles burning in their hands, singing songs of praise and jubilation to Bel.

He recognised the virgin priestesses of Bel, and seeing Adelain among them he stepped down from the chariot and approached her, to wish her well on the completion of her noviciate and her acceptance into the order. She gave him a look that sprang from the very depths of her eyes, with a smile that seemed to combine youthful innocence with turbulence of spirit, and exclaimed:

"You are my God, to you I have dedicated myself and you I shall serve all the days of my life!"

Nejeen also stepped down from the chariot and held out her white hand, and the young priestess clasped the proffered hand tightly, as if it were a life-raft in a stormy sea, and giving her candle to one of her companions, fell into the arms of Nejeen and embraced her fondly, kissing her forehead. Then stepping back, she retrieved her candle and hurried to catch up with the rest of the procession, receding in the distance without a backward glance.

The staff of the King's summer palace sent representatives to meet the new arrivals, among them the chief councillor of Jahanur, Avarnam, a pleasant, silver-haired man who delivered a brief speech of greeting and welcomed them in the customary fashion. And so it was that they entered the township, accompanied by their twelve-strong bodyguards and the chief councillor on his elderly mare, with the steward of the household leading the procession.

At the gates of the palace, all of the King's retainers were gathered – clerks, footmen, cooks, grooms, gardeners, and there was even an aged court jester, who had not wanted to return to Babylon and had asked the King for permission to live out his days in Jahanur, permission which was granted. There was a total of fifty-four servants to maintain the palace with its seventy-eight rooms, halls and chambers.

The deputy steward came out to meet them, bowed low and offered them wine and bread, served on a gold tray covered by a white cloth, to celebrate their arrival. The maids and the servants followed his example, bowing low and holding the pose until the guests had passed them.

He replied to the greetings of the deputy steward and the leader of the town council, and expressed the hope that all would be conducted properly, and he assured them that he had no intention of changing their daily routine, and all the existing arrangements would remain in force. This was reassuring news for his audience, and there were smiles all around.

Out of the plethora of bed-chambers available, lavishly furnished and decorated in all colours known to man with the exception of black – they chose for themselves a spacious room on the upper storey, furnished in pink, with huge windows overlooking a fertile, verdant valley crossed by a foaming river, the rhythmic plash of its waters clearly audible.

She opened the window wide, and the air of the open spaces streamed into the room, bringing with it the light fragrance of wild flowers. At the end of the meadow, to their right, were thickets of pine trees.

"Nashdernach mentioned the scent of resin," he said, "and sure enough, I can smell it now!"

"The air and the atmosphere are both reminiscent of our homeland," she remarked.

"You're right," he agreed. "And the residents of Jahanur, will they be like our fellow-countrymen?"

"We shall have plenty of time to find out," she replied.

"I read some texts in the royal library about the inhabitants of this mountainous region in general and the inhabitants of Jahanur in particular. There is much that is known about them, and even more that is unknown."

Her calm gaze rested on him. Joy flooded his heart. How blessed he was in her!

He was not aware of the walls of the palace, the spaces in the room, all the heavy furniture, the light and pervasive scent of fields and pines, in a dream – of her perhaps, in any thought whatsoever.

The very fact of her presence prevented these things approaching him and disturbing that living depth that people fear to touch, even in imagination, lest they spoil the current of joy that is nourished by it.

The very fact of her presence brought him closer, in a closer communion than any he had known, to the one object of his love, none other than his Father in Heaven and his God, who is the infinite, freedom, love. How can he explain to himself this wonderful thing, that the very presence of someone could set him free from all that surrounds him, give him wings to soar away to the highest firmament, and to touch the Holy of Holies, to melt into it and to become a part of it?

Who is this someone who is setting you free, from herself and from yourself, so that you may awake to know yourself an inseparable part of the one, all-pervading love? Is she not the only object of your love, who is taking on, through the power of her love for you and by virtue of that love – human form?

Their eyes met. And it was only then that he realised that all his former conceptions of the sublime and of the pure were utterly meaningless. For the first time in his life he encountered the truly sublime and the entirely pure, these being nothing other than the inexhaustible, limpid and deep springs of love, the love that draws out from servitude to freedom, and from darkness into a great light.

He did not remember how long they had been standing in the spacious bed-chamber, but somehow he finally became aware that both the sky and the horizon had changed colour, turning through ever deepening shades of blue to the darker hues of regal velvet, studded with diamonds.

His eyes were in hers, and her gaze was his desire and his gaze was her delight, and the world of shapes and names ceased to exist, and with it time subsided, melted away as if it never was.

When he became aware of the knocking at the door, it had ceased to be as decorous and reverential as it was supposed to be. Then he remembered that throughout that day, while they stood by the open window, staring into one another's eyes, his glance melting into hers and her glance vanishing into the infinite freedom of his – in some place or another, under certain circumstances, and definitely without any reference to the time that had ceased to exist for them – there had indeed been persistent knocking, properly decorous and reverential at the start, but as the changes unfolded in the timeless void, so the knocking exceeded its normal limits, abandoning the last vestiges of respect and veering towards clamorous cacophony.

"Come in!" he cried.

The tall, wide door opened slowly, inch by inch, and one of the housemaids, the one responsible for the bed-chambers, peered inside and on seeing them froze where she stood, eyes gaping and tongue stuck to her palate. She remained there, petrified and dumbstruck, until he addressed her again, his voice gentle and reassuring:

"Are you the chambermaid?"

The tone of his voice did its blessed work.

"That is so, Sir!" she replied, her voice unsteady and still reflecting the shock that she had experienced on opening the door and looking into the room.

"That is so, Sir!" she repeated, this time with some of the balance restored to her voice. "Since this morning we..." she began awkwardly, paused and then resumed: "Your worships did not tell us what times would be convenient... for preparing the bed-chamber. And in the dining room too they are awaiting instructions. Clearly it is too late for the midday meal, but whatever your worships desire, so it shall be done. This is the time that we usually serve the evening meal, but we are ignorant folk, unfamiliar with the ways of the royal palace in the capital city, and we would be delighted if you would enlighten us! After all – it is dark outside, and the stars are in the sky and yet in this bed-chamber, there is light! Not a light such as candles give, nor the light of torches nor the light of a fire burning in the grate. A light such as we do not know and perhaps – it is only I, foolish and ignorant serving maid that I am, that does not know this light and has never seen the like!" Her voice shook and she was close to tears.

Nejeen hastened to say:

"You're neither stupid nor ignorant, and what happened here, really happened! And as my lord and husband has told you – the arrangements to which you are accustomed are not to be changed. We are running a little late, and in just a few moments we shall come down to eat our evening meal. This room is entirely to my satisfaction, and you need do nothing more here until tomorrow. What is your usual time for cleaning and tidying rooms?"

"Noon," replied the chambermaid, her confidence restored.

"Come back here tomorrow then, at noon!"

They did not part that night, or go to separate rooms. The night passed like a dream, or a fairy-tale that has never been told, or written.

The bright light of morning streamed in through the broad window that had been left open all night. A light, gusting breeze woke them with a caress, as a mother wakes her baby. He watched the white clouds drifting slowly, in ceremonious procession, across the deep blue of the sky, and they both admired once again the vista of meadows, river and groves of pine. The air shone, and the horizon sparkled in the distance like molten silver.

Having risen, they took turns bathing in the bath-house, with its three-fold arrangement of pools; the cold water of the final stage refreshed and invigorated them.

They broke their fast in an improvised dining room adjacent to the bath-house, and after thanking their attendants, went down to the stables to choose horses for themselves. Having so much time at their disposal, they could choose at their leisure. All the horses were of the finest quality, flawless thoroughbreds, well fed and properly trained.

They left the walls of the palace behind and spurred along the ridge of a gently sloping hill, on whose northern flank the inhabitants of Jahanur had built their white, somewhat decorative houses.

Generally these houses were built in the centre of a plantation or alongside an orchard or at the edge of a cultivated field. Beside each house, without exception, was a fig-tree in full bloom, and a number of the local residents were sitting at this early hour of the morning beneath their fig-trees, eating their morning snack in the shade of the branches.

It seemed that some of them noticed the two strange riders and hurried to inform the leader of the council, the silver-haired and agreeable Avarnam. He was not slow to arrive on the scene, his elderly and rather overweight mare panting and wheezing as if every step was an effort. He met them as they descended from the ridge, heading for one of the most picturesque streams they had ever seen.

"Be blessed in the name of God the most High!" Avarnam greeted them, raising his arm in an unconventional gesture, his face aglow.

"Blessings and all good things to you and to the good people of Jahanur!" he answered him cordially.

"If I may be of any service to your worships, it will be my delight and my most profound satisfaction!"

And before anyone could respond to these words, startling in their sincerity, Avarnam went on to say:

"As for the census of residents of Jahanur, it has already been done – a scroll has been prepared and will be delivered to you this very day, at the palace, by a representative of the community. According to this scroll, we have a population today of one thousand two hundred and sixty-one souls, men and women. And they are all the privileged descendants of those twelve ancient families, who lived in the past, the distant past I should say, in the ancient city of Ur, Ur of the Chaldees that is," he explained, and added: "In the aftermath of a certain episode, they abandoned the place and came to these hills and built the fertile and the prosperous township of Jahanur, the happy and the peace-loving settlement that you see today!"

At the mention of Ur of the Chaldees, the two of them exchanged bemused glances.

"This Ur of the Chaldees that you describe as 'ancient' – was it not prosperous in its time, and an agreeable place to live?"

"It seems that not everything was managed as it should be, and they did not all walk in the ways of virtue. And then that episode occurred of which I spoke – and a shattering and traumatic episode it was – and the twelve families, which exist today as they existed then, left their houses on the plain, houses built of clay, and climbed these hills and built for themselves the houses of stone and of wood that you have seen!" He stretched out his short arm in an expansive gesture, pointing to the houses with their friendly white facades, strewn across the slope of the hill at their feet.

"And our flock earned the blessing of Almighty God and flourished by His grace and has prospered ever since to this very day, and with the consent of the Holy One, will continue to flourish and prosper until the end of all generations!"

"Which 'Almighty God' is this?" he asked with great interest.

"The Creator of Heaven and Earth and all that is in them!" Avarnam answered him cheerfully, his resonant voice expressing a childlike innocence.

Hitherto she had refrained from taking any part in the conversation, assuming that in Jahanur, as in most eastern communities, women were excluded from men's conversations, and any contribution they made was likely to be ignored. But seeing the sincerity in Avarnam's face and the pure expression of his eyes, she felt confident enough to ask a question:

"Are the gods of Babylon your gods?"

Avarnam turned to her and without any change in his pleasant manner, in his air of fellowship and willingness to serve, he answered her:

"No, your ladyship! We differ from the Babylonians and their gods are not our gods, and their style of worship is not our style of worship!"

"Meaning?" he asked with mounting interest.

"We are forbidden to set up any image to any god, least of all to our God, Creator of Heaven and Earth and all that is in them. He must not be represented in any physical form."

"Since when has this ordinance existed?"

"Not since yesterday, or the day before!" Avarnam chuckled pleasantly, and while puckering his broad forehead as if trying to calculate times and dates he continued: "It has been our rule for many years, Excellency. And this is not to the liking of the Chaldeans living in the valley of the Tigris and the Euphrates who have claimed, with some justification, that we belong to them and are a part of their nation, as their language is our language. And we for our part claim, also with some justification, that although we have common roots there are also differences that divide us, and no faith is to be forced on us, least of all a faith that is not to our taste, that is fundamentally opposed to our conceptions and to the tradition in which we were nurtured – an ancient tradition indeed!" Avarnam declared with emphasis, still smiling his broad and captivating smile, expressing warmth, innocence and above all, a sincere willingness to serve and to oblige.

They both came to the conclusion, independently of one another, that Avarnam, leader of the council of Jahanur, was a most agreeable companion, and an affable interlocutor.

He went on to say:

"Not everything has proceeded smoothly. The Chaldeans, as is well known, are a people of resolute opinions, a nation of conquerors and valiant warriors, and they do not tolerate dissenters who refuse to accept their discipline, and bear their yoke – even if it is a small and peaceable community such as ours, doing no harm to anyone." Avarnam sighed and his plump mare shifted beneath him impatiently. He soothed her, patting her neck, and added:

"Nevertheless, they have not succeeded in imposing their will on us and we have not changed our religion – the same today as it has always been, although we have experienced setbacks and been treated like outcasts."

"And who has prevented the Chaldeans from imposing their will upon you and forcing you to change your religion?" he asked.

Avarnam turned his snow-white head to stare at him with a look of bewilderment, as if wondering how such a question could even be asked, the answer being so obvious and self-evident, and he replied with two simple words:

"Our God."

After the brief silence that followed, Avarnam went on to say.

"Our God, in whose hands are all things, and from whose hands all things come, He it was who defended our forefathers from the Chaldeans and from all the other troubles of the world, and He it is who guards us to this very day against anyone who would try to induce us to abandon our faith in Him for the sake of another religion."

"And what was the event that prompted your ancestors to dispense with idols and pictorial representations of the divine, to believe in God Most High, Creator of Heaven and Earth and all that is in them – and to abandon the ancient Ur of the Chaldees and move to the hills, founding the new Jahanur?" he asked.

"It is a fascinating story!" Avarnam declared emphatically, the broad, infectious smile returning to his face. "If you would like to know all the details as they are recorded in our ancient texts, you are welcome to visit the office of the community scribe and archivist, who records the chronicles of Jahanur and is an unrivalled expert in the interpretation of ancient writings. And he has it all preserved on parchment scrolls and on clay tablets. And as I said before, I shall be glad to be of service to you in any way I can!"

They made their way down to the building which housed all the municipal offices of the resort town, along narrow tracks winding between groves and orchards, crossing fast-flowing streams and lush meadows.

"What is the livelihood of the people of Jahanur?" he asked.

"Since time immemorial the people of Jahanur have been fruit-growers and tillers of the soil. They made all their own tools, everything needed for the home as well as for the field and the orchard, and sometimes they even traded with the surplus produce. As you see, every effort has been made to avoid contact with the outside world, disturbing no one and being disturbed by no one. Those who trade with other places are a very small minority, and most people born in Jahanur live here happily all their lives, finally being laid to rest in the ground that is celebrated in song. And if you need to know the extent of our loyalty to the Chaldean state and to His Majesty, it has never occurred to us to defy him in any way, and we shall continue to pay the tribute that is levied, punctually and in whatever medium is required – whether it be silver or gold, or textiles or wine or corn or fruit. Just so long as the Chaldeans leave us to ourselves, not stirring up religious dissension, opposing our true faith with their vain superstitions, and persecuting us for no fault of ours!" Avarnam looked back at him with an earnest, inquisitive expression.

And he replied in a tone of calm, genial assurance:

"I shall convey to the King what you have said, and my own impressions too I shall set before him. And how is it that a small town such as this, with a population of one thousand, two hundred and sixty-one, has a scribe and chronicler of its own?"

"Oh, that is a tradition among us, instituted after that extraordinary event that you will soon be hearing about, and it is a noble profession, requiring special skills, dedication and patience and above all, a strong and uncompromising devotion to the truth. It is the duty of the scribe and chronicler," – Avarnam warmed to his theme – "to inquire deeply and without prejudice into events and sayings until he arrives at the truth, and then he must record the truth, even if it is uncomfortable for him. And this is the proud inheritance of the Jaharan family, our family of scribes and copyists, whose scions have never omitted a letter, or added a single dot, or deviated to the tiniest degree from the texts that they transcribe. And all this work is done in a spirit of reverence, for the sake of Heaven, and every father in this family who teaches his son the sacred art, is also serving as a living example for him, of steadfast devotion to the truth."

"And who supports the scribe and his family?" she asked.

Without turning to face her, Avarnam replied:

"They support themselves. They have fields and orchards, and compiling chronicles does not occupy too much of their time. It is something that they do for the sheer pleasure of it – and as an act of reverence."

"And they have no slaves to assist them?" she persisted.

The leader of the council of Jahanur tugged at the reins and brought his mare to a standstill; she was glad of the respite, and took deep gulps of air into her elderly lungs.

"There you have touched on another of the principles that separate us from the Chaldeans and perhaps – from all other nations in the world!" And looking up towards the horizon, he explained:

"This faith of ours in one God, the God Most High, Creator of Heaven and Earth and all that is in them – is incompatible with slavery. It is a known fact that all human beings are brothers, sons of one Father, and how can you allow yourself to enslave your brother, taking from him the crop that he has planted with the sweat of his brow, and harvested with his own hands, allocating a meagre share to him and keeping for yourself the fruits of his labours? This is neither our inclination, nor our tradition!" he declared firmly, adding with an air of cheerful satisfaction: "You see? Without any recourse to slavery, our town has flourished and prospered, and all public matters are properly administered. And something else you should know: not one member of the council, not even the leader of the council, seeks any reward for his services to the public. All are happy to work in the Name of God, and for the sake of Heaven. And there are blessings everywhere!" he concluded, gently coaxing his mare into motion; reluctantly she resumed her clumsy gait.

"So you mean, you lack for nothing?" he asked.

"We lack for nothing, so it has always been and so it will always be, as long as we serve our God in faith and gladly obey His commandments."

Again they exchanged glances, with astonishment and wonderment in their eyes, and something resembling reverence.

Before the sun had risen to its zenith, they halted their horses at the foot of a low building, constructed of stone and freshly plastered, dismounted and hitched the reins to an iron ring beside the door. Avarnam knocked on the wide door, waited a moment and knocked again, this time with more vigour.

"Perhaps the scribe is working today in his field or his orchard, and has no leisure for his other activities," he suggested.

Avarnam smiled pleasantly and assured him:

"He's here! Writing a report on your visit, and your mission! But the moment he sits down at his desk and starts working, he becomes engrossed in the task in hand and detached from everything around him, and it's not easy to draw his attention to anything outside his texts!"

"Perhaps we shouldn't disturb him!" he said, trying to restrain Avarnam who was about to renew his onslaught on the door. "We can come back another time." But his intervention was too late, and the door shuddered under the hail of blows.

Avarnam looked up at him and once again wrinkled his brow, as if pondering his next words, but at that moment there was the sound of cautious movements from inside and the door swung open. On the threshold stood a man, with beard and hair sparse and flecked with grey, stooped posture and bright eyes, blinking in the sunlight.

For a long moment the man stood immobile, not sure what was happening, and then turned to them, smiled, bowed courteously, muttered something that sounded like "Welcome!" between thin and tight lips, then asked in a throaty, yet clear voice:

"How can I help you?"

Avarnam answered him:

"This is the King's envoy, who has come to inspect Jahanur. I'm sure you have already recorded the event in one of your scrolls."

The stooping man bowed again, in token of assent.

And Avarnam continued:

"We were talking of that episode that forced our ancestors to leave Ur of the Chaldees on the plain and settle in the hills, founding our beloved Jahanur. And they have expressed an interest in hearing more."

"Do they want me to read it to them from the old scrolls, which aren't easy to read, or would they rather hear it in my own words, in the oral tradition as is passed down from father to son and from teacher to pupil?"

"We'd like to hear it from you!" he said.

"I'll fetch some chairs and we can sit in the sun, which is pleasant at this time of year. It is dark inside, and the air dank and cold."

The scribe turned and bowed three times – once for each of the guests, and disappeared again behind the door with its mezuzah, returning a moment later with four stools. Then he fetched a tray with four apples on it, and a scroll wrapped in leather that had lost its original colour and turned black.

"These apples," he asked Avarnam, "were they grown here?"

"They were," he answered, not without pride. "The truth is," he added, "such fruit doesn't usually grow in places like this. But not everything depends on climate and quality of soil. In fact, very little depends on climate and quality of soil. A man and his work – they are the essence. If a man's work is done for the sake of Heaven – his labour is blessed and his fruit plentiful, and if a man's work is not done for the sake of Heaven, his work is cursed and his fruit blighted."

"There is no truth more holy than that!" he agreed.

"Part of the story," the scion of the Jaharan family began, his voice lucid and carefully modulated – "was recorded in this scroll by our ancestors. Anyone who knows how to decipher the language that preceded Chaldee is free to make use of this text – without taking it away of course, which is strictly forbidden. The script isn't easy to read, and the copying is in itself time-consuming. I myself have been making repeated efforts to transcribe the text onto fresh parchment, and even with the blessing and the help of God, the task will occupy a year of my time. Perusal is allowed only in my office, and with my help and supervision . One way or the other, the following is what is known to the people of Jahanur, regarding the ancient times."

Jaharan Ben Jaharan pronounced a brief blessing, bit

into the juicy apple, and munching contentedly, resumed his account:

"Many generations ago the inhabitants of ancient Ur of the Chaldees, our ancestors, were worshippers of idols, like other nations and races in that locality. Their lives were apparently uneventful, as they did not stand out from their neighbours in any way. Like them they lived by rearing sheep and cattle, like them they worshipped innumerable idols and knew no serenity in their lives, neither joy nor satisfaction. And there were some who quarrelled with others over matters of religion or the distribution of land, and sometimes disputes erupted and often these turned into petty wars between tribe and tribe, between settlement and settlement, household and household, family and family. These wars claimed victims, and the relatives of the victims swore to avenge the deaths of their loved ones, and so it went on and on. And the idol-worshippers of Ur of the Chaldees, like the idol-worshippers of other places, carved their images out of wood and brass and stone, and bowed down to them and worshipped them, and offered them sacrifices and poured out before them their bitterness of heart – and all this to no avail. Until one day the son of one of the most illustrious sculptors arose and did something unheard of: he smashed the idols that his father had made and said to him: If these are really gods, let them avenge their injury!

"The father, who at first was seething with wrath at the impetuous act of his young son, was suddenly assailed by fits of laughter, wild and resounding laughter, for he saw with his own eyes that this young son of his was wiser than all the citizens of Ur of the Chaldees, with their reverence for images, images which he himself had created. But the sculptor soon stopped laughing, realising that his neighbours, friends and relatives were liable to see this act of his son as a very serious matter, and would vent their wrath on him, even stone him to death. So the sculptor called his clever son, gave him food and water and ordered him to go out to the desert and hide for a few days, allowing time for passions to cool and the affair to be forgotten. The son obeyed his father, took his knapsack and went away to hide in one of the caves in the desert, to the east of Ur of the Chaldees.

"No sooner had the son disappeared from his father's view, when the neighbours, his friends and relatives, having heard the sound of the idols breaking, came hurrying to discover the source of the terrible commotion – had some disaster occurred? And when they saw the shattered images, a great cry went up, and they flew into a panic and a rage, and began frantically wailing, tearing at their hair and their beards, ripping their clothes and scattering dust on their heads. And the rumour sprouted wings, and almost the entire population of Ur of the Chaldees came streaming to the door of the sculptor's house. And they demanded that the sculptor come out and admit the sin he had committed, and submit to the judgment of the crowd and receive his just deserts, meaning – death by stoning. And the sculptor was terrified, although relieved to know that his son was safe, and he came to the door of his house and promised to tell them the whole story, from beginning to end, omitting no detail, however small. And then his neighbours and relations and friends and fellow-citizens could decide what was to be done with him – whether it was to be life or death.

"Hearing the measured words of the sculptor the crowd was hushed, and in the tense silence that reigned in the open space before the house, the sculptor gave his version of events, revealing that last night, just after midnight, he heard a terrible din coming from his workshop and a deafening uproar, and he was jolted from his sleep and hurriedly went down to the workshop to see what was causing the racket, and he approached the door of the workshop, and though his heart was scared to death, he forced himself to touch the door, and opened it a crack, and stooped and peered through the crack. And what was revealed to him there was so dreadful, so terrifying, he immediately closed the door again and was minded to flee for his life while he still could. But knowing full well that in the morning he would definitely be summoned by the burghers and sages of Ur of the Chaldees to explain what had happened, and he would need a plausible account, he steeled himself again, opened the door and saw – Heavens above! – all the idols fighting one another, locked in vicious combat: the god of vineyards detached his stone arm and killed the god of rice with a single blow, and the god of rain held his heavy stone head in his hands and battered all his envoys and minions until they were wrecked beyond repair, and then the god of the forest attacked the god of vineyards and knocked him to the ground with a single blow, to be felled in his turn by the god of frost, who was killed by the god of the bears. The god of pregnant and nursing mothers slew at least a dozen minor deities, with the half of his body that he wielded as a weapon, but before the witness could identify the victims, the goddess of mammon took on all those who were still standing and laid them dead on the ground, and then she turned and saw the sculptor peering in at the doorway, shaking with fear, and she stormed upon him in a rage, but as she had been seriously injured in the course of the battle, she collapsed on the pile of slain gods and gave up the ghost too.

"For a long moment there was silence in the crowd

listening attentively to the words of the sculptor, until one of the renowned sages plucked up the courage to stand on a table and address all the citizens of Ur of the Chaldees, saying:

'How ridiculous we have been in our worship of wood and clay and iron and stone, and then here comes this wise sculptor, and he shows us how foolish we are, how incomparably ignorant!'

"And all at once the inhabitants of Ur of the Chaldees burst into gales of laughter, loud and long.

"And the sculptor asked for permission to conclude his story, for it had a conclusion, and the crowd respected his wish and was hushed. The sculptor admitted frankly that he was neither sage nor prophet nor thinker; such things were the prerogative of his young son, whom he had sent to hide in the desert until such time as the passions had subsided.

"The crowd laughed again, and the elders and the sages and the worthies of the community decided to send a deputation to bring the wise young man back to their city, as he was a precious asset to his community and his people, deserving to be their leader and their mentor, whose every command should be obeyed.

"The burghers of the town were as good as their word, and a dignified delegation set out and found the wise young man hiding in his cave, and they brought him back with great honour to his city and to his father. And the wise young man did indeed become their leader and their mentor and their governor, his every command obeyed. And in the fullness of time the young man revealed to them the existence of one God – Creator of Heaven and Earth and of all that is in them, who bears them only good will and shows them the way they should walk if they are to be saved, and to be the happiest of all men.

"And the boy, who grew in stature and in wisdom, gave then certain laws, which later the Chaldeans tried to copy and to adopt for themselves. These laws spoke of purification of the heart from the unclean, and its cleansing from every idolatrous or malicious or covetous thought. And the people of Ur of the Chaldees began studying these laws and adhering to them. And then it became known to them, to their grief and deep sorrow, that their neighbours were looking at them with a jealous eye and plotting against them and thinking ill of them, and hating them and informing against them. And it was at about this time, that God, the true God, commanded the son of the sculptor who had grown up and was a man and a leader of his people, to leave Ur of the Chaldees, his hometown, and never to return, and go to a place that He, his God, would show him:

"Go from your homeland and your father's house, God commanded, and the man, whose name was Abram, obeyed, and bade farewell to his fellow citizens and his community, who respected him greatly, and he told them that Ur of the Chaldees was no longer a place for believers in the true God, and they should apply their minds to this and move to another place, and God would bless them, and afford them His protection, and defend them against their enemies and against all evil.

"And so indeed it was – Abram left his homeland and his father's house at God's command and twelve families of Ur of the Chaldees, believers in his God, followed his example, went up into the hills and founded Jahanur, and served the true God with all their hearts and minds, with all their souls and strength.

"This is the story as it is recorded in our writings," – Jaharan Ben Jaharan concluded, and held out to him the blackened scroll.

Slowly and carefully he untied the wrapper, which had stiffened over the course of the years, opened it and unrolled it until the first signs of writing appeared; this was one ancient language that even Denur-Shag had never taught. He rolled up the scroll again, wrapped it and handed it to Jaharan, who took it back into his office, and returned. Taking his seat again, he resumed:

"We have heard tell of what became of Abram, son of our little nation, and we know that he changed his name at God's command to Abraham, meaning 'Father of a great people', and this is not recorded in our writings as we didn't hear it from first hand, but it has been handed down from father to son and from teacher to pupil.

"There are sages among us," Jaharan explained "who teach the young the right path that they should follow. And these sages have much to say regarding the revelation of the Son of God, who will bring about the salvation of the human race, and who will be chastised and rejected and persecuted by many. And from hearsay we know that a great prophet arose to preach to the race of Abraham, and he heard the voice of God, and gave them laws, called the Torah. According to this Torah, men are commanded not to covet and not to commit adultery and not to bear false witness, commandments that we too accept, the difference being that we place more emphasis on purity of heart, so that adultery for example is forbidden not only in deed or in word, but above all – in the heart, in thought. And we believe with absolute faith that if the heart has not been purified – the Torah and the laws are nothing more than idle incantation."

He fell to his knees, bowing to the scribe of Jahanur and to the leader of the council and kissing the ground at their feet. Then he rose, shook their hands warmly and said:

"I wish there were many more like you!" – and taking his leave of Avarnam and Jaharan he mounted his horse and with Nejeen beside him, rode back to the King's summer palace. In their hands they held the apples they had been given, steadfast proof that all they had seen and been told was the truth.

In the room that he had set aside for an office, the scroll that Avarnam had mentioned was waiting for him.

He untied the ribbon and opened it: in clean, and cursive script – to the extent that Chaldean letters allowed for cursive forms – were the names of all the inhabitants of Jahanur, divided among the twelve families. There were also detailed notes relating to the history of the community and giving the names of its founders. The exceptional form of religion practised in Jahanur was also mentioned, and summed up in a single sentence: "They believe in the one, Almighty God, Creator of Heaven and Earth and of all that is in them."

He rolled up the scroll and placed it with the bundles they had brought with them.

An extensive veranda opened off the guest-room next to the bed-chamber, and they went out to inspect it. Like all the verandas of Babylon, this too was awash with flowers, their freshness testifying to the devoted care lavished upon them. They sat at a heavy table, of highly polished walnut wood, and with matching chairs. For a long time they were silent, trying to digest the riot of sensations stirring their minds. As the sun turned towards the west she began:

"How is it that this wonderful community of faithful upholders of tradition – and I say 'faithful' rather than 'fanatical' which is perhaps where they differ from our own people – has survived over the years untouched by destruction or neglect or the erosion of time, time which, it seems, has not changed it at all?"

Instead of answering her, he added a question of his own:

"If this community has indeed been preserved in this way, why has it not increased and multiplied, like any other community which has been spared from destruction, and grown inevitably into a great and populous nation? Think of our forefathers – seventy men who went down to Egypt, and their numbers grew and multiplied despite the yoke of servitude, and they returned to their land no longer a tiny band, but a race and a nation of some sixty thousand!"

She answered him equably:

"That is because of the strength of their faith, and the grace of God that rests upon them! They have remained as they are, neither suffering destruction nor growing and multiplying – and this because they have no interest in carnal pursuits for their own sake, and all the satisfaction that they need they find in their love of their God, loving him with all their hearts and minds, all their souls and all their strength."

"This marvellous community," he began, as if his thoughts and his mood were identical to hers, and his speech an extension of hers – "is a symbol of great hope and an example to all humanity of the faithful way of life. This community will never cease to exist, and no one will ever dare to attack and destroy it, as that would be tantamount to making war on God Himself!"

"And King Nebuchadnezzar," she said with no change in the tone of her voice, "did not send you here merely for rest and recuperation. This was a mission with a purpose!"

"That is indeed so!" he agreed. "Before I came here I read documents and scrolls, everything ever written about the community of Jahanur, and I found that it was all vague and elusive and unconvincing, because the compilers of reports simply did not have the mentality to comprehend the truth that the community of Jahanur embodies. And the King was exasperated by these unsatisfactory accounts, lines revealing less than they concealed, and when the opportunity arose to send someone on a tour of inspection, he took it."

They both looked out at the calm, pastoral landscape of Jahanur, bright with the radiance of the sunset.

"It is the grace of God that lights everything here!" she declared, and he added, as if to continue this train of thought:

"As our friends here in Jahanur have pointed out, blessing prevails where man is worthy of it. Regrettably, it can't be said of our compatriots that they have been blessed with that innocent and steadfast faith, faith for its own sake, that is rewarded by the grace of God!" There was bitterness in his voice and distant sadness. She turned to look at him, her calm gaze pouring into his eyes the unbounded freedom of her love, and he looked back at her, repaying her with the same love and the same freedom.

"Do you remember the wonderful story of the house of the Rechabites?" she asked.

He searched his memory for the name, but could not find it.

"At the beginning of his ministry Jeremiah the prophet was commanded to go down to the house of the Rechabites," she reminded him, and quoted:

"Go to the house of the Rechabites and speak to them, and bring them to one of the rooms in the house of the Lord

and offer them wine to drink. So I fetched Jaazaniah son of Jeremiah son of Habaziniah, with his brothers and all his sons and all the family of the Rechabites. I brought them into the house of the Lord to the room of the sons of Hanan son of Igdaliah, the man of God, that adjoins the rooms of the officers above that of Maaseiah son of Shallum, the keeper of the threshold. I set bowls full of wine and goblets before the Rechabites and invited them to drink wine, but they said: We shall not drink wine, as our forefather Jonadab son of Rechab laid this commandment upon us, saying, You shall never drink wine, neither you nor your children. And you shall not build houses or sow seed or plant vineyards, and you shall have none of these things, but shall stay in tents all your lives, so that you may live long in the land in which you dwell. And we have obeyed all that our forefather Jonadab son of Rechab commanded us and have drunk no wine all our lives, neither we nor our wives, nor our sons, nor our daughters. We have not built houses to live in, or planted vineyards or fields. We have lived in tents, and obeyed all the commandments of our forefather Jonadab...

"And here with your permission I shall omit a few lines," she said without turning to him, "and move on to the end: *And to the house of the Rechabites Jeremiah said: These are the words of the Lord of Hosts the God of Israel, because you have obeyed the commandments of Jonadab your forefather, and followed his instructions and done all that he told you to do, therefore, says the Lord of Hosts the God of Israel – Jonadab the son of Rechab will not be deprived of a descendant, to stand before me for all time.*"

After a short pause he responded:

"Hope is not yet lost for the people of Judah!"

The days passed one by one, and their tranquil

radiance strengthened something in their hearts, but this was not faith, as their faith was already so steadfast it was beyond compare. Rather, it was what was shared between them that grew stronger and blossomed, striking deep roots and becoming an element of unity astonishing in its enduring vigour.

Most of the time they spent together and most of the time they kept their silence and did not converse between themselves, speech being superfluous. They did not need the voice to convey their feelings to one another, and the thoughts of one were revealed to the other without a word spoken. And the lasting pleasure prevailed over everything, even over mere satisfaction, and this was a pleasure that had nothing to do with the fleeting day or with the tender night. And their hearts beat with the same rhythm, until it seemed they were not two hearts divided one from the other but one heart alone – perceiving, feeling and thinking for two.

Often they went out on horseback, ascending to the low ridge or following the winding goat-track leading from one end of the settlement to the other. There was silence all around them, save for the steady murmur of the eddying streams which did nothing to impair it but rather accentuated it, as did the sound of their horses' hooves. There were days too when they went out walking, and their impressions then were sharper, as if closer to the primeval sources. Sometimes on their way they met a man or a woman of the locality who blessed them, and they never ceased to be amazed by the look of sincere humility, innocence and friendship. After meeting a woman advanced in years, her wrinkled face beaming, who urged them to take some of the nuts that she carried in her basket, and would brook no refusal, he said to Nejeen:

"From my father I heard a legend, or not so much a legend as a prophecy," – and as they climbed that winding goat path he continued: "The human race will destroy itself by driving God away, and all that will be left will be a tiny minority, people of simple ways who never considered themselves worthy of any distinction or prize, like the people of Jahanur for example, or the family of the Rechabites that you spoke of. And their precise number will be twelve thousand times twelve. And it isn't of the chosen ones that we speak, but those who have known God and delighted in Him secretly, and loved Him, and will not deny Him whatever the circumstances. In those one hundred and forty-four thousand souls God will reveal Himself in all His glory, and those souls shall be saved, turning from mortal to immortal, and God in them, and they in Him."

"So this is what lies ahead for the community of Jahanur, and for the future offspring of the family of the Rechabites!" she declared. "But what is to become of our people, which is astray in the ways of chaos and is far from God?"

"As the prophet said," he replied with a sadness that he could not hide: *"Would that my head were water and my eyes a fountain of tears, so I might weep day and night for the slain of my people!"*

THE BLAZING FURNACE

Midway through the month allotted to him, he felt a heavy weight growing in his heart, and he knew that disaster was imminent. She shared his premonition but revealed nothing to him – nor he to her – and both tried not to speak of what was in their minds, smiling at one another as if their smiles could instil confidence and equanimity. Until one morning he rose and said to her:

"We are returning to Babylon!"

And without saying a word in reply she set to packing their belongings, and felt some relief, knowing there was to be no more delay; trouble lay ahead and so long as they stayed here, they could do nothing to avert or forestall it.

He approached the steward of the household and ordered him to harness their chariot and to prepare the baggage wagon. In a few words he expressed gratitude for the hospitality that they had enjoyed, and declared himself fully satisfied, and the steward bowed to him, assured him that his commands would be obeyed, and gave instructions to his underlings.

About an hour before noon everything was packed and ready in the wagon, and they boarded their chariot, bidding hurried farewells to the staff of the household, slaves and serving-maids, and to Avarnam, who heard of their impending departure just in time and arrived in haste to give them his blessing. And as the royal chariot left the courtyard, Avarnam ran behind, calling out obscure words which at the time he did not understand:

"Accept the Son of the living God!"

On the way a vision was revealed to him, and he saw

his three friends, Mishael, Hananiah and Azariah, standing in a ring of fire, laughing.

King Nebuchadnezzar made an image of gold, sixty cubits in height and six cubits in width. He had it set up in the valley of Dura in the province of Babylon. And the King sent out a summons to assemble the satraps, prefects, viceroys, counsellors, treasurers, judges, constables and all governors of provinces to attend the dedication of the image which he had set up. So they assembled – the satraps, prefects, viceroys, counsellors, treasurers, judges, constables and all governors of provinces – for the dedication of the image which King Nebuchadnezzar had set up, and they stood before the image, that Nebuchadnezzar had set up. Then the herald loudly proclaimed: O peoples and nations of every tongue, you are commanded, when you hear the sound of horn, pipe, zither, triangle, dulcimer, music and singing of every kind, to prostrate yourselves and worship the golden image which King Nebuchadnezzar has set up. Whosoever does not prostrate himself and worship shall forthwith be thrown into a blazing furnace. Accordingly, no sooner did all the peoples hear the sound of horn, pipe, zither, triangle, dulcimer, music and singing of every kind, then all the peoples and nations of every tongue prostrated themselves and worshipped the golden image which King Nebuchadnezzar had set up.
It was then that certain Chaldeans came forward and informed against the Jews. They said to King Nebuchadnezzar: O King, live for ever! Your Majesty has issued an edict that every man who hears the sound of horn, pipe, zither, triangle, dulcimer, music and singing of every kind shall fall down and worship the image of gold. Whosoever does not do so shall be thrown into a blazing furnace. There are certain Jews, whom you have appointed

to serve in the administration of the state of Babylon – Shadrach, Meshach and Abed-Nego – and these men have paid no heed to Your Majesty's command. They do not serve your god, nor do they worship the golden image which you have set up.

Then in rage and fury Nebuchadnezzar ordered Shadrach, Meshach and Abed-Nego to be fetched and they were brought before the King. Nebuchadnezzar said to them: Is it by design, Shadrach, Meshach and Abed-Nego, that you do not serve my god or worship the golden image which I have set up? You have heard the commandment, that when you hear the sound of horn, pipe, zither, triangle, dulcimer, music and singing of every kind, you are to worship the image that I have made, and if you do not worship, you shall forthwith be thrown into the blazing furnace, and who is the god who can deliver you from my power?

Shadrach, Meshach and Abed-Nego said to King Nebuchadnezzar: We are not afraid to answer you in this matter. We have a God whom we serve, and he can save us from the blazing furnace, and deliver us from your power, O King. And even if we are not saved, be it known to Your Majesty that we will neither serve your God nor worship the golden image that you have set up.

Then the King was filled with rage against Shadrach, Meshach and Abed-Nego and he commanded that they be thrown into the blazing furnace. So these men were bound, in their cloaks and their breeches and their turbans and their other garments, and thrown into the blazing furnace. Because the King's command was urgent, and the furnace exceedingly hot, the men who threw Shadrach, Meshach and Abed-Nego into the furnace were themselves killed by the flames. And those three men, Shadrach, Meshach and Abed-Nego, fell bound into the blazing furnace.

Then King Nebuchadnezzar was amazed, and he rose in haste and said to his counsellors: Did we not throw three men bound into the fire? And they answered the King: Yes, Your Majesty. He answered: Yet I see four men walking about in the fire free and unharmed, and the fourth looks like the son of God. Nebuchadnezzar went to the door of the blazing furnace and said: Shadrach, Meshach and Abed-Nego, servants of God the Most High, come out, come here! And then Shadrach, Meshach and Abed-Nego came out from the fire. And the satraps, prefects, viceroys and royal counsellors gathered around and saw how the fire had not the power to harm the bodies of these men, and their hair was not singed and their garments were unchanged, and there was not even the smell of fire about them.

Then Nebuchadnezzar spoke out: Blessed is the God of Shadrach, Meshach and Abed-Nego, who has sent His angel to save His servants who trusted in Him, who disobeyed the royal edict, and would rather yield their bodies to the fire than worship any god other than their God. And it is my decree that any man, of whatever race or nation or tongue, who speaks ill of the God of Shadrach, Meshach and Abed-Nego, shall be cut in pieces and his house laid waste, for there is no other god who could save men in this way. And the King promoted Shadrach, Meshach and Abed-Nego in the service of the state of Babylon.

King Nebuchadnezzar to all nations and peoples and tongues in the world: may you ever prosper. It is my pleasure to tell of the signs and wonders that God the Most High has worked for me. How great are his signs, how mighty his wonders! His kingdom is an everlasting kingdom, and his dominion shall stand for all generations.

The vision that was revealed to him as he rode in the chariot, before arriving in Babylon, at once eased his heart and soothed his spirit. He smiled at her and said:

"Our God who is love has rescued his loyal servants from the King's furnace, namely Hananiah, Mishael and Azariah."

Her face reflected the relief that lit up his face, and the oppression that had tormented them lifted, melting away as if it had never been. As a field of wheat glows in the sunlight after a ferocious storm, so her face shone before him now, in all its youthful radiance.

He found Babylon in a ferment. Nashdernach was sitting in his office, his face ashen grey as the face of a corpse, his gloomy eyes sunk deep into their sockets, framed by the wrinkles of many sleepless nights.

Nashdernach rose to meet him and stood before him silent for a long moment, as if he did not recognise him or had lost his wits, but then he recovered himself, bowed low and vacated his place behind the broad table.

"It's all my fault!" he mumbled as if talking to himself, almost in a whimper, and then he clutched his outstretched hand, hugged him briefly and stood back, staring at him curiously, as the dilated pupils of his eyes gradually returned to their habitual state.

"I never imagined, it never occurred to me that the King's decree would apply to them as well, your three friends Meshach, Shadrach and Abed-Nego, and even when the decree was issued and they were forced to go to that valley and to follow the example of all the others, there was still hope that with all the confusion, and the noise and the crowds this would not be noticed – a few people defying the edict and not bowing down to that image. But there was jealousy in the hearts of the enemies of those three. The Chaldeans are by no means a people innocent of jealousy, but the Chaldeans were not the first to see them. Someone drew their attention, and he was neither a Chaldean nor a Sidonian nor a Mede. Someone pointed to those three, who were standing firm and not bowing to the image, in defiance of the King's command, and he whispered in the ears of the Chaldeans.

"So the matter was reported and they were brought before the King, who tried to mitigate their offence, asking them if it was 'by design' that they did what they did. If the three of them were to fall at his feet now, and confess that they had acted not by design but out of error and in all innocence, and now they were begging his forgiveness and appealing to his mercy, knowing he was generous of heart and great of spirit, showing mercy to all who deserve mercy – then they would be dismissed with a rebuke, and perhaps also relieved of some of their official duties, but their lives would be spared. They responded with vehemence that was utterly unexpected, defying that awesome King, Nebuchadnezzar, His Majesty, in the style of great warriors or saints, fearlessly and unequivocally, and thereby dealt a mortal blow to the King's pride, and his wrath was kindled.

"And I, who had thought of coming before him and falling at his feet and appealing for clemency on their behalf – I stopped myself just in time, realising that I would be doomed and they would not be helped! My death would be to nobody's advantage, least of all my own! And then, oh, then!" Nashdernach exclaimed, his eyes bulging wide open – "Then the miracle happened! Incredible to relate, a real miracle before our very eyes. The fire in the furnace didn't touch them at all, didn't even singe a hair of their heads or their beards. With my own eyes I saw," – the narrator pointed to his eyes – "and I couldn't believe what I was seeing. Even at this moment, I find myself shuddering, awe-struck, wondering if this was a dream that I dreamed or is my mind unhinged – did these things really happen? They did! And all praise and glory be to God the Most High, who saved His loyal servants from the fire. As King Nebuchadnezzar himself said, no other god could have done this. It happened, it happened before these eyes of mine. I saw and I witnessed. And once again I give thanks to the God of the Jews, to your God. Were it not for the miracle that He performed – I could not have endured the shame and the disgrace, of having deceived myself and deceived you, however innocently and unintentionally. Unforgivable – and my life would not have been worth living!

"I was sure your companions would not be forced to attend the ceremony of dedication of that image. And since it happened I have been wondering – why does your God, the true, the one God, the all-powerful – not deliver your people, rescue the whole of your race from the clutches of King Nebuchadnezzar, from the clutches of all the conquerors and kings of the world, as he has done for your three friends, Meshach, Shadrach and Abed-Nego?" He looked up at him with an air of innocent curiosity.

"Because my compatriots are not as devoted to Him as are Meshach, Shadrach and Abed-Nego, and they do not serve Him as Meshach, Shadrach and Abed-Nego serve Him, or trust in Him as they trust in Him!" he replied in a voice of remarkable serenity, a voice he hardly recognised as his own.

At his home, Denur-Shag was waiting for him. He rejected all offers of hospitality or refreshment and seemed in an agitated mood, quaking in every limb of his body, pacing this way and that, and mumbling to himself. For the first time since he had known him, he was not tripping on the flaps of his long, shabby cloak.

"The whole of this business," he said, sitting down opposite him and shaking his big, balding head to a rhythm all of his own, "has left me feeling utterly helpless, completely lost! It was a fateful moment, I should say – a moment of truth! You may find this hard to believe, but I actually tried to force my way through the crush and get to the King, with the idea of talking him into a compromise, exerting all my eloquence and persuading him to show mercy – and then this soldier comes along and clubs me over the head!" Denur-Shag touched his scalp gingerly, and he noticed a fresh, blue bruise.

"I lost consciousness," Denur-Shag continued, "but after that ignominious episode it suddenly became clear to me as daylight that deep down, I had no confidence at all in my ability to reach the King, stand before him, put my argument forward and drown him in a tidal wave of erudite words, thus attaining my goal. This being the case, it wasn't by chance that I passed so close to that coarse, rough-tempered soldier. In fact, I was hoping to be hit, and the man didn't disappoint me, he did a thorough job. This is the part of it that I just can't fathom out, and I reckon the best thing for me is a spell of voluntary exile, leaving Babylon and sorting some things out for myself. Perhaps I'll go to the countryside, stay with that estranged wife of mine – and suffer at her hands until I've atoned for my cowardice!

"And as for you," – he looked up at him, his eyes still troubled – "I'm sure you realised that that small community, the community of Jahanur, is distinct from all others, differing from its neighbours in an unbridgeable sense, not like, let us say, the difference between the Chaldean people and the Jewish people or any people you care to name. And the past of the community of Jahanur is shrouded in mystery, and other peoples have a strong interest in this past remaining hidden and shrouded in mystery. For if the past of the Jahanurians were ever to come into the light of day and be revealed before the eyes of all – then all wars and conquests and pomp and glory and lucre would cease to exist! And it is the opinion of these peoples, and of the leaders and chieftains they have chosen for themselves, that without these things their lives would be utterly pointless. Anyway, these peoples worship their gods, any gods, out of fear and hatred, and cannot bring themselves to believe that there is a God who is real and all-powerful, who will defend those whom He chooses to defend, and no one can do any harm to the one who is defended by the hand of God!

"The true God, oh yes!" cried Denur-Shag. "The true God!" he sighed and gave him a long look, a faint glow of distant hope beginning to take the place of the fear and unease. "We saw him in the fire of the furnace! I fall to my knees in fear and reverence and bow down to him!" and Denur-Shag knelt and raised joined hands towards the ceiling, crying "How good it is to know that You, the one God, the creator and the all-powerful – are real!"

Denur-Shag stood up from his kneeling posture, returned to his seat, gave him a sharp and uncharacteristically earnest look, and went on to say:

"And He, the true God, has taught me a lesson. He has proved to all of us, simpletons that we are, floundering around in all kinds of superstition and calling it 'faith' – that He is reality itself, the one and the only. And it is well that it happened the way it happened, and well that we were witnesses to the miracle, and well that our King, His Majesty, Nebuchadnezzar the valiant and the wise, at once acknowledged the true God, and repented of his anger, and declared the God of Meshach, Shadrach and Abed-Nego to be this God, and anyone daring to cast the slightest shadow of a doubt on this – his flesh shall be 'cut to pieces' and his home destroyed. A right royal decree indeed! And now, I'm ready to accept a cup of honey-water!"

That very evening he met Mishael, Hananiah and Azariah, sitting in Hananiah's spacious house. They had just finished their prayers. Their faces, which seemed to have matured almost beyond recognition, glowed. They held out their hands to him and took turns embracing him warmly, and weeping on one another's shoulder, shedding tears that were pure and purged of any hint of self-pity, like the spring rain that cleanses the fields and the plain.

And then the four of them sat and spent a long time looking into one another's eyes, inspecting one another, their looks expressing by turns wonder, reverence and joy, all the stronger for being held in check.

"The most marvellous thing of all," Hananiah began in a calm, controlled voice, welling up from the depths and not his own voice at all, "was that figure that descended into the furnace and was with us in the fire, untouched by the flames and driving them back!"

It was then he noticed that Hananiah's hair, including his beard and eyebrows, had turned completely white, like bleached wool.

He turned to look at Azariah and Mishael. Their hair too was streaked with grey, but was not like Hananiah's.

"You are wondering," Hananiah noted his expression and interpreted it correctly – "why my hair is all white, and the hair of Mishael and Azariah is merely turning grey. Listen then," Hananiah leaned towards him, pronouncing every word with emphasis. "My hair has turned white, because I am the one who spoke with him!"

"With whom?" he asked, taken aback.

"With the being in human form who came down into the furnace and rescued us from the fire. A figure of wondrous beauty, radiating love, speaking wisdom and bestowing freedom. We were so astonished at the sight we forgot where we were and all that we wanted – was to be with him until the end of all days. And he turned to me, and in that moment as we stood face to face, the light of his eyes sinking into mine, I was suddenly seized by an overwhelming sense of perplexity, wracked by shudders and spasms such as I never knew before, such as I never experienced nor ever will again! In fact, this wasn't so much perplexity as awe, and blended with it a feeling of joy from an unknown source, and a sensation of flying and soaring beyond the highest Heavens and becoming nothing, as insubstantial as the dust, and all of this – at one and the same time! And then I knew for sure that my hair had turned white and would never return to its former colour, though that was the least of my concerns! This divine figure, for it surely was divine, turned to me and asked me:

"Do you know me, Hananiah?" – and his voice was deep and clear, and keen, and painful.

"No, Master," I answered him sadly, for then I would have paid any price, given up my life even, if only I could have answered him gladly with words such as: "Yes, Master! I have always known you, and you I have served, serve and shall serve all the days of my life, in this world and the next!

"So," Hananiah continued – "my answer was 'No, Master'. And in spite of the grief that this answer caused me, or perhaps because of it, I asked: 'Who are you, Master?' And the answer was not slow in coming:

'I am the one who will be known in the fullness of time as the Son of God, and I shall be the touchstone for your people and for all other peoples! A tiny minority of your people will believe in me and be saved, and the majority that has neither purity nor truth, that will reject me, hate me and persecute me, slay me in the flesh and deny me – the majority shall not know salvation. And you, Hananiah, do you believe in the Son of the living God?'

"And I fell to my knees and said to him: 'I believe in the son of the living God with all my heart, as do my companions!' And he turned to Azariah and Mishael with his glorious light and they knelt at his feet and said to him: 'We believe!'"

He glanced at Azariah and Mishael and they nodded their heads as if in confirmation, their faces still aglow.

"And finally," Hananiah went on to say, "the Son of God revealed to us that the afflictions of the Children of Israel and of Judah will not come to an end until they believe in Him and accept Him. And at that moment the door of the furnace opened and King Nebuchadnezzar stood there staring at us, his whole body trembling as he declared: 'There is no God on the earth beneath or in the Heavens above other than the God of Meshach, Shadrach and Abed-Nego'."

Hananiah's story was told, and silence reigned in the room. Then Hananiah turned to him and asked:

"And you Daniel, do you believe in the Son of the living God?"

And without any hesitation he replied:

"With all my heart and soul!" – and only then did he remember the strange cry of Avarnam, the chief councillor of Jahanur: "Accept the Son of the living God!"

"Who do you think he is, this Son of God?" Azariah asked him.

"The future saviour of mankind."

"So how is he related to our God, who is one and one

alone?" asked Mishael.

And he answered him, knowing it was the voice of another speaking through his lips:

"He is His embodiment!"

THE REBELLION

A year later, King Zedekiah rebelled. The Chaldean tax-collectors, coming to Jerusalem as they did every year, were sent away empty-handed.

The royal palace of Babylon was in uproar. Preparations were made for the dispatching of a punitive expedition, to be led, so it was rumoured, by none other than King Nebuchadnezzar himself.

Contacts between Babylon and the homeland were disrupted, and finally broken off altogether. In spite of this, there were still Jews arriving from Jerusalem. They saw themselves as refugees in the full sense of the word rather than exiles, and they told of what was happening there.

And so it was that he heard how the prophet Jeremiah had been assaulted by Zedekiah's minions, and had narrowly escaped stoning to death by the mob. Some of the elders and sages of the people had stood up and spoken out on his behalf, drawing attention to the similarities between his prophecies and those of his predecessors, and saying it should not be doubted it was God speaking through him; he was not to be persecuted or imprisoned lest the King and his ministers and the populace of Judah find themselves at war with God. But the words of the elders and the sages were to no avail, and there were instances when the inflamed mob turned its anger against them and attacked them, and some of them did as the prophet advised, packing a few possessions and leaving the rebellious city of Jerusalem, making their way, after many vicissitudes, to Babylon. After giving their reports to the King's representatives, who questioned them closely about the mood in Jerusalem, the activities of Zedekiah and his ministers and the common people, and the prophecies of Jeremiah, to which no one was listening – they recognised them as refugees and settled them in huts outside the walls. Those who had experience of agriculture were given plots of land to farm, skilled craftsmen were employed in the royal workshops, and scholars and intellectuals became clerks in the palace.

The newcomers were satisfied with their reception and grateful for everything, saying that all Jeremiah's predictions were coming true before their eyes, in spirit and in letter, including his assertion that anyone not rising in revolt against the Chaldeans would retain life and property intact; they had no reason to complain and nothing more to say – except to give praise and thanks to the King of Babylon – the envoy of God, according to Jeremiah.

And so it was that the four of them – Mishael, Hananiah, Azariah and he – happened to be together in Hananiah's office, listening to the report of one of the refugees, a clerk in the royal treasuries. He told them of the activities of an officer named Irijah, son of Shelemiah son of Hananiah, who detained Jeremiah at the Benjamin Gate as he was leaving the city, meaning to go to the land of Benjamin and hide there from the anger of the crowd and the machinations of the King's courtiers, and from the King himself, that unpredictable youth forever changing his mind and his policies.

And this man, Irijah son of Shelemiah son of Hananiah, raised a commotion in the marketplace and denounced Jeremiah as a traitor saying: "You mean to defect to the Chaldeans!" and Jeremiah replied: "That is a lie! I have no intention of defecting to the Chaldeans!" And the man did not believe him, nor did most of the crowd gathered there in the market-place, and they manhandled Jeremiah the prophet and put him in chains and brought him before the King. And the King disowned him, telling the ministers and the commoners: "Do with him as you see fit!"

And they threw Jeremiah into a pit in the prison yard. And there was no water in the pit, only mud, and Jeremiah began sinking into the mud.

King Zedekiah had a Negro servant, a eunuch, who well knew his master's mind, and how changeable it was. He was also, secretly, a supporter and a disciple of the prophet. And when the King's Negro servant heard that Jeremiah had been thrown into the pit in the prison yard, and was sinking into the mud, and did not have long to live, he approached the King and appealed to his compassion, saying: "My Lord the King, these men have done wrong in their dealings with Jeremiah the prophet, throwing him into a pit where he will sink and die!"

And the King commanded his Negro servant: "Take thirty men with you and haul Jeremiah the prophet out of the pit before he dies." And the servant assembled the men and went to the store-room of the palace under the treasury and took from there some cast-off clothing which he threw down to Jeremiah, with a rope. And the King's Negro servant said to Jeremiah: "Put these rags under your armpits, to ease the chafing of the ropes," and the prophet followed his advice. So they pulled Jeremiah out of the pit with ropes, and he stayed in the prison yard.

Then King Zedekiah had Jeremiah the prophet brought to him by the third entrance of the House of the Lord, and the King said to Jeremiah: "I have a question to ask you – speak and hide nothing from me!" And Jeremiah said to Zedekiah: "If I speak out you will kill me, and if I give you advice, you will ignore it!" And King Zedekiah swore a secret oath to Jeremiah: "As the Lord lives who gave us our lives, I shall not kill you, or hand you over to those men who seek your life!"

And Jeremiah said to Zedekiah: "This is the word of the Lord of Hosts, the God of Israel. If you go out and surrender to the officers of the King of Babylon, your life will be spared and this city will not be set on fire, you and your family shall live. And if you do not go out and surrender to the officers of the King of Babylon, this city will fall into the hands of the Chaldeans who will burn it to the ground – and there will be no escape for you!"

And here the story was suspended, as the refugee-narrator had urgent duties to attend to in his new post.

The four young men exchanged glances, all of them utterly perplexed and deeply worried by what they had heard.

"I suppose," said Mishael, "there is a chance that reason may prevail, when a ruler seeks to know what is the will of God, and God does not withhold His word from him, but informs him through His prophet what he must do if he is to live. And the ruler holds his fate in his own hands, his fate and the fate of his family and the fate of his people. All that is then required of the wise ruler is that he comply with the word of God and put an end to all his troubles and come out from darkness into a great light. Yet in this case, he does the opposite. The first step is sensible and gives grounds for hope – and yet without the second step it is worthless! It is an undeniable fact that the first step does not invariably lead to the second!"

"And why do those who take the first step not go on to take the second, which according to logic should follow from it?" Azariah queried.

He looked up at the ceiling and stared at it for a while,

before lowering his eyes and saying, without addressing anyone in particular:

"Lack of faith."

And Mishael asked him:

"And is there no way to increase their faith and strengthen it?"

"There is," he declared, and added – "It's a question of repentance. This was an option that was offered to Zedekiah the King of Judah, and he rejected it out of hand."

"And what are we to do in these perilous times – and how can we help our compatriots and our families in Judah, and the unfortunate King, who is astray and leading others astray?"

"We must remain firm in our own faith, and strengthen it, and trust in Him, the Blessed One, and love Him with all our hearts and minds, our spirits and our might!"

"And this strengthening of faith and love of Him – will that help our compatriots and the hapless King Zedekiah, and our families in Judah?" asked Azariah.

"Increase of our faith and our love of Him will set out before every man, inasmuch as he is a man, the path to repentance, which leads on to salvation."

"So it is pointless, turning to God and asking for His guidance, if the one who turns and asks for guidance is lacking in faith!"

"As pointless as lighting a way in the darkness for one who has been blind from birth!"

They left Hananiah's office and went their separate ways – all of them in a mood of the most profound gloom.

Or-Nego sat facing him. It seemed that he had changed somewhat, having grown older and more circumspect. This was no longer the army commander who had boasted of punishing rebellious peasants and burning down their homes. Sitting there before him was a restrained man in the prime of life, who knew what lay before him and was determined to do the right thing, who was loyal to whatever seemed to him worthy of his loyalty. He remembered Adelain's story of the vows which Or-Nego made to his wife before she died – vows which he had kept. Truly, Nebuchadnezzar knew how to choose his men! If his army had a dozen more officers like Or-Nego, that army would be invincible.

The passage of the years had left their mark on his face and his body as well. This body had lost some of its litheness while gaining solidity. Two deep furrows scored his cheeks, as if to underline his firmness, while his gentle eyes had receded further into their sockets, their look of serenity, courage and congenial intelligence unimpaired.

Or-Nego had asked for this interview, in his capacity as a senior officer, but had insisted on waiting for his turn. As it turned out, the meeting was taking place a week after the original approach was made. They sat for a while in companionable silence, while he looked into those eyes that reminded him of Adelain's eyes – a little dry, and their lustre restrained – and made mental note of the more obvious changes that had come about since last he saw him. It was Or-Nego who eventually broke the silence:

"I'm supposed to be joining the King's army for the campaign against Judah, and I thought it right to come and see you beforehand and perhaps bid you farewell, even though the expedition won't be setting out for some time yet. And above all, the main purpose of my visit is to ask if you have any particular requests regarding your native city and your homeland."

"What do you mean, Or-Nego?" he asked him, sensing

a faint awkwardness in the other, in that deep, benevolent look that reminded him so vividly of Adelain.

"If you like..." he hesitated momentarily, before continuing in a clear, steady voice: "I could use my discretion where your relatives are concerned. Tell me where they live – and I can deploy my troops in such a way that they're not harmed, they and their neighbours! I shall be glad to be of service – and Adelain will be glad too. This idea, of coming to you and offering my modest services appealed to her very strongly and perhaps," Or-Nego paused and pondered briefly, before revealing something that surprised him – though not the most shattering of surprises – "it was she who suggested it in the first place, knowing that nothing would give me greater pleasure... so, do you have any favours to ask of me, anything that's within my power to grant?" The soldier looked up and regarded him steadily.

He was in no hurry to reply. His eyes were fixed on Or-Nego's hands, laid on the polished table – good, broad hands, and most important of all – reliable.

"If you can't decide just now, I'll come back in two weeks or three, a month even. The expedition won't be setting out for at least another three months, possibly four, because the season has to be right and it takes time organising such a large and heavily-equipped force. Anyway, as you well know – it's all in the hands of Heaven!" He raised his hand and the look of serenity left him, to be replaced by that blend of reverence and hope that is the hallmark of the soldier and devout believer. "So think it over," he went on to say, "make up your mind and let me know. I shall return at a time of your choosing, and whatever you ask, I shall carry out with the utmost pleasure!" He bowed his head respectfully, as he concluded. And it was then that the voice was heard, emerging from his throat:

"You must do as King Nebuchadnezzar commands!"

Both men knew this was a commandment that could not be disobeyed, and it was not he who spoke but One whose will was incumbent upon both, to be done gladly.

Or-Nego stood up from his seat, took a step back and bowed to him, a full, deep bow of friendship, reverence and admiration, and so, still stooping, he retreated backwards towards the door, bowed again and went out without another word spoken.

Shortly after this he heard that Adoniah had returned from Jerusalem, and was brimming over with news and information about the rebellious city and its inhabitants, King Zedekiah and his court, and the prophet Jeremiah.

They met at Azariah's house. Beside a table that was laden with food and drink – ranging from honey-water to the choicest of wines – Adoniah reclined at his ease in a padded chair. He did not rise to greet him as the others did, but held out his fleshy hand as if dispensing a favour, smiling that characteristic smile of his – always hiding something behind the mask of ostentatious scorn.

"In your honour," he drawled, "your friends have chosen not to serve meat on their table!"

"Not just in his honour," Azariah objected hastily. "Since coming to Babylon, we too have willingly abstained from eating meat."

"Is that any reason to deny me, a meat-eater, my favourite food? What kind of hospitality is this?"

"It's precisely for reasons of hospitality, and the well-being of our guests, that we serve no meat on our tables!" Azariah retorted with a smile, this time succeeding in reproducing a hint of 'Adoniah-style' irony.

"A strange way of looking at things, in my opinion!"

Adoniah replied, and for a moment it seemed that the sarcasm was wiped from his fleshy lips, as his round, ruddy head, with its dense fringe of beard and hair, moved slowly up and down in token of disapproval. "I have no choice then," he sighed, putting on an injured expression, "but to sample your menu and be like that lion, which at the end of time will eat straw for its prey and delight in wild herbs!" He took the goblet that the house-slave had filled with yellow wine, pure as a tear, cried "To life!" and took a long gulp. Laying down his goblet, he wiped his lips on a cloth that the slave handed him, and finally turned to the topic of the day:

"If you saw Jerusalem now, you wouldn't believe your eyes! It isn't the place we knew in our youth. Another Jerusalem has arisen to take its place, a proud and defiant city, the capital of a mighty kingdom, a city that will stand up to defend its honour, that is all splendour and valour. And all its citizens, young and old alike, are rushing to arms and joining Zedekiah's army, to fight the Chaldean oppressor. And I tell you truly – they will fight like lions and they will prevail! Be sure to remember what I say. The great and the confident kingdom of Babylon will burst like a soap-bubble, and great days will return to Judah. A glorious future beckons, more glorious than anything man can imagine!" Adoniah reached for his goblet again and drank from it thirstily.

"And what of the prophet Jeremiah?" he asked, keeping his feelings in check.

"Our land is no stranger to cowards and traitors..."

"Watch your tongue! You have no right to judge the prophet of God!" His stern words reverberated around the room.

Adoniah was silent, flinching as if a whip had struck him, his tongue lolling from his mouth, and for a moment it seemed he had lost the power of speech. The next moment he regained some composure, and having tried to revert to his broad, sarcastic smile and failed, went on to say in a conciliatory tone:

"Forgive me, but I don't think that Jeremiah is serving his King, or showing any love for his people. Time will tell!" he added hurriedly, to forestall any interruption, and he resumed self-righteously: "If it really is God who is putting into his mouth the things that he says, preaching from morning to evening in the House of the Lord, in the market-places and the streets of Jerusalem – why do they arouse such anger?" He added, in an abrupt change of subject: "The King's servant saved him from certain death, and the King is holding him to witness what is yet to happen, when the day comes that Judah is liberated from the Chaldean yoke, and we storm Babylon and tear down its strongholds. And then it will finally be proved, for all to see, that the words of Jeremiah are not the words of the living God, but tales that he has made up for himself, for reasons known only to him..."

"Time will tell!" This time it was Hananiah who interrupted him, the tone of his voice much sharper than it had ever been known before, his face glowing in its frame of snow-white hair.

"You're right of course," Adoniah agreed, but went on to say: "Anyway, this Jeremiah that you call a 'prophet' has suffered so much violence and abuse that he's been uttering heart-breaking laments, even regretting the day he was born:

"Cursed be the day, he says, *when I was born, and be it ever unblessed, the day my mother bore me! A curse on the man who brought word to my father saying, a child is born to you, a son, rejoice! That man shall fare like the cities, which the Lord overthrew without mercy, and he shall hear*

225

cries of alarm in the morning and uproar at noon, because death did not claim me in the womb and my mother did not become my grave. Why did I come forth from the womb, to know toil and grief and end my days in shame?

"It wasn't because of the blows and the insults he received that the prophet said what he said," he pointed out in a steady voice that would brook no interruption, "but because of the violence and the ruin on the way, the destruction to come!"

"Permit me to disagree with you!" Adoniah answered him, after draining the entire contents of his goblet, wiping his lips again and signalling to the slave for a refill. "I don't believe that violence and ruin are the future of our people, this wise and wondrous, dauntless people! On the contrary, glory and praise are in store for it, and unbounded dominion over the earth and its fullness!" Adoniah cried, the enthusiasm flashing in his eyes. He sipped from the goblet, put it down again in front of him and declared with vehemence, unable to control his feelings:

"This is the golden age of Israel and Judah! Zedekiah is not standing idle, and envoys from Egypt are coming and going, and there are caravans of camels and countless wagons bringing weapons and provisions, and all the granaries are full, and if the city were to be besieged for ten years it could withstand it and not capitulate! But this time there will be no need to withstand a siege, for the Lord will deliver His people and lay His hand on the one whom Jeremiah calls His faithful servant, and fight him and destroy him long before there is any siege of Jerusalem, the Holy City, and his intentions shall be foiled and his conspiracy frustrated, and Babylon shall fall, never to rise again!"

"That kind of talk is liable to bring disaster upon our

people, forcing Nebuchadnezzar to exact brutal reprisals and conquer our homeland and raze Jerusalem to the ground, as no foreign king has ever done before!" he insisted.

"That kind of talk, as you call it, is going to prove to be the truth, as you are all going to find out! Still, time will tell – and that's one thing on which we can agree! And now, if you have no objection, let's drink a toast to Zedekiah, King of Judah, and tomorrow's victor!"

He raised his cup, but they were slow to follow his example. They looked at him. Slowly he held out his hand, took his cup, raised it smoothly and said, in a voice that was not his:

"Long live Jeremiah, holy prophet of the Lord!"

This was a toast that they were glad to drink. Even Adoniah joined in – a triumph of thirst over principle, perhaps.

He barely tasted any of the fine and abundant foods on offer, tastefully prepared though it all was and attractively presented. Azariah was fortunate in having the services of a first-rate chef, from the northern provinces of the state of Babylon, regions renowned for fine craftsmanship and culinary skills.

"So here you are in Babylon, alongside this King, and you're singing his praises and extolling his wisdom," Adoniah began again, in a voice thickened by wine, "and you're impressed by his power and you speak of him with reverence and respect. And you give no thought to all the things that are happening out there in the world. Do you reckon that the whole universe is wrapped up within the lofty walls of this pagan Babylon? That is what you think, isn't it? Oh yes, and by the way," – and he raised his hand to forestall any interruption – "I've heard about that stunt with the furnace, and the miracle that you experienced, an impressive miracle by any standards, the finger of God, no less!" He nodded his round, hairy head, in token of wonderment. "And this naïve and gullible king, the pagan and gentile Nebuchadnezzar, falls in humble submission at your feet, and declares that your God is the only God. And I've heard talk too about the Son of God, the one who's going to split the Jewish people and set faction against faction. And I won't ask how you did it, and how the King was duped, and how you created the illusion of being inside the fire when in fact you were outside it, no doubt with the help of your accomplice, posing as the Son of God. No, I won't ask and I won't pry!"

The four of them exchanged glances, their eyes reflecting bemusement and perplexity, and something faintly resembling anger, resentment even. All at once they realised there was no purpose to be served by becoming embroiled in argument with him, and the best response to such slander was silence. And this thought nipped their anger in the bud and erased their resentment, giving way to sorrow and pity, and the four of them smiled barely perceptible smiles at one another and kept their silence, while their guest ranted on, piling words upon words and sentences upon sentences, paying no attention to his surroundings, and seeming at times to be talking to himself:

"And what have you gained from all this? What did you demand in exchange for this so-called miracle, performed before the goggling eyes of that ignorant pagan king, who was in such a hurry to proclaim yours the only God, and to threaten anyone denying this with summary execution. What did you ask him for?" – and without waiting for an answer – "He wouldn't have dared refuse you anything, he'd have done whatever you wanted, in the spirit and in the letter! Did it occur to you to ask him to liberate Judah from the yoke of his slavery, and ease the burden of his taxes? Did such a thought ever enter your heads, my dear friends?" he asked, and answered for himself exclaiming "No, no, of course not! You were content with your comfortable jobs and smart offices, and swanky houses, and all the precious gifts that the pagan King has been lavishing on you, holding you in such awe and reverence. And what do you expect to be called, other than pursuers of power and worldly glory? Is this how you serve your God – who rescued you, so you say, from the flames of the furnace – and whose deadly enemy you have been cosseting so courageously, King Nebuchadnezzar the pagan? Or perhaps you're relying on what your friend said, that nice Jeremiah:

These are the words of the Lord of Hosts, the God of Israel, to all the exiles whom I carried off from Jerusalem to Babylon: Build houses and live in them, plant gardens and eat their fruits. Marry wives and beget sons and daughters, and take wives for your sons and give your daughters to husbands, so they may increase and not dwindle away. Seek the welfare of the city to which you are exiled and pray for it to the Lord, since on its welfare your welfare depends. These are the words of the Lord: when a full seventy years have passed over Babylon, I will take up your cause and fulfil the promise of good things that I made to you, and bring you back to this place.

"Do you believe those words, are those the principles you live by? Oh, don't tell me, I'm really not that interested!" he exclaimed, waving a restraining arm in a gesture that was quite superfluous, as no one had any intention of responding.

"So you sit around idly, amassing wealth and acquiring ornate houses, your tables are creaking under the weight of fine foods, you wear the medals of pagan authority around your necks, you have grown fat, whereas I have been constantly on the move, forever devising strategies to elude my enemies, ignorant boors that they are – and me, you ignore, me you have left outside, left behind, like a severed limb that's no use to anyone. No one remembers me, no one calls on me – not even to bow to that ridiculous image set up by the idol-worshipping King! But I was there, I went on my own initiative, in person. And I saw the three of you," he pointed to Mishael, Hananiah and Azariah, "standing there and not bowing down, as stiff as statues and as proud as peacocks! You made me so angry! And I actually bowed down, made a point of bowing down, because of you! Or I should say, to be different from you, apart, untouched by your smug arrogance, close to the people rather than the ruling class!

"No one has ever offered me a prestigious job – to this very day. No one has ever put a necklace around my neck – let alone one of those pendants with the royal seal. I'm the one they forget, the one you've forgotten! And I'll tell you something – I'm grateful for this! In days to come you'll pay a high price for what you've been doing, and your joy will turn to grief, your pleasure to depression!

"Have I hurt your feelings?" – it was both a question and an exclamation, and the guest continued in a wheedling voice: "Can't you tell that I'm only joking! I have a sharp tongue, an errant tongue, and as the wisest of all men said, the tongue has the power of life and death! Anyway, at least here I can be myself, open the secrets of my heart to my friends and comrades... just a moment," he paused as if thinking something through – "when were you my friends and comrades? We met for the first time in that jolting wagon on the way to Babylon. Still, I shall call you my friends and ask you to forgive this provocative tongue of mine, that sometimes strays beyond the bounds of good taste. Anyway, accept my thanks and my warmest compliments, renowned miracle-workers and interpreters of dreams that you are, and be neither hurt nor offended. Pardon and forgive me. Even in the presence of the women I have dallied with, and there have been many of them, I could never confess and be my true self. Please, let me be a member of your group again, and don't think badly of me!" Again, the four of them exchanged baffled glances.

At a late hour of the night, Adoniah was finally defeated by the strong wine. His servants arrived, and carried him home.

IN THE DEAD OF NIGHT

He parted from Nejeen and went to his room for his night's rest. After a while, he heard Oshrich's soft knocking.

"Enter!" he cried and the door opened without a sound. Oshrich bowed low, and rising he said:

"Lord Denur-Shag is asking to see you, Sir!"

"Ask him to come in," he replied, wondering what urgent business had brought the dependable Denur-Shag knocking on his door at such a late hour of the night.

"Greetings and blessings!" Denur-Shag entered and immediately tripped on the flaps of his cloak and fell. He hurriedly took a step forward to catch him, but the guest managed to grab the back of a chair just in time.

"As usual!" exclaimed Denur-Shag, adding in the mock-serious tone that always brought a genial smile to the lips of his hearers – "The sense of balance of a one-day old baby who hasn't yet learned to walk on two legs! And it's a compliment, without a shadow of a doubt – a compliment!" he insisted, and in characteristic style, veered off at a tangent: "The baby, as you know, is distinguished by his innocent thoughts and purity of heart, and his trust in everything and in all people, and if it were possible for him to rule any people, he would bring it peace and happiness and most important of all – true equality and a final end to slavery. Yes, in my vision of the end of days, the rulers of all nations will be babies!"

Denur-Shag sat on the padded chair beside the broad table, covered with a white cloth and as a centre-piece, a crystal vase containing a rare flower of delicate fragrance, then took out from under his cloak a flask of wine, and laying it on the cloth, commented without looking up:

"From your homeland! Old Jerusalem wine, from the years before the crises and the conflicts. This was looted from the palace of King Jehoiakim, a renowned lover of fine wines who made a point of keeping a well-stocked cellar even when his granaries were empty. Anyway," Denur-Shag continued, looking up, "without the proper cups, glass ones I mean, this drink loses its special allure – its fragrance and the whole of that infusion of ancient flavours!"

He sat down opposite Denur-Shag, who seemed intent on drowning him in a deluge of words as a prelude, or a tentative overture, to the main point at issue, a weapon as yet unsheathed.

He clapped his hands and Oshrich appeared, bowed and awaited his instructions.

"Two glass goblets, please!"

There was silence in the room.

Denur-Shag treated him to a long, probing, inquisitive look, with, as always, an undercurrent of irony bordering on whimsy. He derived a strange pleasure from gauging the reactions of other people to the challenges that he set before them. Nevertheless, in this look of his, playful and challenging as it was, there was a sense of the warmth and the fellowship which are expressed in the willingness to share both in another's joy and in another's tribulation.

He responded to the challenge with a broad smile, and then noticed that those eyes, with the ironical and inquisitive look that was also warm and sympathetic – were weary, weary not in a casual or a temporary fashion, and for the first time in all the years that he had known his teacher, he feared for him.

Oshrich returned and placed before them a pair of

thin-stemmed goblets of fine Egyptian glass, edged with a kind of tracery that was harmonious and of considerable aesthetic appeal.

Denur-Shag tugged at the wooden bung with its deerskin wrapper, and not without some effort, pulled it from the long neck of the flask. A thin vapour rose from the mouth of the flask. Carefully, almost reverently, Denur-Shag tilted the neck of the flask over the goblet set before the host and filled it half-full, then, with a similar flourish, repeated the process with his own. The clear, rosy liquid glided smoothly into the elegant glassware.

Having completed the task of pouring, Denur-Shag plugged the flask again, with deliberate movements, as if cautious of something, set it down beside him, raised his goblet and said:

"In your homeland, they drink a toast 'to life', meaning the true life in the realm of the legendary King-Messiah! Let's hope that in this story there is a spark of truth and optimism for the future, and let's drink in honour of the King-Messiah, urging him to come with all possible speed and put an end to strife and error. So, to life!"

"To life!" – he raised his goblet in turn and took a sip of the amber-coloured liquid. Denur-Shag was right – the wine was fine indeed, retaining its fragrance and with delicate flavours that refreshed the body and infused a sense of lightness and lustre. He was reminded of his homeland, the hills surrounding the Holy City, the road to Anathoth, the grove and the valleys, the enchanted air at nightfall, the paved streets, the temple of the Lord and the palace of the King, proud Jerusalem – long since trampled under the feet of foreign armies.

"All Jerusalem," the guest said softly, "the glory and the sanctity that hover above its temples and its houses and its alleyways, and give the air its special savour, and the hopes that have faded into nothing – all are embodied in this wine!"

"Denur-Shag, you have seen my thoughts and read my mind!"

The other did not respond.

They took up their goblets again and sipped from them with a strange sensation of loss and longing, blended with a distant hint of hope.

Denur-Shag wiped his lips, put down the goblet, and looked up at him, his little eyes dry and serious, and ominously acute.

"As you know," he began in a thoroughly practical tone, "our King, King Nebuchadnezzar, intends to march against rebellious Jerusalem and establish order there 'once and for all'. Obviously, 'once and for all' is a purely rhetorical expression. And although a dauntless warrior and a divinely appointed conqueror like this King of ours, is far removed from anything even remotely resembling literature or art or suchlike – he too cannot resist using borrowed expressions, by which I mean those that hover in the ether, with neither depth nor substance to them. 'Once and for all', at best, may be regarded as extending over one lifetime, no more, and there are various rogue elements that will, naturally, do everything possible to frustrate the purposes of this King of ours, His Majesty. And there can be no doubt that the King and his entourage are aware of this. And establishing order in Jerusalem on a 'once and for all' basis will not be achieved without pain and suffering and without the sacrifice of many lives, in other words – without war. And war usually begins before it is officially declared, *before the arrow is loosed and the shield wards it off,* as your prophet Isaiah puts it so well. And this war has already started, meaning here, in glorious Babylon. Zedekiah, the Jewish King, who reveres everything except God, refusing to hear His voice as conveyed to him by the prophet Jeremiah – is sly and cunning, as has been typical of losers since this world was created and will be so until its final destruction." Denur-Shag sighed, put the goblet to his lips and took a minute sip, replaced the goblet on the table and went on to say, broaching a subject apparently unrelated to all that had gone before:

"There are here, in Babylon, a number of Jewish families, citizens of long-standing to be sure, but Jewish in every respect. And they live in certain houses, built in the space between the walls, as a sign and a symbol that on the one hand they do not belong to Babylon, and on the other, they cannot afford to ignore it.

"And this strange community has put a proposition to King Zedekiah, or King Zedekiah has approached its elders with a proposition. One way or the other, and without the parties ever meeting face to face, something is being hatched between them that in any language would be called 'intrigue' or 'conspiracy', and this with the active collusion of those merchants, itinerant traders and wayfarers, who are the bridge between Babylon and Judah. And the plan is – to lie in wait for the King, who means to set out, two or three months from now, to bring Jerusalem to heel 'once and for all' – and strike him a mortal blow, thus making life easier for King Zedekiah, although all this is in defiance of the will of God, and the warnings uttered constantly, from morning to evening, by His prophet, Jeremiah.

"Everyone has his own plans," Denur-Shag stressed, going on to explain in the same tone, "and one of the couriers in the service of the Jewish community has a plan and an agenda of his own, or at least, that is the conclusion of my elderly brain." Denur-Shag raised his round hand, finger lightly touching his temple.

"It is possible that this courier, who is also attached to the royal trade mission, is eager to curry favour in the eyes of his King, and for this reason has chosen the route he has taken. In any case, the plan is known in all details and particulars to the soldiers of the royal guard and to the King himself. It has also been brought to my attention, but *that*, the King and his guard do not know. According to this ambitious plan, frightfully naïve in my opinion and for that reason, all the more dangerous and likely to succeed, a young man, an incorrigible fanatic, will arrive tomorrow, as darkness falls, at the south-eastern wall of the palace, a section of the wall that is overgrown with vegetation," the guest explained – "and not regularly patrolled. A narrow path, also neglected and overgrown, leads from the wall directly to the King's apartments and his private office. The young man is supposed to infiltrate this office, with a dagger concealed under his cloak, and if his luck holds and the King is present – attack him with the dagger and thus abort the whole of this expedition and the imposition of order 'once and for all' upon Jerusalem, which has been groaning under a heavy yoke since the day of its foundation to this very day. And confusion shall fall upon Babylon and someone will see in this the finger of God, and Zedekiah will be declared the winner of this war. We should also take into account the possibility – admittedly remote but just the kind of thing to inflame fanatical imaginations – that when Zedekiah marches in triumph through the land of the Chaldeans and takes Babylon by storm with his small but highly effective army, then that forgotten and outcast community will emerge from its anonymity, and they will exchange their hovels between the walls for the royal apartments, and rule over the pagan and dim-witted Chaldeans with a heavy hand and a firm purpose, and chastise them severely, as is written in one of the sacred books of that community. One way or the other," Denur-Shag sighed, fidgeting with his elegant goblet and twisting it between his fingers but not drinking any of the wine, the wine with its pleasant, twinkling reflections of the bright candle-light – "this young man, brave and resourceful as he may be, and armed with his dagger, will be awaited by heavies from the guard detachment, Chaldeans through and through, their swords drawn and clubs in their hands, the shackles for his wrists and ankles set out ready on the thorny ground. And all that remains for us is to finish the consecrated wine from the chosen land, and hope that the chosen people will come to its senses in time and listen, solemnly, to the voice of God and not to the voice of weak-minded novices or crafty tradesmen."

Denur-Shag raised his goblet and calmly sipped his wine. Rising from his seat, he shook the hand of his host and left the room without another word.

A few moments later he rode into the night, calmly and steadily urging on his horse, which needed little encouragement but bore him swiftly over streets now emptied of people, as the stars flicked in the violet, infinite void.

A little after midnight he came to the familiar houses between the two walls, all swathed in utter darkness.

Without dismounting from his horse, he knocked hard on the door of the family home of Joseph Hanaggid. It was not long before somebody called:

"Who is there?"

"Daniel! Open the door! This is urgent!"

The door opened. Saul, the father of Havatzelet, stood

in the doorway, an oil-lamp in his hand.

"I must speak to you!" he said, jumping down from his horse and tying him to the hitching-post, and without waiting for an invitation, he rushed inside.

Saul closed the door behind him, and ushered him along the hallway and into the main living room of the house. Here he lit a dozen large oil-lamps, and every corner of the room was bathed in bright light.

"Speak!" Saul demanded. His face glowered, his voice was aggressive – but there was deep fear in his eyes.

"In the royal court there is talk of some kind of plot to murder the King, tomorrow at nightfall. The soldiers of the royal guard know when and where and how the assassin will strike. An ambush has been set for him and he has no chance of either doing the deed or evading capture. Take this to heart and act accordingly. And don't forget, it's the whole community that you're endangering, including women and children and the old."

"Wait here a moment!" Saul cried, clearly shaken. He took a lamp and left the room.

A few moments later he returned with Raphael, his elder brother, and a youth – lean, tall and wiry, with a pointed beard, black as pitch, lank hair and flashing eyes.

"This is Eleazar, of the family of Nehemiah the priest," Saul introduced him and added: "Please, respected Sir, tell him what you just told me!"

In a few words he repeated all that he knew.

For a long moment the four men stood in silence. No one sat. The bright flames of the lamps swayed calmly, this way and that.

Suddenly the young man turned away, and when he turned back a split-second later, he had a dagger in his hand.

"Death to the traitor!" he cried and lunged at him.

The two other men managed to restrain him, and with Daniel's help they wrested the dagger from his hand.

"I have done my part!" he said. He moved to the door and before leaving turned and blessed them: "May God have mercy upon you and upon your household!"

He went to his bed before daybreak and slept for a while, but fitfully. He got up finally and went to the window, feeling weary and heavy-hearted. The garden was in darkness and the sky turning pale, the last of the stars flickering and fading.

He was pleasantly surprised to find that the slave had already prepared a bath for him, and he spent some time lounging in the warm water. When he emerged and dressed in shirt and breeches of soft blue fabric, with a white sash, and entered the dining-room – the table was set. On the other side of the table sat Nejeen, in a pink robe. Her smile was radiant, and her face spoke of tenderness, her eyes – of love. She greeted him and rose as he approached the table. He returned her greeting mechanically, and did not seem to notice she was standing. She sat after he had taken his seat, and asked the maid who was serving drinks to fill his goblet with light wine. For herself she poured a cup of the mountain spring water that was brought down to Babylon in great wooden barrels.

He sipped the wine and felt its warmth restoring the vitality to his body and flushing his cheeks. How apt she was at guessing what he wanted and silently satisfying his desires, always finding a way of comforting him!

He looked up at her with eyes filled with gratitude.

She said as if answering a question:

"I saw you riding out in the night and I waited for you to return."

"What were you doing all that time?" he asked.

"I was praying," she smiled at him, a smile that opened up again before him a wondrous world of soft radiance, of song and harmony.

"Was it you who ordered the hot bath?"

She nodded. "Did you enjoy it?" she asked.

"It restored my strength."

"Praise be to God!" she exclaimed joyfully.

"Amen and amen!" he confirmed her blessing.

He was offered rye bread, a honeycomb, milk and butter. He felt his strength returning, with a healthy hunger that gratified him.

He offered her a buttered slice and took one for himself.

She thanked him and said:

"One morning, not long before the Chaldeans came, at the end of spring, you invited me to stroll with you to the grove of pines on the road to Anathoth. We walked along a path that could hardly be called a path because of the long, fresh grass that covered it. Once we had gone a certain distance, you held my hand, as if you wanted to protect and reassure me. I tried to convey to you that I wasn't afraid and your concern for me was unnecessary. We found the cave of a bear, or more precisely, a she-bear, and there were three little cubs there, full of energy and mischief. You had what was left of a honeycomb with you, and you gave it to me to share out among the cubs. I was the happiest girl in the world! And the main reason for this – I sensed how happy you were too, and what a delightful experience it was for you. At that moment – do you remember?" she asked curiously.

"I remember!" he exclaimed, going back to relive that exceptional, thrilling moment.

"At that very moment," she continued, putting the slice

back on the plate in front of her, "we both sensed something strange, a heavy and clumsy presence, but not hostile. And then, I'm sure you remember, we slowly turned round and found ourselves standing, face to face, with the mother-bear, looking into her placid eyes."

"I remember!"

"She rubbed her muzzle, with more delicacy than you'd believe such a clumsy creature was capable of – on your shoulder and mine, and then she put out her tongue and licked your face and mine, and then she withdrew with a kind of contented purr and curled up in her corner, glancing at us with a look that seemed to say:

You play with my cubs! They're happy with you, and I'm happy to see them happy, and to see you happy!"

"And that's just what we did!" he reminded her. "We played and played for ages, we chased them and they chased us, and they climbed all over us and challenged us to catch them as they hid behind bushes and climbed trees. And all this time the mother was lying there contentedly, grooming her fur with her long, red tongue."

His marvellous wife had detected the tension that was troubling him and the fear that had penetrated deep into his heart, disturbing his rest and perhaps also souring his mood, and she had found just the right antidote, to assuage this fear and ease his depression – with the healing story of the she-bear and her cubs.

His face shone with warmth and gaiety, as did hers, and each of them had no desire other than to share this gaiety and this warmth with the other, rejoicing in the other's happiness, and finding relief and contentment in the relief and contentment of the other.

When he rose and passed by her, he kissed her silky hair, gathered at the back of her neck, as well as the hand that was held out to clutch his, and before he had time to say another word she kissed the back of his hand, a kiss that was tender and at the same time, deliberate and protective.

He worked in his office until evening, and after dining with his wife, invited her to join him for a stroll in the royal gardens. The walk refreshed them both, and they climbed the steps to their bed-chambers hand in hand.

When they woke the next morning, the palace was in a ferment, like an ant-hill turned upside down. It emerged that the prospective assassin had not abandoned his plan but only changed it – and had simply entered the palace by the main entrance. The man approached the gate and when asked to stand back in the customary manner and await clearance he pretended to obey, but the moment that one of the guards stepped forward to search him, he slipped past him and made a run for it, succeeding in getting as far as the royal gardens.

A pursuit followed, ending with the would-be assassin cornered in one of the felt-covered tool-sheds, some distance from the royal compound. The shed was surrounded by a tight ring of guardsmen, who called upon the fugitive to surrender of his own accord rather than wait to be taken by force. The summons was repeated, but there was no response. Just as the soldiers were about to launch an attack, a pillar of thick smoke was seen rising from the roof of the felt building, and immediately after it a massive flame leapt into the sky, and within moments the whole of the shed was ablaze. The soldiers did not lose their nerve, but found buckets, pans and other utensils and ran to fetch water from the nearby well. As they were busy dowsing the fire, a figure emerged from among the panels of felt, a human figure wreathed in flames and burning like a torch, shouting with the last remnants of his strength:

"Long live King Zedekiah! Long live Judah! Death to Nebuchadnezzar! Death to the ungodly Chaldeans!" – and a blazing hand still brandished a long dagger.

Still yelling, the burning figure fell, collapsed there and then and lay inert. As no one had any intention of intervening, the figure burned on to the end, until only ashes were left.

The day after the distasteful episode of the would-be assassin who was burned alive, there came to the royal palace a delegation of worthies from the ancient Jewish community of Babylon, and among them were Simeon and Raphael, Benjamin and Saul, who had been instigators of the assassination plot and its most ardent supporters. After they had been kept waiting for two days at the palace gate, the King agreed to receive them.

The members of the delegation all fell at the King's feet, and prostrated themselves reverently. After they had spent some considerable time kissing the cold floor of the reception hall the King commanded them to rise, and they rose to their feet one by one, assuring the King of their utter abhorrence of the criminal act committed by that deranged young man, whose sole intention had been to damage the exemplary relations, relations of peace, friendship, brotherhood and mutual trust that had always prevailed between the Chaldean people and the Jewish people, peoples which after all had shared roots and even similar laws, legal traditions mutually nourished – and they had come here to bow down before the King and affirm once more their unbounded loyalty to the Chaldean state and monarchy in general, and to King Nebuchadnezzar in particular. As was well known, since time immemorial they had spared no effort in demonstrating their fervent support of the Chaldean administration and glorious Babylon, which they saw as their homeland and their patrimony. And they offered the King an ancient sword which they said had once belonged to King Solomon himself, and one thousand gold shekels, of Babylonian coinage, as a contribution to the Chaldean war effort against the disloyal Zedekiah, and they welcomed this opportunity to denounce him publicly and disown any connection with him.

With a cynical sneer that he made no attempt to hide, the King rejected the sword and commanded that the thousand shekels be distributed among the poor and the needy of Babylon. He was minded to have the delegation forcibly ejected, but in the end he relented and let them go in peace, much to their relief. He had no quarrel with the Jewish community of Babylon as a whole, and besides, he reckoned that these men had humiliated themselves quite adequately without any help from him.

ADONIAH

Adoniah called upon Rafsi, the eunuch responsible for the east wing of the harem:

"I need to speak urgently with Anabil, the Egyptian woman that I brought here for His Majesty the King! Just for a few moments!" And before the giant could respond and send him on his way, he touched his swarthy arm and drew out a bulging purse from beneath his purple cloak. "One hundred gold shekels!" he whispered.

The eunuch seemed to be reconsidering his next move, his protuberant eyes fixed on that purse, and then, after inspecting his surroundings to be sure that the corridor was empty, with no living soul in sight, he snatched the purse as it was offered him and quickly hid it under his broad sash.

"Tomorrow, at sunset, in the perfumery, for a short time only! And I know nothing!" he whispered, adding emphatically: "The responsibility is all yours!" And with his head held high, and eyes scanning the ceiling with its carvings of cattle in bronze and lions in wood, he swept away in stately style, as indifferent to Adoniah as if he were a wall or a pillar.

Next day, at sunset, Adoniah slipped into the harem, turned towards the east wing, found the narrow corridor leading to the perfumery, and knocked on the low, white-painted door. A pale hand opened the door and he made a hasty entrance. The door was closed again without a sound.

"You're endangering my life!" Anabil fumed, irritation and impatience reflected in her big, dark eyes – handsome eyes, in which an inexperienced young man might have fancied he saw tenderness and devotion, and boundless submissiveness.

"I need you!" he whispered and added at once: "You are to tell the eunuch responsible for the wing that Belteshazzar, the chief minister and viceroy of the King, entered your bed-chamber at the seventh hour of the evening and tried to rape you!"

"What kind of nonsense is this!" she protested, staring at him coldly.

In his hand he held two bulging purses.

"In each of these," he pointed to the purses – "there are five hundred gold shekels. One of them is yours now, the other you will have when the deed is done."

"Why at the seventh hour?" she asked, still indignant.

"Because at the seventh hour he says his private prayers. No one will see him at that time or testify to that effect!"

"This is going to cost Belteshazzar his head!" she mused, as a broad smile of satisfaction, impossible to disguise, parted her sensual lips and exposed for an instant the flash of her teeth.

"Do you like him?" he asked.

"No!" she declared.

"Has he hurt you?"

"No," she replied grimly,

"He's hurt me!" he asserted.

"How?"

"Through his arrogance!"

"Yes," she agreed, her cold smile reflected now in her eyes as well. "Arrogance – that sounds like him!" and without any further hesitation she held out an eager hand and grabbed one of the two purses.

He turned around, opened the door a crack and

stooped to peer out – the corridor was empty. Nimbly and without a sound, he slipped out and closed the door behind him. And so, unobserved by anyone, he left the harem of King Nebuchadnezzar, the valiant and the wise King, conqueror of the world.

Two days later the palace was shaken to its very foundations, and all those residing there were struck dumb with amazement on hearing reports of the shameful deed committed by Belteshazzar, the King's viceroy and senior counsellor. It seemed he was not immune from guilty passions after all, but had tried his luck with the young Egyptian concubine whom Adoniah had brought for the King a few months before, and who was indeed in the full bloom of her womanhood, sensuous and incomparably seductive, with charms that no man could easily resist. So even Belteshazzar had fallen from grace, and Anabil had rebuffed him and called for the help of the eunuch responsible for the wing, and he feared for his life and fled.

And when the story reached the ears of King Nebuchadnezzar, he ordered that both Belteshazzar and Anabil, his new concubine, be summoned before him. And the two of them came before the King, seated on his high throne of cast gold and ivory.

The viceroy bowed and blessed the King in the accepted manner, while Anabil sprawled on the floor at Nebuchadnezzar's feet and at once burst into bitter tears and loud lamentation.

The King commanded his concubine to stand and tell her story from beginning to end. And still whimpering, the Egyptian concubine described how Belteshazzar, in a frenzy of lust, had invaded her room the night before last at the seventh hour, and had assaulted her. She spurned his advances, but what strength did she have to resist a man? And she called out for help...

"Who answered your call?" the King interrupted her sternly. And she spoke out in praise of the prompt response of the one responsible for the east wing of the harem, none other than Rafsi, the eunuch.

And the King commanded that the eunuch responsible for the east wing of the harem be brought before him.

Rafsi arrived, flustered to the very roots of his soul, sweat glistening on his broad forehead. And he fell at the feet of the King and did not rise until permission was given, and then the King addressed him in a tone that did not bode well:

"Dirty, despicable wretch!" cried Nebuchadnezzar, incensed. "Why did you wait a day and a half before coming to me to report the scandalous activities taking place on your wing? You deserve to have that stupid head of yours removed from your shoulders!"

Rafsi prostrated himself again at the feet of the King and in a quaking and mumbling voice, confessed at once that it was all a fabrication.

Nebuchadnezzar commanded that they both be tortured with red-hot irons but before the irons touched their flesh, the truth came to light, and Adoniah was arrested at the King's command and brought before him in chains.

Adoniah adopted an air of baffled innocence and denied everything, declaring with fervour that he had never spoken to the eunuch or to the Egyptian concubine, and they had hatched a plot to make him a scapegoat. Clearly, they were enemies of the Jews, who felt they had scores to settle with the exiles of Judah. As for Belteshazzar, he was his best and most trusted friend, whom he had never known to do anything but good. It would never occur to him to describe him as "arrogant" – least of all in conversation with a bonded slave-woman!

Adoniah's protestations of innocence failed to convince the King, who silenced him and sentenced him forthwith to death by hanging.

It was then that Belteshazzar bowed to the King and asked for permission to speak. Permission was granted, and he proceeded to say:

"My King, live for ever! No word that His Majesty utters is ever to be ignored, and this wretched man is indeed worthy of the most severe of punishments – if it is proved beyond doubt that he has committed the heinous offence of which these witnesses have accused him, conspiring to incriminate his friend. Indeed, there is enough in the witnesses' accounts to cast a heavy shadow of suspicion on the King's commercial agent, but this is not conclusive, unequivocal proof, however likely it may seem. And because there is doubt, I venture to suggest that the sentence of death be commuted to hard labour in the mines in the mountains, so that no man's conscience needs to be troubled over the unproven guilt of this man, who persists in his claim that his hands are clean."

Belteshazzar's measured words eased some of the tension in the atmosphere, and opened the way to calm reflection and reconsideration.

For a brief moment King Nebuchadnezzar looked down as he pondered what had been said, before looking up again and declaring:

"It shall be as you say! This cunning knave shall have the benefit of the doubt and his head may remain on his shoulders. Instead he shall be sent for twenty-five years into the bowels of the earth, for hard labour in the bronze mines. He is to be bound in shackles which will not be removed until the very last day of his sentence has been served!

"The other two," the King thundered – "shall be put to death, and at once!"

Soldiers of the royal bodyguard swooped on the three malefactors and began dragging them towards the door.

The eunuch and the concubine uttered the most heart-rending shrieks, while Adoniah twisted round in his captor's hands to face the King and cried out to him:

"I have something important to say, my lord the King! Of the greatest importance, please hear me!"

And since the King showed no inclination to hear anything more from him, sentence having been passed, Adoniah shouted:

"I lied to my Lord the King! What these witnesses have said of me – is the absolute truth!"

"Stop!" cried the King, and his agent, in chains, was brought back to him and thrown down at his feet.

Adoniah was agitated, emotional and perhaps in pain as well, but he was not scared. Making no attempt to rise from the floor where he lay, he looked up at Belteshazzar and addressed his remarks to him, while panting heavily:

"All praise be to you! Your efforts to save me from the claws of death touched my heart, but the truth is, my fear of death is as nothing compared to my fear of hard labour and chains! You know how indolent and lazy I am, intent on fleeting pleasures... jealous too, and the most mean-spirited of men. Forget me, if you can, and I'm not asking you to mention me in your prayers! Peace be with you, Daniel, my brother! You are well rid of me – for I am your enemy! And you should know, you have many more enemies, so beware of them! And before I disappear from your life I must confess to another sin that I committed against you – the metal spike under the saddle of your horse, that was supposed to wreck your chances of winning the race, and bring your life to an abrupt end – it was my idea. I thought of it, and Matthew, the unlucky boy who died that day, was the one who carried it out.

"And all these years I have hated you for your success, and this hatred gave meaning to my life! And now, my life is ended, and the hatred is ended too. I am also the one who incited those who informed against Mishael, Hananiah and Azariah, bringing to their attention the way that those three stood erect while all of Babylon bowed to the golden image. Oh, how proud of them I was, and how I envied them! And how I hated them, and how eager I was to put them to the test, the severest of tests, to the end! And sure enough, I did it – and they withstood it! Pass on my warmest congratulations! Even at this moment, my heart is full of pride in you, and envy, at one and the same time. And as for you, peace be with you. I am swarthy, and not the prince of any haughty maiden's dreams!" And suddenly he turned where he lay and kissed the feet of the King's viceroy, and cried in a choking voice: "Forgive me and pardon me – if you can!"

"I forgive you and I pardon you, my brother Adoniah!" he said, and tried to raise him to his feet, but the soldiers of the guard forestalled him, dragged Adoniah up from the floor and made him stand, looking into the purple, enraged face of the King.

"Hang him!" commanded Nebuchadnezzar.

- End of Book II -

To be continued in:
THE CHOSEN Book III: A MAN MUCH LOVED

Made in the USA
Columbia, SC
11 December 2019